All in the family

"What are you looking for in Constantinople?"

I took a deep breath. "To fulfill my destiny, by finding the one whom I am meant to find, the one whom I love."

Pulcheria gasped, crossed her arms chastely over the high mounds of her breasts. "It's impossible."

"Nothing's impossible. A bond holds us together—a bond stretching across all of time. This was fated," I whispered. "It had to be."

"Yes! Yes! Tonight. When Leo is in bed, I'll come to you."

I shivered, thinking of the Time Patrol sword-like above me. The punishment for unauthorized interference in past events was death . . . and having an affair with one's own great-great-multi-great grandmother was about as unauthorized an interference in the past as you could get!

UP THE
LINE

Robert Silverberg

A Del Rey Book

BALLANTINE BOOKS • NEW YORK

A Del Rey Book
Published by Ballantine Books

Copyright © 1969 by Robert Silverberg

All rights reserved under International and Pan-American
Copyright Conventions. Published in the United States by
Ballantine Books, a division of Random House, Inc., New York,
and simultaneously in Canada by Ballantine Books of Canada,
Ltd., Toronto, Canada.

ISBN 0-345-27388-5

Manufactured in the United States of America

First Edition: August 1969
Third Printing: June 1978

Cover art by Murray Tinkelman

For Anne McCaffrey
a friend in deed

1.

Sam the guru was a black man, and his people up the line had been slaves—and before that, kings. I wondered about mine. Generations of sweaty peasants, dying weary? Or conspirators, rebels, great seducers, swordsmen, thieves, traitors, pimps, dukes, scholars, failed priests, translators from the Gheg and the Tosk, courtesans, dealers in used ivories, short-order cooks, butlers, stockbrokers, coin-trimmers? All those people I had never known and would never be, whose blood and lymph and genes I carry—I wanted to know them. I couldn't bear the thought of being separated from my own past. I hungered to drag my past about with me like a hump on my back, dipping into it when the dry seasons came.

"Ride the time-winds, then," said Sam the guru.

I listened to him. That was how I got into the time-traveling business.

Now I have been up the line. I have seen those who wait for me in the millennia gone by. My past hugs me as a hump.

Pulcheria!

Great-great-multi-great-grandmother!

If we had never met—

If I had stayed out of the shop of sweets and spices—

1

If dark eyes and olive skin and high breasts had meant nothing to me, Pulcheria—

My love. My lustful ancestress. You ache me in my dreams. You sing to me from up the line.

2.

He was really black. The family had been working at it for five or six generations now, since the Afro Revival period. The idea was to purge the gonads of the hated slave-master genes, which of course had become liberally entangled in Sam's lineage over the years. There was plenty of time for Massa to dip the wick between centuries seventeen and nineteen. Starting about 1960, though, Sam's people had begun to undo the work of the white devils by mating only with the ebony of hue and woolly of hair. Judging by the family portraits Sam showed me, the starting point was a café-au-lait great-great-grandmother. But she married an ace-of-spades exchange student from Zambia or one of those funny little temporary countries, and their eldest son picked himself a Nubian princess, whose daughter married an elegant ebony buck from Mississippi, who—

"Well, my grandfather looked decently brown as a result of all this," Sam said, "but you could see the strain of the mongrel all over him. We had darkened the family hue by three shades, but we couldn't pass for pure. Then my father was born and his genes reverted. In spite of everything. Light skin and a high-bridged nose and thin lips —a mingler, a monster. Genetics must play its little joke on an earnest family of displaced Africans. So Daddo went to a helix parlor and had the caucasoid genes edited, accomplishing in four hours what the ancestors hadn't managed to do in eighty years, and here I be. Black and beautiful."

Sam was about thirty-five years old. I was twenty-four. In the spring of '59 we shared a two-room suite in Under New Orleans. It was Sam's suite, really, but he invited me to split it with him when he found out I had no place to stay. He was working then part time as an attendant in a sniffer palace.

I was fresh off the pod out of Newer York, where I was supposed to have been third assistant statutory law clerk to Judge Mattachine of the Manhattan County More Supreme Court, Upper. Political patronage got me the job, of course, not brains. Statutory law clerks aren't supposed to have brains; it gets the computers upset. After eight days with Judge Mattachine my patience eroded and I hopped the first pod southbound, taking with me all my earthly possessions, consisting of my toothflash and blackhead remover, my key to the master information output, my most recent thumb-account statement, two changes of clothing, and my lucky piece, a Byzantine gold coin, a nomisma of Alexius I. When I reached New Orleans I got out and wandered down through the underlevels until my feet took me into the sniffer palace on Under Bourbon Street, Level Three. I confess that what attracted me inside were the two jiggly girls who swam fully submerged in a tank of what looked like and turned out to be cognac. Their names were Helen and Betsy and for a while I got to know them quite well. They were the sniffer palace's lead-in vectors, what they used to call come-ons in the atomic days. Wearing gillmasks, they displayed their pretty nudities to the bypassers, promising but never quite delivering orgiastic frenzies. I watched them paddling in slow circles, each gripping the other's left breast, and now and then a smooth thigh slid between the thighs of Helen or Betsy as the case may have been, and they smiled beckoningly at me and finally I went in.

Sam came up to greet me. He was maybe three meters tall in his build-ups, and wore a jock and a lot of oil. Judge Mattachine would have loved him. Sam said, "Evening, white folks, want to buy a dream?"

"What do you have going?"

"Sado, maso, homo, lesbo, inter, outer, upper, downer and all the variants and deviants." He indicated the charge plate. "Take your pick and put your thumb right here."

"Can I try samples first?"

He looked closely. "What's a nice Jewish boy like you doing in a place like this?"

"Funny. I was just going to ask you the same thing."

"I'm hiding out from the Gestapo," Sam said. "In blackface. *Yisgadal v'yiskadash—*"

"*—adonai elohainu,*" I said. "I'm a Revised Episcopalian, really."

"I'm First Church of Christ Voudoun. Shall I sing a nigger hymn?"

"Spare me," I told him. "Can you introduce me to the girls in the tank?"

"We don't sell flesh here, white folks, only dreams."

"I don't buy flesh, I just borrow it a little while."

"The one with the bosom is Betsy. The one with the backside is Helen. Quite frequently they're virgins, and then the price is higher. Try a dream instead. Look at those lovely masks. You sure you don't want a sniff?"

"Sure I'm sure."

"Where'd you get that Newer York accent?"

I said, "In Vermont, on summer vacation. Where'd you get that shiny black skin?"

"My daddy bought it for me in a helix parlor. What's your name?"

"Jud Elliott. What's yours?"

"Sambo Sambo."

"Sounds repetitious. Mind if I call you Sam?"

"Many people do. You live in Under New Orleans now?"

"Just off the pod. Haven't found a place."

"I get off work at 0400. So do Helen and Betsy. Let's all go home with me," said Sam.

3.

I found out a lot later that he also worked part time in the Time Service. That was a real shocker, because I always thought of Time Servicemen as stuffy, upright, hopelessly virtuous types, square-jawed and clean-cut— overgrown Boy Scouts. And my black guru was and is anything but that. Of course, I had a lot to learn about the Time Service, as well as about Sam.

Since I had a few hours to kill in the sniffer palace he let me have a mask, free, and piped cheery hallucinations to me. When I came up and out, Sam and Helen and Betsy were dressed and ready to go. I had trouble recognizing the girls with their clothes on. Betsy for bosoms, was my mnemonic, but in their Missionary sheaths they were indistinguishable. We all went down three levels to Sam's place and plugged in. As the good fumes rose and clothes dropped away, I found Betsy again and we did what you might have expected us to do, and I discovered that eight nightly hours of total immersion in a tank of cognac gave her skin a certain burnished glow and did not affect her sensory responses in any negative way.

Then we sat in a droopy circle and smoked weed and the guru drew me out.

"I am a graduate student in Byzantine history," I declared.

"Fine, fine. Been there?"

"To Istanbul? Five trips."

"Not Istanbul. Constantinople."

"Same place," I said.

"Is it?"

"Oh," I said. *"Constantinople.* Very expensive."

'Not always," said black Sam. He touched his thumb to the ignition of a new weed, leaned forward tenderly, put it between my lips. "Have you come to Under New Orleans to study Byzantine history?"

"I came to run away from my job."

"Tired of Byzantium so soon?"

"Tired of being third assistant statutory law clerk to Judge Mattachine of the Manhattan County More Supreme Court, Upper."

"You said you were—"

"I know. Byzantine is what I *study.* Law clerk is what I *do.* Did."

"Why?"

"My uncle is Justice Elliott of the U.S. Higher Supreme Court. He thought I ought to get into a decent line of work."

"You don't have to go to law school to be a law clerk?"

"Not any more," I explained. "The machines do all the data retrieval, anyway. The clerks are just courtiers. They congratulate the judge on his brilliance, procure for him, submit to him, and so forth. I stuck it for eight days and podded out."

"You have troubles," Sam said sagely.

"Yes. I've got a simultaneous attack of restlessness, Weltschmerz, tax liens, and unfocused ambition."

"Want to try for tertiary syphilis?" Helen asked.

"Not just now."

"If you had a chance to attain your heart's desire," said Sam, "would you take it?"

"I don't know what my heart's desire is."

"Is that what you mean when you say you're suffering from unfocused ambitions?"

"Part of it."

"If you knew what your heart's desire was, would you lift a finger to seize it?"

"I would," I said.

"I hope you mean that," Sam told me, "because if you don't, you'll have your bluff called. Just stick around here."

He said it very aggressively. He was going to force happiness on me whether I liked it or not.

We switched partners and I made it with Helen, who had a firm white tight backside and was a virtuoso of the interior muscles. Nevertheless she was not my heart's desire. Sam gave me a three-hour sleepo and took the girls home. In the morning, after a scrub, I inspected the suite and observed that it was decorated with artifacts of many times and places: a Sumerian clay tablet, a stirrup cup from Peru, a goblet of Roman glass, a string of Egyptian faience beads, a medieval mace and suit of chain mail, several copies of *The New-York Times* from 1852 and 1853, a shelf of books bound in blind-stamped calf, two Iroquois false-face masks, an immense array of Africana, and a good deal else, cluttering every available alcove, aperture, and orifice. In my fuddled way I assumed that Sam had antiquarian leanings and drew no deeper conclusions. A week later I noticed that everything in his collection seemed newly made. He is a forger of antiquities, I told myself. "I am a part-time employee of the Time Service," black Sam insisted.

4.

The Time Service," I said, "is populated by square-jawed Boy Scouts. Your jaw is round."

"And my nose is flat, yes. And I am no Boy Scout. However, I am a part-time employee of the Time Service."

"I don't believe it. The Time Service is staffed entirely by nice boys from Indiana and Texas. Nice white boys of all races, creeds, and colors."

"That's the Time Patrol," said Sam. "I'm a Time Courier."

"There's a difference?"

"There's a difference."

"Pardon my ignorance."

"Ignorance can't be pardoned. Only cured."

"Tell me about the Time Service."

"There are two divisions," Sam said. "The Time Patrol and the Time Couriers. The people who tell ethnic jokes end up in the Time Patrol. The people who invent ethnic jokes end up as Time Couriers. *Capisce?*"

"Not really."

"Man, if you're so dumb, why ain't you black?" Sam asked gently. "Time Patrolmen do the policing of paradoxes. Time Couriers take the tourists up the line. Couriers hate the Patrol, Patrol hates Couriers. I'm a Courier. I do the Mali-Ghana-Gao-Kush-Aksum-Kongo route in January and February, and in October and November I do Sumer, Pharaonic Egypt, and sometimes the Nazca-

Mochica-Inca run. When they're shorthanded I fill in on Crusades, Magna Carta, 1066, and Agincourt. Three times now I've done the Fourth Crusade taking Constantinople, and twice the Turks in 1453. Eat your heart out, white folks."

"You're making this up, Sam!"

"Sure I am, sure. You see all this stuff here? Smuggled right down the line by yours truly, out past the Time Patrol, not a thing they suspected except once. Time Patrol tried to arrest me in Istanbul, 1563, I cut his balls off and sold him to the Sultan for ten bezants. Threw his timer in the Bosphorus and left him to rot as a eunuch."

"You didn't!"

"No, I didn't," Sam said. "Would have, though."

My eyes glistened. I sensed my unknown heart's desire vibrating just beyond my grasp. "Smuggle me up the line to Byzantium, Sam!"

"Go smuggle yourself. Sign on as a Courier."

"Could I?"

"They're always hiring. Boy, where's your *sense?* A graduate student in history, you call yourself, and you've never even thought of a Time Service job?"

"I've thought of it," I said indignantly. "It's just that I never thought of it seriously. It seems—well, too *easy.* To strap on a timer and visit any era that ever was—that's cheating, Sam, do you know what I mean?"

"I know what you mean, but you don't know what you mean. I'll tell you your trouble, Jud. You're a compulsive loser."

I knew that. How did he know it so soon?

He said, "What you want most of all is to go up the line, like any other kid with two synapses and a healthy honker. So you turn your back on that, and instead of signing up you let them nail you with a fake job, which you run away from at the earliest possible opportunity. Where are you now? What's ahead. You're, what, twenty-two years old—"

"—twenty-four—"

"—and you've just unmade one career, and you haven't made move one on the other, and when I get tired of you I'll toss you out on your thumb, and what happens when the money runs dry?"

I didn't answer.

He went on, "I figure you'll run out of stash in six months, Jud. At that point you can sign up as stoker for a rich widow, pick a good one out of the Throbbing Crotch Registry—"

"Yigg."

"Or you can join the Hallucination Police and help to preserve objective reality—"

"Yech."

"Or you can return to the More Supreme Court and surrender your lily-white to Judge Mattachine—"

"Blugh."

"Or you can do what you should have done all along, which is to enroll as a Time Courier. Of course, you won't do that, because you're a loser, and losers infallibly choose the least desirable alternative. Right?"

"Wrong, Sam."

"Balls."

"Are you trying to make me angry?"

"No, love." He lit a weed for me. "I go on duty at the sniffer palace in half an hour. Would you mind oiling me?"

"Oil yourself, you anthropoid. I'm not laying a hand on your lovely black flesh."

"Ah! Aggressive heterosexuality rears its ugly head!"

He stripped to his jock and poured oil into his bath machine. The machine's arms moved in spidery circles and started to polish him to a high gloss.

"Sam," I said, "I want to join the Time Service."

5.

PLEASE ANSWER ALL QUESTIONS

Name: Judson Daniel Elliott III

Place of Birth: Newer York

Date of Birth: 11 October 2035

Sex (M or F): M

Citizen Registry Number: 070=28=3479=xx5=100089891

Academic Degrees—Bachelor: Columbia '55

                 Master: Columbia '56

                 Doctor: Harvard, Yale,

                                Princeton, incomplete

                Scholar Magistrate: ——

                Other: ——

Height: 1 meter (s) 88 centimeters

Weight: 78 kg.

Hair Color: black

Eye Color: black

Racial Index: 8.5 C+

Blood Group: BB 132

Marriages (List Temporary and Permanent Liaisons, in order
    of registration, and duration of each):

            none

_____

_____

_____

_____

_____

_____

_____

Acknowledged Offspring: none

Reason for Entering Time Service (limit: 100 words):

To improve my knowledge of Byzantine

culture, which is my special study area;

to enlarge my acquaintance with human

customs and behavior; to deepen my rela-

tionship to other individuals through

constructive service; to offer the bene-

fits of my education thus far to those in

need of information; to satisfy certain

romantic longings common to young men.

_____

_____

_____

Names of Blood Relatives Currently Employed by Time
Service:

_____

6.

Very little of the foregoing really mattered. I was supposed to keep the application on my person, like a talisman, in case anybody in the Time Service bureaucracy really wanted to see it as I moved through the stages of enrolling; but all that was actually necessary was my Citizen Registry Number, which gave the Time Service folk full access to everything else I had put on the form except my Reason for Entering Time Service, and much more besides. At the push of a node the master data center would disgorge not only my height, weight, date of birth, hair color, eye color, racial index, blood group, and academic background, but also a full list of all illnesses I had suffered, vaccinations, my medical and psychological checkups, sperm count, mean body temperature by seasons, size of all bodily organs including penis both flaccid and erect, all my places of residence, my kin to the fifth degree and the fourth generation, current bank balance, pattern of financial behavior, tax status, voting performance, record of arrests if any, preference in pets, shoe size, et cetera. Privacy is out of fashion, they tell me.

Sam waited in the waiting room, molesting the hired help, while I was filling out my application. When I had finished my paperwork he rose and conducted me down a spiraling ramp into the depths of the Time Service building. Squat hammerheaded robots laden with equipment and documents rolled beside us on the ramp. A door in the wall opened and a secretary emerged; as she crossed

our path Sam gave her a lusty tweaking of the nipples
and she ran away shrieking. He goosed one of the robots,
too. They call it appetite for life. "Abandon all hope, ye
who enter here," Sam said. "I play the part well, don't
I?"

"What part? Satan?"

"Virgil," he said. "Your friendly spade guide to the
nether regions. Turn left here."

We stepped onto a dropshaft and went down a long
way.

We appeared in a large steamy room at least fifty meters high and crossed a swaying rope bridge far above the
floor. "How," I asked, "is a new man who doesn't have a
guide supposed to find his way around in this building?"

"With difficulty," said Sam.

The bridge led us into a glossy corridor lined with
gaudy doors. One door had SAMUEL HERSHKOWITZ
lettered on it in cutesy psychedelic lettering, real antiquarian stuff. Sam jammed his face into the scanner slot and
the door instantly opened. We peered into a long narrow
room, furnished in archaic fashion with blowup plastic
couches, a spindly desk, even a typewriter, for God's
sake. Samuel Hershkowitz was a long, long, lean individual with a deeply tanned face, curling mustachios, sideburns, and a yard of chin. At the sight of Sam he came
capering across the desk and they embraced furiously.

"Soul brother!" cried Samuel Hershkowitz.

"Landsmann!" yelled Sam the guru.

They kissed cheekwise. They hugged. They pounded
shoulders. Then they split and Hershkowitz looked at me
and said, "Who?"

"New recruit. Jud Elliott. Naive, but he'll do for the
Byzantium run. Knows his stuff."

"You have an application, Elliott?" Hershkowitz
asked.

I produced it. He scanned it briefly and said, "Never
married, eh? You a pervo-deviant?"

"No, sir."

"Just an ordinary queer?"

"No, sir."

"Scared of girls?"

"Hardly, sir. I'm just not interested in taking on the permanent responsibilities of marriage."

"But you *are* hetero?"

"Mainly, sir," I said, wondering if I had said the wrong thing.

Samuel Hershkowitz tugged at his sideburns. "Our Byzantium Couriers have to be above reproach, you understand. The prevailing climate up that particular line is, well, steamy. You can futz around all you want in the year 2059, but when you're a Courier you need to maintain a sense of perspective. Amen. Sam, you vouch for this kid?"

"I do."

"That's good enough for me. But let's just run a check, to be sure he isn't wanted for a capital crime. We had a sweet, clean-cut kid apply last week, asking to do the Golgotha run, which of course requires real tact and saintliness, and when I looked into him I found he was wanted for causing protoplasmic decay in Indiana. And several other offenses. So, thus. We check." He activated his data outlet, fed in my identification number, and got my dossier on his screen. It must have matched what I had put on my application, because after a quick inspection he blanked it, nodded, keyed in some notations of his own, and opened his desk. He took from it a smooth flat tawny thing that looked like a truss and tossed it to me. "Drop your pants and put this on," he said. "Show him how, Sam."

I pressed the snap and my trousers fell. Sam wrapped the truss around my hips and clasped it in place; it closed seamlessly upon itself as though it had always been one piece. "This," said Sam, "is your timer. It's cued in to the master shunt system, synchronized to pick up the waves of transport impulses as they come forth. As long as you don't let it run out of phlogiston, this little device is capable of moving you to any point in time within the last seven thousand years."

"No earlier?"

"Not with this model. They aren't allowing unrestricted travel to the prehistoric yet, anyway. We've got to open this thing up era by era, with care. Attend to me, now. The operating controls are simplicity itself. Right here, just over your left-hand Fallopian tubes, is a microswitch that controls backward and forward motion. In order to travel, you merely describe a semicircle with your thumb against this pressure point: from hip toward navel to go back in time, from navel toward hip to go forward. On this side is your fine tuning, which takes some training to use. You see the laminated dial—year, month, day, hour, minute? Yes, you've got to squint a little to read it; that can't be helped. The years are calibrated in B.P.—Before Present—and the months are numbered, and so on. The trick lies in being able to make an instant calculation of your destination—843 years B.P., five months, eleven days, and so on—and setting the dials. It's mostly arithmetic, but you'd be surprised how many people can't translate February 11, 1192 into a quantity of years, months, and days ago. Naturally you'll have to master the knack if you're going to be a Courier, but don't worry about that now."

He paused and looked up at Hershkowitz, who said to me, "Sam is now going to give you your preliminary disorientation tests. If you pass, you're in."

Sam strapped on a timer also.

"Ever shunted before?" he asked.

"Never."

"We gonna have some fun, baby." He leered. "I'll set your dial for you. You wait till I give the signal, then use the left-hand switch to turn the timer on. Don't forget to pull your pants back up."

"Before or after I shunt?"

"Before," he said. "You can work the switch through your clothes. It's never a good idea to arrive in the past with your pants around your knees. You can't run fast enough that way. And sometimes you've got to be ready to run the second you get there."

7.

Sam set my dial. I pulled up my pants. He touched his hand lightly to the left-hand side of his abdomen and vanished. I described an arc from my hip to my navel on my own belly with two fingertips. I didn't vanish. Samuel Hershkowitz did.

He went wherever candle flames go when they're snuffed, and in the same instant Sam popped back into view beside me, and the two of us stood looking at each other in Hershkowitz' empty office. "What happened?" I said. "Where is he?"

"It's half-past eleven at night," said Sam. "He doesn't work overtime, you know. We left him two weeks down the line when we made our shunt. We're riding the time-winds now, boy."

"We've gone back two weeks into the past?"

"We've gone two weeks up the line," Sam corrected. "Also half a day, which is why it's nighttime now. Let's go take a walk around the city."

We left the Time Service building and rose to the third level of Under New Orleans. Sam didn't seem to have any special destination in mind. We stopped at a bar for a dozen oysters apiece; we downed a couple of beers; we winked at tourists. Then we reached Under Bourbon Street and I realized suddenly why Sam had chosen to go back to this night, and I felt the tingle of fear in my scrotum and started suddenly to sweat. Sam laughed. "It always gets the new ones right around this point, Jud-baby. This is where most of the washouts wash out."

"I'm going to meet myself!" I cried.

"You're going to *see* yourself," he corrected. "You better take good care not to *meet* yourself, not ever, or it'll be all up for you. The Time Patrol will use you up if you pull any such trick."

"Suppose my earlier self happens to see me, though?"

"Then you've had it. This is a test of your nervous system, man, and you better have the juice turned on. Here we go. You recognize that dumb-looking honky coming up the street?"

"That's Judson Daniel Elliott III."

"Yeah, man! Ever see anything so stupid in your life? Back in the shadows, man. Back in the shadows. White folks there, he ain't smart, but he ain't *blind*."

We huddled in a pool of darkness and I watched, sickbellied, as Judson Daniel Elliott III, fresh off the pod out of Newer York, came wandering up the street toward the sniffer palace on the corner, suitcase in hand. I observed the slight slackness of his posture and the hayseed outturning of his toes as he walked. His ears seemed amazingly large and his right shoulder was a trifle lower than his left. He looked gawky; he looked like a rube. He went past us and paused before the sniffer palace, staring intently at the two nude girls in the tank of cognac. His tongue slid forth and caressed his upper lip. He rocked on the balls of his toes. He rubbed his chin. He was wondering what his chances were of spreading the legs of one or the other of those bare beauties before the night was over. I could have told him that his chances were pretty good.

He entered the sniffer palace.

"How do you feel?" Sam asked me.

"Shaky."

"At least you're honest. It always hits them hard, the first time they go up the line and see themselves. You get used to it, after a while. How does he look to you?"

"Like a clod."

"That's standard too. Be gentle with him. He can't help not knowing all the things you know. He's younger than you are, after all."

Sam laughed softly. I didn't. I was still dazed by the impact of seeing myself come up that street. I felt like my own ghost. Preliminary disorientations, Hershkowitz had said. Yes.

"Don't worry," said Sam. "You're doing fine."

His hand slipped familiarly into the front of my pants and I felt him make a small adjustment on my timer. He did the same to himself. He said, "Let's shunt up the line."

He vanished. I followed him up the line. A blurry half instant later we stood side by side again, on the same street, at the same time of night.

"When are we?" I asked.

"Twenty-four hours previous to your arrival in New Orleans. There's one of you here and one of you in Newer York, getting ready to take the pod south. How does that catch you?"

"Crosswise," I said. "But I'm adapting."

"There's more to come. Let's go home now."

He took me to his flat. There was nobody there, because the Sam of this time slot was at work at the sniffer palace. We went into the bathroom and Sam adjusted my timer again, setting it 31 hours forward. "Shunt," he said, and we went down the line together and came out still in Sam's bathroom, on the next night. I heard the sound of drunken laughter coming from the next room; I heard hoarse gulping cries of lust. Swiftly Sam shut the bathroom door and palmed the seal. I realized that I was in the next room sexing with Betsy or Helen, and I felt fear return.

"Wait here," Sam said crisply, "and don't let anybody in unless he knocks two longs and a short. I'll be right back, maybe."

He went out. I locked the bathroom door after him. Two or three minutes passed. There came two long knocks and a short, and I opened up. Grinning, Sam said, "It's safe to peek. Nobody's in any shape to notice us. Come on."

"Do I have to?"

"If you want to get into the Time Service you do."

We slipped out of the bathroom and went to sightsee the orgy. I had to fight to keep from coughing as the fumes hit my unready nostrils. In Sam's living room I confronted acres of bare writhing flesh. To my left I saw Sam's huge black body pounding against Helen's sleek whiteness; all that was visible of her beneath him was her face, her arms (clasped across his broad back) and one leg (hooked around his butt). To my right I saw my own prior self down on the floor entwined with busty Betsy. We lay in a kamasutroid posture, she on her right hip, I on my left, her upper leg arched over me, my body curved and pivoted at an oblique angle to hers. In a kind of cold terror I watched myself having her. Although I've seen plenty of copulation scenes before, in the tridim shows, on the beaches, occasionally at parties, this was the first time I had ever witnessed myself in the act, and I was shattered by the grotesqueness of it, the idiot gaspings, the contorted features, the sweaty humpings. Betsy made bleating sounds of passion; our thrashing limbs rearranged themselves several times; my clutching fingers dug deep into her meaty buttocks; the mechanical thrustings went on and on and on. And my terror ebbed as I grew accustomed to the sight, and I found a cold clinical detachment stealing over me, and my fear-born perspiration dried and at last I stood there with my arms folded, coolly studying the activities on the floor. Sam smiled and nodded as if to tell me that I had passed a test. He reset my timer once more and we shunted together.

The living room was empty of fornicators and free of fumes. "When are we now?" I asked.

He said, "We're back thirty-one hours and thirty minutes. In a little while now, you and I are going to come walking into the bathroom, but we won't stay around to wait for that. Let's go up on top of the town."

We journeyed uplevel to Old New Orleans, under the starry sky.

The robot who monitors the comings and goings of the eccentrics who like to go outdoors made note of us, and we passed through, into the quiet streets. Here was the real Bourbon Street; here were the crumbling buildings of the authentic French quarter. Spy-eyes mounted on the lacy grillwork balconies watched us, for in this deserted area the innocent are at the mercy of the depraved, and tourists are protected, through constant surveillance, against the marauders who prowl the surface city. We didn't stay long enough to get into trouble, though. Sam looked around, considering things a bit, and positioned us against a building wall. As he adjusted my timer for another shunt, I said, "What happens if we materialize in space that's already occupied by somebody or something?"

"Can't," Sam said. "The automatic buffers cut in and we get kicked back instantly to our starting point. But it wastes energy, and the Time Service doesn't like that, so we always try to find a nonconflicting area before we jump. Up against a building wall is usually pretty good, provided you can be fairly sure that the wall was in the same position at the time you're shunting to."

"When are we going to now?"

"Shunt and see," he said, and jumped. I followed.

The city came to life. People in twentieth-century

clothes strolled the streets: men wearing neckties, women with skirts that came down to their knees, no real flesh showing, not even a nipple. Automobiles crashing along emitting fumes that made me want to vomit. Horns honking. Drills digging up the ground. Noise, stench, ugliness. "Welcome to 1961," Sam said. "John F. Kennedy has just been sworn in as President. The very first Kennedy, dig? That thing up there is a jet airplane. That's a traffic light. It tells when it's safe for you to cross the street. Those up here are street lights. They work by electricity. There are no underlevels. This is the whole thing, the city of New Orleans, right here. How do you like it?"

"It's an interesting place to visit. I wouldn't want to live here."

"You feel dizzy? Sick? Revolted?"

"I'm not sure."

"You're allowed. You always feel a little temporal shock on your first look at the past. It somehow seems smellier and more chaotic than you expect. Some applicants cave in the moment they get into a decently distant shunt up the line."

"I'm not caving."

"Good boy."

I studied the scene, the women with their breasts and rumps encased in tight exoskeletons under their clothing, the men with their strangled, florid faces, the squalling children. Be objective, I told myself. You are a student of other times, other cultures.

Someone pointed at us and screamed, "Hey, looka the beatniks!"

"Onward," Sam said. "They've noticed us."

He adjusted my timer. We jumped.

Same city. A century earlier. Same buildings, genteel and timeless in their pastels. No traffic lights, no drills, no street lights. Instead of automobiles zooming along the streets that bordered the old quarter, there were buggies.

"We can't stay," said Sam. "It's 1858. Our clothes are

too weird, and I don't feel like pretending I'm a slave. Onward."

We shunted.

The city vanished. We stood in a kind of swamp. Mists rose in the south. Spanish moss clung to graceful trees. A flight of birds darkened the sky.

"The year is 1382," said the guru. "Those are passenger pigeons overhead. Columbus' grandfather is still a virgin."

Back and back we hopped. 897. 441. 97. Very little changed. A couple of naked Indians wandered by at one point. Sam bowed in a courteous way. They nodded affably to us, scratched their genitals, and sauntered on. Visitors from the future did not excite them greatly. We shunted. "This is the year A.D. 1," said Sam. We shunted. "We have gone back an additional twelve months and are now in 1 B.C. The possibilities for arithmetical confusion are great. But if you think of the year as 2059 B.P., and the coming year as 2058 B.P., you won't get into any trouble."

He took me back to 5800 B.P. I observed minor changes in climate; things were drier at some points than at others, drier and cooler. Then we came forward, hopping in easy stages, five hundred years at a time. He apologized for the unvarying nature of the environment; things are more exciting, he promised me, when you go up the line in the Old World. We reached 2058 and made our way to the Time Service building. Entering Hershkowitz' empty office, we halted for a moment while Sam made a final adjustment on our timers.

"This has to be done carefully," he explained. "I want us to land in Hershkowitz' office thirty seconds after we left it. If I'm off even a little, we'll meet our departing selves and I'll be in real trouble."

"Why not play it safe and set the dial to bring us back five minutes later, then?"

"Professional pride," Sam said.

We shunted down the line from an empty Hershkowitz office to one in which Hershkowitz sat behind his desk, peering forward at the place where we had been—for him —thirty seconds earlier.

"Well?" he said.

Sam beamed. "The kid has balls. I say hire him."

8.

And so they took me on as a novice Time Serviceman, in the Time Courier division. The pay wasn't bad; the opportunities were limitless. First, though, I had to undergo my training. They don't let novices schlep tourists around the past just like that.

For a week nothing much happened. Sam went back to work at the sniffer palace and I lounged around. Then I was called down to the Time Service headquarters to begin taking instruction.

There were eight in my class, all of us novices. We made a pretty disreputable crew. In age we ranged from early twenties to—I think—late seventies; in sex we ranged from male to female with every possible gradation between; in mental outlook we were all something on the rapacious side. Our instructor, Najeeb Dajani, wasn't much better. He was a Syrian whose family had converted to Judaism after the Israeli conquest, for business reasons, and he wore a glittering, conspicuous Star of David as an insignia of his faith; but in moments of abstraction or stress he was known to evoke Allah or swear by the Prophet's beard, and I don't know if I'd really trust him on the board of directors of my synagogue, if I had a synagogue. Dajani looked like a stage Arab, swarthy and sinister, with dark sunglasses at all times, an array of massive gold rings on twelve or thirteen of his fingers, and a quick, amiable smile that showed several rows of very white teeth. I later found out that he had been taken off the lucrative Crucifixion run and demoted to this instructorship for a period of six months, by orders of the Time Patrol, by way of punishment. It seems he had been conducting a side business in fragments of the True Cross, peddling them all up and down the time lines. The rules don't allow a Courier to take advantage of his position for private profit. What the Patrol especially objected to was not that Dajani was selling fake relics, but that he was selling authentic ones.

We began with a history lesson.

"Commercial time-travel," Dajani said, "has been functioning about twenty years now. Of course, research into the Benchley Effect began toward the end of the last century, but you understand that the government could not permit private citizens to venture into temponautics until it was ruled to be perfectly safe. In this way the government benevolently oversees the welfare of all."

Dajani emitted a broad wink, visible through the dark glasses as a corrugation of his brow.

Miss Dalessandro in the front row belched in contempt.

"You disagree?" Dajani asked.

Miss Dalessandro, who was a plump but curiously small-breasted woman with black hair, distinct Sapphic urges, and a degree in the history of the industrial revolution, began to reply, but Dajani smoothly cut her off and continued, "The Time Service, in one of whose divisions you have enrolled, performs several important functions. To us is entrusted the care and maintenance of all Benchley Effect devices. Also, our research division constantly endeavors to improve the technological substructure of time transport, and in fact the timer now in use was introduced only four years ago. To our own division —the Time Couriers—is assigned the task of escorting citizens into the past." He folded his hands complacently over his paunch and studied the interlocking patterns of his gold rings. "Much of our activity is concerned with the tourist trade. This provides our economic basis. For large fees, we take groups of eight or ten sightseers on carefully conducted trips to the past, usually accompanied by one Courier, although two may be sent in unusually complex situations. At any given moment in now-time, there may be a hundred thousand tourists scattered over the previous millennia, observing the Crucifixion, the signing of the Magna Carta, the assassination of Lincoln, and such events. Because of the paradoxes inherent in creating a cumulative audience for an event located at a fixed position in the time stream, we are faced with an increasingly difficult task, and limit our tours accordingly."

"Would you explain that, sir?" said Miss Dalessandro.

"At a later meeting," Dajani replied. He went on, "Naturally, we must not confine time travel exclusively to tourists. Historians must have access to all significant events of the past, since it is necessary to revise all existing views of history in the light of the revelation of the real story. We set aside out of the profits of our tourist business a certain number of scholarships for qualified historians, enabling them to visit periods of their research without cost. These tours, too, are conducted by Courier. However, you will not be concerned with this aspect of our work. We anticipate assigning all of you who qualify as Couriers to the tourist division.

"The other division of the Time Service is the Time Patrol, whose task it is to prevent abuses of Benchley Effect devices and to guard against the emergence of paradoxes. At our next lesson we will consider in detail the nature of these paradoxes and how they may be avoided. Dismissed."

We had a small social session after Dajani left the room. Miss Dalessandro, moving in a determined whirl of hairy armpits, closed in on blonde, delicate Miss Chambers, who promptly fled toward Mr. Chudnik, a brawny, towering gentleman with the vaguely noble look of a Roman bronze. Mr. Chudnik, however, was in the process of trying to reach an accommodation with Mr. Burlingame, a dapper young man who could not possibly have been as homosexual as he looked and acted. And so, seeking some other shelter from the predatory Miss Dalessandro, Miss Chambers turned to me and invited me to take her home. I accepted. It developed that Miss Chambers was a student of later Roman imperial history, which meant that her field of interest dovetailed with mine. We sexed in a perfunctory and mechanical way, since she was not really very interested in sex but was just doing it out of politeness, and then we talked about the conversion of Constantine to Christianity until the early hours of the morning. I think she fell in love with me. I gave her no encouragement, though, and it didn't last. I admired her scholarship but her pale little body was quite a bore.

9.

At our next lesson we considered in detail the nature of the time-travel paradoxes and how they may be avoided.

"Our greatest challenge," Dajani began, "lies in maintaining the sanctity of now-time. The development of Benchley Effect devices has opened a Pandora's Box of

potential paradoxes. No longer is the past a fixed quantity, since we are free now to travel up the line to any
given point and alter the so-called 'real' events. The results of such alteration would of course be catastrophic,
creating a widening vector of disruption that, by the time
it had reached our own era, might transform every aspect
of society." Dajani yawned politely. "Consider, if you
will, the consequences of permitting a time-traveler to
journey to the year 600 and assassinate the youthful Mohammed. The whole dynamic movement of Islam will
thus be arrested at its starting point; there will be no
Arab conquest of the Near East and southern Europe; the
Crusades will not have taken place; millions who died as
a result of the Islamic invasions will now not have died,
and numerous lines of progeny that would not otherwise
have existed at all will come into being, with incalculable
effects. All this stems simply from the slaying of a certain
young merchant of Mecca. And therefore—"

"Perhaps," suggested Miss Dalessandro, "there's a Law
of Conservation of History which would provide that if
Mohammed didn't happen, some other charismatic Arab
would arise and play precisely the same role?"

Dajani glowered at her.

"We do not care to risk it," he said. "We prefer to see
to it that all 'past' events, as recorded in the annals of history as compiled prior to the era of time-travel, go untouched. For the past fifty years of now-time the entire
previous span of history, thought to be fixed, has been
potentially fluid; yet we struggle to keep it fixed. Thus we
employ the Time Patrol to make certain that everything
will happen in the past exactly as it *did* happen, no matter how unfortunate an event it might be. Disasters, assassinations, tragedies of all kinds must occur on schedule,
for otherwise the future—our now-time—may be irrepar-
ably changed."

Miss Chambers said, "But isn't the very fact of our
presence in the past a changing of the past?"

"I was about to reach that point," said Dajani, displeased. "If we assume that the past and present form a single continuum, then obviously visitors from the twenty-first century *were* present at all the great events of the past, unobtrusively enough so that no mention of them found its way into the annals of the fixed-time era. So we take great care to camouflage everyone who goes up the line in the costume of the time being visited. One must watch the past without meddling, as a silent bystander, as inconspicuous as possible. This is a rule that the Time Patrol enforces with absolute inflexibility. I will discuss the nature of that enforcement shortly.

"I spoke the other day of cumulative audience paradox. This is a severe philosophical problem which has not yet been resolved, and which I will present to you now purely as a theoretical exercise, to give you some insight into the complexities of our undertaking. Consider this: the first time-traveler to go up the line to view the Crucifixion of Jesus was the experimentalist Barney Navarre, in 2012. Over the succeeding two decades, another fifteen or twenty experimentalists made the same journey. Since the commencement of commercial excursions to Golgotha in 2041, approximately one tourist group a month—or 100 tourists a year—has viewed the scene. Thus about 1800 individuals of the twenty-first century, so far, have observed the Crucifixion. Now, then: each of these groups is leaving from a different month, but *every one of them is converging on the same day!* If tourists continue to go up the line at a rate of 100 a year to see the Crucifixion, the crowd at Golgotha will consist of at least 10,000 time-travelers by the middle of the twenty-second century, and—assuming no increase in the permissible tourist trade—by the early thirtieth century, some 100,000 time-travelers will have made the trip, all of them necessarily congregating simultaneously at the site of the Passion. Yet obviously no such crowds are present there now, only a few thousand Palestinians—when I say 'now,' I mean of course the time of the Crucifixion relative to now-time 2059—and just as obviously those crowds will continue to grow in the centuries of now-time. Taken to its ultimate, the cumulative audience paradox yields us the picture of an audience of billions of time-travelers piled up in the past to witness the Crucifixion, filling all the Holy Land and spreading out into Turkey, into Arabia, even to India and Iran. Similarly for every other significant event in human history: as commercial time-travel progresses, it must inevitably smother every event in a horde of spectators, yet at the original occurrence of those events, *no such hordes were present!* How is this paradox to be resolved?"

Miss Dalessandro had no suggestions. For once, she was stumped. So were the rest of us. So was Dajani. So are the finest minds of our era.

Meanwhile, the past fills up with time-traveling sightseers.

Dajani tossed one final twister at us before he let us go. "I may add," he said, "that I myself, as a Courier, have done the Crucifixion run twenty-two times, with twenty-two different groups. If you were to attend the Crucifixion yourselves tomorrow, you would find twenty-two Najeeb Dajanis at the hill of Golgotha simultaneously, each of me occupying a different position at the event explaining the happening to my clients. Is this multiplication of Dajanis not a fascinating thing to consider? Why are there not twenty-two Dajanis at loose in now-time? It stretches the intellect to revolve such thoughts. Dismissed, dear ladies and gentlemen, dismissed."

10.

I was troubled about those twenty-one extra Dajanis, but the smart alecks in the class quickly figured out why they hadn't all jammed up together here in now-time. It had to do with the fundamental limitations of the Benchley Effect in achieving down-the-line, or forward, travel.

My classmate Mr. Burlingame explained it all to me after class. It was his quaint way of trying to seduce me. He didn't score, but I learned a little time theory.

When you go down the line, he told me, you can come forward only as far as you had previously jumped up the line, *plus* the amount of absolute time elapsed during your stay up the line. That is, if you jump from March 20, 2059, say, to the spring of 1801, and spend three months in 1801, you can come forward again as far as June 20, 2059. But you can't jump down the line to August, 2059, nor can you jump to 2159 or 20590.

There is no way at all to get into your own future.

I don't know why this is so. Mr. Burlingame placed his pale palm on my knee and gave me the theoretical substructure for it, but I was too busy fending him off to follow it.

In fact, although Dajani later spent three sessions simply instructing us on the mechanics of the Benchley Effect, I still can't say for sure how the whole thing works, or why, or even if. At times I suspect I've dreamed it all.

Anyway, there aren't twenty-two Dajanis in now-time

because whenever Dajani made the Crucifixion run, he always jumped back to now-time at a point somewhat prior to his next departure for the past. He couldn't help himself about that; if you go up the line in January, spend a couple of weeks in an earlier era, and come back, you've got to land in January or maybe February of the year you started from. And if your next jump isn't scheduled until March, there's no way you can overlap yourself.

So the Dajani who escorted tourists to Golgotha was always the "same" one, from the point of view of people in now-time. At the other end of the jump, though, a couple dozen Dajanis have been piling up, since he keeps jumping from different points in now-time to the same point in then-time. The same happens to anybody who makes repeated jumps to one spot up the line. This is the Paradox of Temporal Accumulation. You can have it.

When not wrestling with such paradoxes I passed my time pleasantly in pleasure, as usual. There were always plenty of willing girls hanging around Sam's place.

In those days I chased crotch quite a bit. Obsessively, even. The pursuit of cunt occupied all my idle hours; it seemed a night wasted if I hadn't slid down that slippery slope at least once. It never occurred to me that it might be worthwhile for me to seek a relationship with a member of the opposite sex that was more than six inches deep. What they call "love."

Shallow, callow youth that I was, I wasn't interested in "love."

On the other hand, maybe I wasn't so shallow. For now I've tried "love" and I don't see where I'm the happier for it. I'm a lot worse off than before, as a matter of fact.

Of course, nobody told me to fall in love with someone who lived up the line.

11.

Lieutenant Bruce Sanderson of the Time Patrol came to our class one day to explain to us the perils of daring to meddle with the fixity of past time.

The lieutenant looked his part. He was the tallest man I had ever seen, with the widest shoulders and the squarest jaw. Most of the girls in the class had instant orgasms when he entered, as did Mr. Chudnik and Mr. Burlingame. He took a spread-legged stance, back to the wall, ready for trouble. His uniform was gray. His hair was red and cut very short. His eyes were a soulless blue.

Dajani, himself guilty of transgressing, himself a victim of the Time Patrol's diligence, slithered into a corner of the classroom and yielded the floor. I saw him peering balefully at the lieutenant through his dark glasses.

"Now then," Lieutenant Sanderson said, "you know that our big job involves maintaining the sanctity of now-time. We can't let all kinds of random changes get introduced into our past, because that'll mess up our present. So we have a Time Patrol that monitors the whole territory up the line and makes sure that everything happens according to the books. And I want to say, God bless the men who legislated the Time Patrol into existence."

"Amen," said the penitent Dajani.

"Mind you, it isn't that I'm thankful for the job I have," the lieutenant continued. "Although I am, because I think it's the most important job a human being can have, preserving the sanctity of his now-time. But when I say God bless the men who said we had to have a Time Patrol, it's because those men are responsible for saving everything that is true and good and precious about our existence. Do you know what might have happened without a Time Patrol? What sort of things unscrupulous villains might have done? Let me give you a few examples.

"Such as going back and killing Jesus, Mohammed, Buddha, all our great religious leaders, when they were still children and hadn't had time to formulate their wonderful and inspiring ideas.

"Such as warning the great villains of our history of trouble in store for them, and thus allowing them to cheat destiny and continue doing harm to humanity.

"Such as stealing the art treasures of the past and preventing millions of people over many centuries from enjoying them.

"Such as engaging in fraudulent financial operations resulting in the bankrupting of millions of innocent investors who happened not to have information on future stock prices.

"Such as giving false advice to great rulers and leading them into terrible traps.

"I mention all these examples, my friends, because they are things that have *actually happened*. They all come from the files of the Time Patrol, believe it or not! In April, 2052, a young man from Bucharest used an illegally obtained timer to shunt up the line to A.D. 11 and poison Jesus Christ. In October, 2043, a citizen of Berlin traveled back to the year 1945 and rescued Adolf Hitler just before the Russians entered the city. In August, 2049, a woman from Nice jumped to the era of Leonardo da Vinci, stole the unfinished *Mona Lisa,* and hid it in her beach cabaña. In September, 2055, a New York man journeyed to the summer of 1929 and netted close to a billion dollars by selling stock short. In January, 2051, a professor of military history from Quebec journeyed to

1815 and, by marketing to the British what purported to be the French strategic program, caused the defeat of the Duke of Wellington by the forces of Napoleon at the Battle of Waterloo. And therefore—"

"Wait a second!" I heard myself say. "Napoleon *didn't* win at Waterloo. Christ *wasn't* poisoned in A.D. 11. If the past was really changed as you just said, how come no effects of it have been felt in now-time?"

"Aha!" cried Lieutenant Sanderson. He was the best crier of *"Aha!"* I have ever heard. "The fluidity of the past, my friend, is a double-edged blade. If the past can be changed once, it can be changed many times. Now we come to the role of the Time Patrol.

"Let us consider the case of the deranged person who assassinated the young Jesus. As a result of this shocking deed, Christianity did not emerge, and much of the Roman Empire was ultimately converted to Judaism. The Jewish leaders of Rome were able to steer the empire away from its collapse of the fourth and fifth centuries A.D., turning it into a monolithic theocratic state that controlled all of western Europe. However, the Byzantine Empire did not develop in the East, which instead was ruled from Jerusalem by a schismatic Hebrew sect. In the tenth century a cataclysmic war between the forces of Rome and those of Jerusalem resulted in the annihilation of civilization and in the takeover of all of Europe and Asia by Turkish nomads, who proceeded to construct a totalitarian state that, by the twenty-first century, had become the most repressive in human history.

"You can see from this how devastating it can be to meddle with the past."

"Yes," I said, "but—"

Lieutenant Sanderson gave me a frigid smile. "You are about to observe that we do not, in fact, live under a repressive Turkish tyranny. I agree. Our present pattern of existence was saved by the following procedure:

"The murder of the young Jesus was detected by a

Time Courier who went up the line late in April, 2052, escorting a party of tourists to witness the Crucifixion. When the group arrived at the time and place of the Crucifixion, they found two thieves undergoing execution; no one, however, had heard of Jesus of Nazareth. The Courier instantly notified the Time Patrol, which began a paradox search. Jesus' time line was followed from birth through boyhood and was seen to be unchanged; but no trace of him could be found after mid-adolescence, and inquiry in the neighborhood finally turned up the information that he had died suddenly and mysteriously in the year 11. It was a simple matter then to maintain surveillance until we observed the arrival of the illegal time-traveler.

"What do you think we did then?"

Hands went up. Lieutenant Sanderson recognized Mr. Chudnik, who said, "You arrested the criminal five minutes before he could give the poison to Jesus, thus preventing the changing of history, and took him back down the line for trial."

Lieutenant Sanderson smiled genially. "Wrong," he said. "We let him give the poison to Jesus."

Uproar.

The Time Patrol man said benignly, "As you surely know, the maximum penalty for unauthorized interference in past events is death—the only capital offense now recognized in law. But before so severe a penalty can be invoked, absolute proof of the crime is necessary. Therefore, whenever a crime of this kind is detected, Time Patrolmen allow it to proceed and surreptitiously make a full record of it."

"But how," Miss Dalessandro demanded, "does the past get unchanged that way?"

"Aha!" cried Lieutenant Sanderson. "Once we have a proper record of the commission of the crime, we can obtain a quick conviction and secure permission to carry out sentence. This was done. The Time Patrol investigators returned with their evidence to the night of April 4, 2052. This was the date of the departure up the line of the would-be murderer of Jesus. They presented their proof of the crime to the Time Patrol commissioners, who ordered the execution of the criminal. Time Patrol executioners were dispatched to the home of the criminal, seized his timer, and painlessly put him to death an hour before his intended trip into the past. Thus he was erased from the time-stream and the main current of the past was preserved, for in fact he did not make his trip and Jesus lived on to preach his creed. In this way—through detection of unlawful changes and eradication of the changers in advance of their departure up the line—we preserve the sanctity of now-time."

How beautiful, I thought.

I'm too easily satisfied. Miss Dalessandro, that archtroublemaker, put up her fleshy hand, and when called on, said, "I'd like one clarification, though. Presumably when your Time Patrolmen returned to April, 2052, with the evidence of the crime, they were returning to a changed world run by Turkish dictators. Where would they find Time Patrol commissioners? Where would they even find the murderer? He might have ceased to exist as a consequence of his own crime, because by murdering Jesus he set in motion some train of events that eliminated his own ancestors. For that matter, maybe timetravel itself was never invented in that world where Jesus didn't live, and so the moment Jesus was killed all Time Patrolmen and Time Couriers and tourists would become impossibilities, and cease to exist."

Lieutenant Sanderson did not look pleased.

"You bring up," he said slowly, "a number of interesting subsidiary paradoxes. I'm afraid that the time at my disposal isn't sufficient to deal with them properly. Briefly, though: if the timecrime of 11 A.D. had not been detected relatively quickly, the focus of change would indeed have widened over the centuries and eventually

transformed the entire future, possibly preventing the
emergence of the Benchley Effect and the Time Patrol itself, leading to what we call the Ultimate Paradox, in
which time-travel becomes its own negation. In fact,
though, the vast potential consequences of the poisoning
of Jesus never occurred because of the detection of the
crime by the Time Courier visiting the Crucifixion. Since
that event took place in A.D. 33, only the years 11 to 33
were ever affected by the timecrime, and the changes
created by the absence of Jesus from those years were insignificant, because Jesus' influence on history emerged
only long after the Crucifixion. Meanwhile the retroactive
deletion of the timecrime canceled even the slight changes
that had taken place in the 22-year period affected; those
two decades were pinched off into another track of time,
inaccessible to us and in effect nonexistent, and the basic
and authentic track was restored in full continuity from
A.D. 11 to the present."

Miss Dalessandro wasn't satisfied. "There's something
circular here. Shouldn't the Ultimate Paradox have occurred all the way down the line, the instant Jesus was
poisoned? How did any of the Couriers and Patrolmen
manage to continue to exist, let alone to remember how
the past *should* have gone? It seems to me that there
ought not to be any way of correcting a timecrime sweep-
ing enough to bring on the Ultimate Paradox."

"You forget, or perhaps you don't yet know," said Sanderson, "that time-travelers currently up the line at the
moment of a timecrime are unaffected by *any* change in
the past, since they're detached from their time matrices.
A time-traveler in transit is a drifting bubble of now-time
ripped loose from the matrix of the continuum, immune
to the transformations of paradox. This means that anyone currently up the line may observe and correct an alteration of the true past, and will continue to retain
memories both of the temporary false condition and of
his role in correcting it. Of course, any time-traveler leav-

ing the sanctuary of the transit state is vulnerable once he comes back to his starting point down the line. That is, if you go up the line and kill your grandfather before his marriage, you won't instantaneously wink out of existence, since you're shielded from paradox by the Benchley Effect. But the moment you return to the present you will cease *ever to have existed,* since as a result of your alteration of your own past you no longer have a time-link to the present. Clear?"

No, I thought. But I kept quiet.

Miss Dalessandro pressed onward. "Those in transit are protected by—"

"The Paradox of Transit Displacement, we call it."

"The Paradox of Transit Displacement. They're encapsulated, and as they travel they're free to compare what they see with what they remember true time to have been like, and if necessary they can make changes to restore the true order if it's been changed."

"Yes."

"Why? Why *should* they be immune? I know I keep coming back to this point, but—"

Lieutenant Sanderson sighed. "Because," he said, "if they were affected by a past-change while they were in the past themselves, this would be the Ultimate Paradox: a time-traveler changing the era that produced time-travel. This is even more paradoxical than the Paradox of Transit Displacement. By the Law of Lesser Paradoxes, the Paradox of Transit Displacement, being less improbable, holds precedence. Do you see?"

"No, but—"

"I'm afraid I can't dwell on this in greater detail," said the Patrolman. "However, no doubt Mr. Dajani will go into these matters at later instruction sessions."

He gave Dajani a sickly smile and excused himself fast.

Dajani, you can bet on it, didn't deal with Miss Dalessandro's paradoxes properly, or at all. He found cunning ways to sidetrack her every time she brought up the issue.

"You can be sure," he said, "that the past *is* restored whenever it is changed. The hypothetical worlds created by unlawful change cease retroactively to exist the moment the changer is apprehended. Q.E.D."

That didn't explain a damned thing. But it was the best explanation we ever got.

12.

One thing they made clear to us was that *good* changes in the past are also forbidden. Dozens of people have been eliminated for trying to persuade Abe Lincoln to stay home from the theater that night, or for trying to tell Jack Kennedy that he should for God's sake put the bulletproof bubble on his car.

They get wiped out, just like the murderers of Jesus and the rescuers of Hitler. Because it's just as deadly to the fabric of now-time to help Kennedy serve out his term as it would be to help Hitler rebuild the Third Reich. Change is change, and even the virtuous changes can have unpredictably catastrophic results. "Just imagine," said Dajani, "that because Kennedy was not assassinated in 1963, the escalation of the Vietnamese War that in fact did take place under his successor did not occur, and so the lives of thousands of servicemen were spared. Suppose now that one of those men, who otherwise would have died in 1965 or 1966, remained alive, became President of the United States in 1992, and embarked on an atomic war that brought about the destruction of civilization. You see why even supposedly beneficial alterations of the past must be prevented?"

We saw. We saw it over and over again.

We saw it until we were scared toothless of going into the Time Service, because it seemed inevitable that we would sooner or later do something up the line that would bring down on us the fatal wrath of the Time Patrol.

"Don't worry about it," Sam said. "The way they talk, the death penalty is inflicted a million times a day. Actually I don't think there have been fifty executions for timecrime in the past ten years. And all of those were real nuts, the kind whose mission it is to murder Mohammed."

"Then how does the Patrol keep the past from being changed?"

"They don't," said Sam. "It gets changed all the time. Despite the Time Patrol."

"Why doesn't our world change?"

"It does. In little ways." Sam laughed. "If a Time Courier gives Alexander the Great antibiotics and helps him live to a ripe old age, that would be an intolerable change, and the Time Patrol would prevent it. But a lot of other stuff goes on all the time. Couriers recovering lost manuscripts, sleeping with Catherine the Great, collecting artifacts for resale in other eras. Your man Dajani was peddling the True Cross, wasn't he? They found out about him, but they didn't execute him. They just suspended him from his profitable run for a while and stuck him in a classroom. Most of the petty tinkering never even gets discovered." He let his glance rove meaningfully over his collection of artifacts from the past. "As you get into this business, Jud, you'll find out that we're in constant intersection with past events. Every time a Time Courier steps on an ant in 2000 B.C., he's changing the past. Somehow we survive. The dumb bastards in the Time Patrol watch out for structural changes in history, but they leave the little crap alone. They have to. There aren't enough Patrolmen to handle everything."

"But that means," I said, "that we're building up a lot of tiny alterations in history, bit by bit, an ant here and a butterfly there, and the accumulation may someday cause a major change, and nobody will then be able to trace all the causes and put things back the way they ought to be!"

"Exactly."

"You don't sound worried about it," I said.

"Why should I be? Do I own the world? Do I give a damn if history gets changed?"

"You would if the change involved seeing to it that you had never existed."

"There are bigger things to worry about, Jud. Like having a good time from day to day."

"Doesn't it scare you that someday you might just pop out of existence?"

"Someday I will," Sam said. "No maybes about it. If not sooner, then later. Meanwhile I enjoy myself. Eat, drink, and be merry, kid. Let the yesterdays fall where they will."

13.

When they were finished hammering the rules into our heads, they sent us on trial runs up the line. All of us had already been into the past, of course, before beginning the instruction sessions; they had tested us to see if we had any psychological hangups about time-traveling. Now they wanted us to observe Couriers in actual service, and so they let us go along as hitchhikers with tour groups.

They split us up, so there wouldn't be more than two of us to each six or eight tourists. To save expense, they assigned us all to visit events right in New Orleans. (In order to shoot us back to the Battle of Hastings, say, they would have had to fly us to London first. Time-travel doesn't include space travel; you have to be physically present in the place you want to reach, before you jump.)

New Orleans is a fine city, but it hasn't had all that many important events in its history, and I'm not sure why anybody would want to pay *very* good money to go up the line there when for about the same fee he could witness the signing of the Declaration of Independence, the fall of Constantinople, or the assassination of Julius Caesar. But the Time Service is willing to provide transport to any major historical event whatever—within certain limits of taste, I mean—for any group of at least eight tourists who have the stash for tickets, and I suppose the patriotic residents of New Orleans have every right to sightsee their city's own past, if they prefer.

So Mr. Chudnik and Miss Dalessandro were shipped to 1815 to cheer for Andrew Jackson at the Battle of New Orleans. Mr. Burlingame and Mr. Oliveira were transported to 1877 to watch the last of the carpetbaggers thrown out. Mr. Hotchkiss and Mrs. Notabene went off to 1803 to see the United States take possession of Louisiana after buying it from the French. And Miss Chambers and I went up the line to 1935 to view the assassination of Huey Long.

Assassinations are usually over in a hurry, and nobody goes up the line just to watch a quick burst of gunfire. What the Time Service was really offering these people was a five-day tour of Louisiana in the early twentieth century, with the gunning down of the Kingfish as its climax. We had six fellow travelers: three well-to-do Louisiana couples in their late fifties and early sixties. One of the men was a lawyer, one a doctor, one a big executive of Louisiana Power & Light Company. Our Time Courier was the right sort to shepherd these pillars of the establishment around: a sleek, bland character named Madison Jefferson Monroe. "Call me Jeff," he invited.

We had several orientation meetings before we went anywhere.

"These are your timers," said Jeff Monroe. "You keep them next to your skin at all times. Once you put them on in Time Service headquarters, you don't remove them again until you come back down the line. You bathe with them, sleep with them, perform—ah—all intimate functions while wearing them. The reason for this should be obvious. It would be highly disruptive to history if a timer were to fall into the hands of a twentieth-century person; therefore we don't allow the devices out of your physical possession even for an instant."

("He's lying," Sam told me when I repeated this to him. "Somebody up the line wouldn't know what the hell to do with a timer. The real reason is that sometimes the tourists have to get out of an area in a hurry, maybe to avoid being lynched, and the Courier can't take the risk that some of his people may have left their timers in the hotel room. But he doesn't dare tell them that.")

The timers that Jeff Monroe distributed were a little different from the one I had worn the night Sam and I went jumping up the line. The controls were sealed, and functioned only when the Courier sounded a master frequency. Sensible enough: the Time Service doesn't want tourists slipping away for time-jaunts on their own.

Our Courier spelled out at great length the consequences of changing the past, and begged us repetitiously not to rock any boats. "Don't speak unless spoken to," he said, "and even then confine any conversations with strangers to a minimum of words. Don't use slang; it won't be comprehensible. You may recognize other time-tourists; under no condition are you to speak to them or greet them in any way, and you should ignore any attention you may get from them. Anyone who breaks these regulations, no matter how innocently, may have his shunting permit revoked on the spot and may be returned at once to now-time. Understood?"

We nodded solemnly.

Jeff Monroe added, "Think of yourselves as Christians in disguise who have been smuggled into the holy Moslem city of Mecca. You're in no danger so long as you're not discovered; but if those about you find out what you are, you're in big trouble. Therefore it's to your advantage to keep your mouths shut while you're up the line, to do a lot of seeing and a minimum of saying. You'll be all right as long as you don't call attention to yourselves."

(I learned from Sam that time-tourists very frequently get themselves into muddles with people living up the line, no matter how hard their Couriers try to avoid such incidents. Sometimes the trouble can be patched up with a few diplomatic words, often when the Courier explains apologetically to the offended party that the stranger is really a mental case. Sometimes it's not so easy, and the Courier has to order a quick evacuation of all the tourists; the Courier must remain behind until he has sent all his people safely down the line, and there have been several fatalities to Couriers in the line of duty as a result. In extreme cases of tourist bungling, the Time Patrol steps in and cancels the jump retroactively, plucking the careless traveler from the tour and thereby undoing the damage. Sam said, "It can really get one of these rich bastards furious when a Patrolman shows up at the last minute and tells him that he can't make the shunt, because if he does he'll commit some ferocious faux pas up the line. They just can't understand it. They promise to be good, and won't believe that their promise is worthless because their conduct is already a matter of record. The trouble with most of the dumb tourists is that they can't think four-dimensionally." "Neither can I, Sam," I said, baffled. "You will. You'd better," said Sam.)

Before we set out for 1935 we were given a quick hypnocourse in the social background of the era. Pumped into us were data on the Depression, the New Deal, the Long family of Louisiana, Huey Long's rise to fame, his "Share Our Wealth" program of taking from the rich and giving to the poor, his feud with President Franklin Roosevelt, his dream of taking the Presidency himself in 1936, his flamboyant disregard for traditions, his demagogic appeal to the masses. We also got enough incidental details on life in 1935—celebrities, sports developments, the stock market—so we wouldn't feel hopelessly out of context there.

Lastly, they fitted us out in 1935 wardrobes. We strutted around giggling and quipping at the sight of ourselves in those quaint rigs. Jeff Monroe, checking us out, reminded the men about zipper flies and how to use them, reminded the women that it was sternly prohibited to reveal the breasts from the nipple down, and urged us strenuously to keep in mind at all times that we were entering a staunchly puritanical era where neurotic repression was regarded as a virtue and our normal freedoms of behavior were looked upon as sinful and shameless.

Finally, we were ready.

They took us uplevel to Old New Orleans, since it wouldn't have been healthy to make our jump from one of the underlevels. They had set up a room in a boardinghouse on North Rampart Street for shunting to the twentieth century.

"Here we go up the line," said Madison Jefferson Monroe, and gave the signal that activated our timers.

14.

Suddenly, it was 1935.

We didn't notice any changes in the dingy room we were in, but yet we knew we were up the line.

We wore tight shoes and funny clothes, and we carried real cash money, United States dollars, because our thumbprints weren't legal tender here. The advance man of the tour had booked us into a big New Orleans hotel on Canal just at the edge of the old French quarter, for the first part of our stay, and after Jeff Monroe had given us a final warning to be circumspect, we went out and walked around the corner to it.

The automobile traffic was fantastic for this supposedly "depressed" year. So was the din. We strolled along, two by two, Jeff leading the way. We stared at things a lot, but no one would get suspicious about that. The locals would simply guess that we were tourists just down from Indiana. Nothing about our curiosity marked us particularly as tourists just down from 2059.

Thibodeaux, the power company man, couldn't get over the sight of power lines right out in the open, dangling from post to post. "I've read about such things," he said several times, "but I never really believed them!"

The womenfolk clucked a lot about the fashions. It was a hot, sticky September day and yet everybody was all covered up. They couldn't understand that.

The weather gave us trouble. We had never been exposed to real humidity before; there isn't any in the undercities, of course, and only a lunatic goes up to surface level when the climate is sour. So we sweated and labored.

There wasn't any air-conditioning in the hotel, either. I think it may not have been invented yet.

Jeff checked us all in at the hotel. When he was through signing the register, the desk clerk, who of course was human and not a computer terminal, banged a bell and yelled, "Front!" and a platoon of friendly black bellhops came over to get our luggage.

I overheard Mrs. Bienvenu, the lawyer's wife, whisper to her husband, "Do you think they're slaves?"

"Not here!" he said fiercely. "The slaves were freed seventy years ago!"

The desk clerk must have overheard that. I wonder what he made of it.

The Courier had booked Flora Chambers and me into one room. He explained that he had registered us as Mr. and Mrs. Elliott, because it wasn't permissible to let an unmarried couple share the same hotel room even if they were part of the same tour party. Flora gave me a pale but hopeful smile and said, "We'll pretend we're on a temporary."

Monroe glared at her. "We don't talk about down-the-line customs here!"

"They don't have temporary liaisons in 1935?"

"Shut *up!*" he hissed.

We unpacked and bathed and went out to see the town. We did Basin Street and heard some respectable primitive jazz. Then we walked a few blocks over to Bourbon Street for drinks and a strip-tease. The place was full; and it amazed us all that grown men and women would sit around for a full hour, enduring a lot of indifferent music and polluted atmosphere, simply to wait for a girl to come out and take off some of her clothes.

When she got undressed, finally, she kept little shiny caps on her nipples and a triangular patch of cloth over her pubic region, too. Anybody who has a serious interest in nudity can see more than that any day at a public bathhouse. But of course this was a repressive, sexually strangled era, we reminded ourselves.

Our drinks and other nightclub charges were all put on one bill, which Jeff Monroe always paid. The Time Service didn't want us ignorant tourists handling unfamiliar currencies except when absolutely necessary. The Courier also deftly fended off drunks who kept invading our group, beggars, soliciting prostitutes, and other challenges to our ability to handle the social situations 1935 presented.

"It's hard work," Flora Chambers observed, "being a Courier."

"But think of all the free traveling you get to do," I said.

We were profoundly awed by the ugliness of the people up the line. We realized that there were no helix parlors here, that cosmetic microsurgery was unknown, and that esthetic genetics, if it had been heard of at all in 1935, would have been regarded as a Fascist or Communist conspiracy against the right of free men to have ugly children. Nevertheless, we couldn't help registering surprise and dismay at the mismatched ears, the pockmarked skins, the distorted teeth, the bulging noses, of these unprogrammed and unedited people. The plainest member of our group was a theatrical beauty, compared to the 1935 norm.

We pitied them for having to live in their cramped, dark little era.

When we got back to our hotel room, Flora took all her clothing off, and sprawled out wildly on the bed with legs spread. "Do me!" she shrieked. "I'm drunk!"

I was a little drunk too, so I did her.

Madison Jefferson Monroe had carefully allotted each of us one alcoholic drink during the whole evening. Despite all temptations, we weren't allowed a second, and had to stick to soft drinks the rest of the time. He couldn't take the risk that we might say something dangerous under the influence of alcohol, a substance we weren't really accustomed to. As it is, even that one drink was enough to loosen some tongues and melt some brains, and a few remarks slipped out which, if they had been overheard, could have caused trouble.

It astounded me to see the twentieth-century people drink so much without collapsing.

("Get used to alcohol," Sam had urged me. "It's the favorite mind-poison in most places up the line. Develop a tolerance for it or you may have problems." "No drugs?" I asked. "Well, you'll find some weed here and there, but nothing really psychedelic. No sniffer palaces anywhere. Learn to drink, Jud. Learn to drink.")

Later that night Jeff Monroe came to our room. Flora lay in an exhausted heap, unconscious; Jeff and I talked for a long while about the problems of being a Courier. I rather got to like him for all his slickness and blandness.

He seemed to enjoy his work. His specialty was twentieth-century United States, and the only thing he regretted was the wearying routine of covering the assassinations. "Nobody wants to see anything else," he complained. "Dallas, Los Angeles, Memphis, New York, Chicago, Baton Rouge, Cleveland, over and over again. I can't tell you how sick I am of muscling into the crowd by that overpass, and pointing out that window on the sixth floor, and watching that poor woman crawling onto the back of that car. At least the Huey Long thing is reasonably untouched. But there are twenty of me in Dallas by now. Don't people want to see the *happy* parts of the twentieth century?"

"Were there any?" I asked.

15.

We had breakfast at Brennan's and dinner at Antoine's, and had a tour of the Garden District, and came back to the old town to visit the cathedral in Jackson Square, and then we walked down to have a look at the Mississippi. We also went to see Clark Gable and Jean Harlow in *Red Dust* at a movie house, visited the post office and the public library, bought a lot of newspapers (which are permissible souvenirs), and spent a few hours listening to the radio. We rode the Streetcar Named Desire, and Jeff took us motoring in a hired automobile. He offered to let us drive, but we were all terrified of taking the wheel after watching him going through the intricate routines of changing gears. And we did a lot of other twentieth-century things. We really soaked up the flavor of the era.

Then we went up to Baton Rouge to watch Senator Long get killed.

We got there on Saturday, September 7, and took rooms in what Jeff swore was the finest hotel in the city. The legislature was in session, and Senator Huey had come down from Washington to run things. We hovered around town aimlessly until late Sunday afternoon. Then Jeff got us ready to see the show.

He had donned a thermoplastic disguise. His pink, regular face was now pocked and sallow, he had a mustache, and he wore dark glasses that he might have borrowed from Dajani. "This is the third time I've conducted this tour," he explained to us. "I think it might look bad if somebody noticed identical triplets standing in the corridor when Huey gets shot." He warned us to pay no attention to any of the other Jeff Monroes we might see at the assassination; he, pockmarks and mustache and glasses, was our authentic Courier and the other two were not to be approached.

Toward evening we strolled over to the colossal 34-story state capitol building and casually wandered in—sightseers, here to admire Huey's $5,000,000 edifice. Unobtrusively we entered. Jeff checked the time every few seconds.

He positioned us where we'd have a good view while still keeping out of range of the bullets.

We couldn't help noticing other groups of sightseers slouching into positions nearby. I saw a man who was unmistakably Jeff Monroe standing with one group; another group was clustered around a man of the same size and physique who, however, wore metal-rimmed glasses and had a plum-colored birthmark on one cheek. We made an elaborate show of not looking at these other people. They worked hard at not looking at us.

I worried about the Cumulative Paradox. It seemed to me that everybody who would ever come up the line to witness Huey Long's assassination should be right here now—thousands of people, maybe, all crowding round, jostling for a view. Yet there were only a few dozen, representing those who had set out from 2059 and earlier. Why weren't the others here? Was time so fluid that the same event could be played off infinitely often, for a larger audience each time?

"Here he comes," Jeff whispered.

The Kingfish hurried toward us, his bodyguard close behind. He was short and chubby, with a florid face, a snub nose, orange hair, heavy lips, a deeply cleft chin. I told myself that I could sense the power of the man, and wondered if I might be deluding myself. As he approached he scratched his left buttock, said something to a man to his left, and coughed. His suit was slightly rumpled; his hair was unruly.

Since we had been coached by our Courier, we knew where to look for the assassin. On a murmured signal from Jeff—not before!—we turned our heads and saw Dr. Carl Austin Weiss detach himself from the crowd, step up to the Senator, and push a .22 automatic pistol into his stomach. He fired one shot. Huey, surprised, fell back, mortally wounded. His bodyguards instantly drew their guns and killed the assassin. Gleaming puddles of blood began to form; people screamed; the red-faced bodyguards pushed at us, hammered at us, told us to get back, get back, get back!

That was it. The event we had come to see was over.

It had seemed unreal, a playback of ancient history, a clever but not quite convincing tridim. We were impressed with the ingenuity of the process, but we were not awed by the impact of the event.

Even while the bullets had been flying, none of it had seemed completely true to us.

Yet those bullets had been real bullets, and if they had hit us, we would have died real deaths.

And for the two men lying on the capitol's polished floor, it had been an extremely real event.

16.

I went on four more training missions before they certified me as a Time Courier. All my jumps were made in the New Orleans area. I got to know the history of that area a lot better than I ever thought I would.

The third of these trips was to 1803, the Louisiana Purchase run. I was the only trainee. There were seven tourists. Our Courier was a hard-faced little man named Sid Buonocore. When I mentioned his name to Sam, Sam guffawed and said, "That shady character!"

"What's shady about him?"

"They used to have him on the Renaissance run. Then the Time Patrol caught him pimping lady tourists to Cesare Borgia. The tourist gals paid him nicely, and so did Cesare. Buonocore claimed he was just doing his job— letting his girls get a deeper experience of the Renaissance, you know. But they pulled him back here and stuck him on Louisiana Purchase."

"Is a Courier supposed to supervise the sex life of his tourists?" I asked.

"No, but he isn't supposed to encourage transtemporal fornication, either."

I found the encourager of transtemporal fornication to be an engaging rakish sort. Buonocore was a long way from handsome, but he had an aura of omnivorous sexuality about him that I had to admire. And his high regard for his own welfare was so obvious that it had a certain rapacious charm. You can't applaud a skulking pickpocket, but you can cheer an out-and-out brigand. That was what Sid Buonocore was.

He was a capable Courier, besides. He slipped us cunningly into 1803 New Orleans in the guise of a party of Dutch traders making a market tour; as long as we didn't meet a real Hollander we were safe, and our "Dutch" label covered the oddities of our futuristic accents. We strode around town uncomfortably garbed in early nineteenth-century clothing, feeling like refugees from a costume drama, and Sid showed us the sights in fine fashion.

On the side, I quickly discovered, he was carrying on a flourishing trade in gold doubloons and Spanish eight-real pieces. He didn't bother to conceal what he was doing from me, but he didn't talk about it, either, and I never really figured out all the intricate details. It had something to do—maybe—with taking advantage of variable exchange rates. All I know is that he swapped United States silver dollars for British gold guineas, used the guineas to buy French silver currency at a big discount, and met with Caribbean buccaneers by night on the banks of the Mississippi to trade the French coins for Spanish gold and silver. What he did with his doubloons and eight-real pieces I never knew. Nor could I see where the profit in the deal was coming from. My best theory was that he simply was trying to switch as many currencies around as possible, in order to build up a stock of coins for sale to collectors down the line; but somehow that seemed too simple-minded an operation for someone of his style. He didn't offer explanations and I was too shy to ask.

He was also a busy sexman. That isn't unusual for a Courier. ("The lady tourists are fair game," Sam said. "They fall all over themselves to submit to us. It's like the white-hunter thing in Africa.") But Sid Buonocore didn't just confine himself to plugging romance-hungry tourists, I discovered.

Late one night in our 1803 trip I was bothered with some procedural point and went to the Courier's bedroom to ask him about it. I knocked and he said, "Come in," so I went in, but he wasn't alone. A tawny maiden with long black hair was sprawled on the bed, naked, sweat-shiny, rumpled. Her breasts were hard and heavy and her nipples were chocolate-colored. "Excuse me," I said. "I didn't mean to intrude." Sid Buonocore laughed. "Crap," he said. "We're finished for now. You aren't interrupting things. This is Maria."

"Hello, Maria," I said tentatively.

She giggled drunkenly. Sid spoke to her in the Creole patois and she giggled again. Rising from the bed, she performed an elegant nude curtsy before me and murmured, *"Bon soir, m'sieu."* Then she fell on her face with a gentle swooning fall.

"She's lovely, isn't she?" Sid asked proudly. "Half Indian, half Spanish, half French. Have some rum."

I took a gulp from the flask he proffered. "That's too many halves," I said.

"Maria doesn't do anything in a petty way."

"So I see."

"I met her on my last trip through here. I'm timing things very carefully so that I can have her for a little while each night, and still not deprive my other selves of her. I mean, I can't predict how often I'll be doing this goddam run, Jud, but I might as well set myself up nicely each time I go up the line."

"Should you be saying such things in front of—"

"Doesn't speak a word of English. Absolutely safe."

Maria stirred and moaned. Sid took the rum flask from me and let some splash down onto her chest. She giggled again, and sleepily began to rub it into her breasts like a magic growth ointment. She didn't need any ointment.

Sid said, "She's quite passionate."

"I'm sure."

He said something to her and she lurched to her feet and came toward me. Her breasts swayed like bells. Fumes of rum and fumes of lust rose from her. Unsteadily she reached her hands toward me, but she lost her balance and slipped once again to the planked floor. She lay there chuckling.

"Want to try her?" Sid asked. "Let her sober up a little, and take her back to your room and have some fun."

I said something about the interesting diseases she might be carrying. Sometimes I break out all over with fastidiousness at funny moments.

Buonocore spat scornfully. "You've had your shots. What are you worrying about?"

"They immunized us against typhoid and diphtheria and yellow fever and all that," I said. "But syphilis?"

"She's clean. Believe me. Anyway, if you're nervous, you can take a thermobath the minute you go down the line." He shrugged. "If something like that scares you, maybe you better not be a Courier."

"I didn't—"

"You saw that *I* was willing to ball her, didn't you? Jud, do you think I'm an ordinary fool or a goddam fool? Would I go to bed with a syphilitic? And then offer her to you?"

"Well—"

"There's only one thing you do have to worry about," he said. "Have you had your pill?"

"My pill?"

"Your *pill*, stupid! Your monthly pill!"

"Oh. Yes. Yes, of course."

"That's vital, if you're going to go up the line. You don't want to run around fertilizing other people's ancestors. The Time Patrol will really scrape you for a thing like that. You can get away with a little fraternization with up-the-line people—you can do some business with them, you can go to bed with them—but you damned well better not plant any babies in them. Got it?"

"Sure, Sid."

"Remember, just because I fool around a little, that doesn't mean I'm willing to risk changing the past in a big way. Like fouling up the genetic flow by making babies up the line. Go you and do likewise, kid. Don't forget your pills. Now take Maria and clear out."

I took Maria and cleared out.

She sobered up fast in my room. She couldn't speak a word of any language I understood. I couldn't speak a word of any language she understood. But we made out all right anyway.

Even though she was 250 years older than me, there was nothing wrong with any aspect of her performance. Some things don't change much.

17.

After I qualified as a Time Courier, and just before I departed to go on the Byzantium run, Sam gave a farewell party for me. Just about everyone I had known in Under New Orleans was invited, and we all crammed into Sam's two rooms. The girls from the sniffer palace were there, and an unemployed oral poet named Shigemitsu who spoke only in iambic pentameter, and five or six Time Service people, and a peddler of floaters, and a wild green-haired girl who worked as a splitter in a helix parlor, and others. Sam even invited Flora Chambers, but she had shipped out the day before to fill in on the Sack of Rome run.

Everyone was given a floater as he arrived. So things turned on fast. Instants after the buzz of the floater's snout against my arm I felt my consciousness expanding like a balloon, stretching until my body could no longer contain it, bursting the confines of my skin. With a *pop!* I broke free and floated. The others were going through the same experience. Liberated from our chains of flesh, we drifted around the ceiling in an ectoplasmic haze, enjoying the slinkiness of the sensation. I sent foggy tentacles off to curl around the floating forms of Betsy and Helen, and we enjoyed a tranquil triple conjugation of the psychedelic sort. Meanwhile, music came seeping from a thousand outputs in the wall paint, and the ceiling screen was tuned to the abstraction channel to enhance the effects. It was a very sweet scene.

"We grieve that you must take your leave of us," said Shigemitsu tenderly. "Your absence here creates an aching void. Though all the world now opens to your knock—"

He went on like that for at least five minutes. The poetry got really erotic toward the end. I wish I could remember that part of it.

We floated higher and higher. Sam, hosting it to the full, saw to it that nobody wore off even for a minute. His huge black body gleamed with oil. One young couple from the Time Service had brought their own coffin along; it was a lovely job, silk-lined, with all the sanitary attachments. They climbed in and let us monitor them on the telemetry line. Afterward, the rest of us tried it, in twos or threes, and there was a great deal of laughter over some of the couplings. My partner was the floater peddler, and right in the middle of things we turned on all over again.

The sniffer palace girls danced for us, and three of the Time Couriers—two men and a fragile-looking young woman in an ermine loincloth—put on an exhibition of biological acrobatics, very charming. They had learned the steps in Knossos, where they watched Minos's dancers perform, and had simply adapted the movements to modern tastes by grafting in the copulations at the right moments. During the performance Sam distributed input scramblers to everybody. We plugged them in and beautiful synesthesia took hold. For me this time, touch became smell; I caressed Betsy's cool buttocks and the fragrance of April lilacs came to me; I squeezed a cube of ice and smelled the sea at high tide; I stroked the ribbed wall fabric and my lungs filled with the dizzying flavor of a pine forest on fire. Then we did the pivot and for me sound became texture; Helen made passion-sounds in my ear and they became furry moss; music roared from the speakers as a torrent of thick cream; Shigemitsu began to moan in blank verse and the stabbing rhythms of his

voice reached me as pyramids of ice. We went on to do
things with color, taste, and duration. Of all the kinds of
sensory pleasures invented in the last hundred years, I
think scrambling is by far my favorite.

Later Emily, the helix-parlor girl, came over. She was
starvation-slim, with painfully sharp cheekbones, a
scraggly mop of tangled green hair, and the most beautiful piercing green eyes I have ever seen. Though she was
high on everything simultaneously, she seemed cool and
self-possessed—an illusion, I quickly discovered. She was
floating. "Listen carefully to what she says," Sam advised
me. "She goes clairvoyant under the influence of floaters.
I mean it: she's the real thing."

She toppled into my arms. I supported her uncertainly
a moment while her mouth sought mine. Her teeth nipped
lightly into my lips. Delicately we toppled to the carpet,
which emitted little thrumming sounds when we landed.
Emily wore a cloak of copper mesh strips interlaced at
her throat. I searched patiently beneath it for her breasts.
She said in a hollow, prophetic voice, "You will soon
begin a long journey."

"Yes."

"You will go up the line."

"That's right."

"In—Byzantium."

"Byzantium, yes."

"That is no country for old men!" cried a voice from
the far side of the room. "The young in one another's
arms, birds in the trees—"

"Byzantium," murmured an exhausted dancer spread-
eagled near my feet.

"The golden smithies of the Emperor!" Shigemitsu
screamed. "Spirit after spirit! The smithies break the
flood! Flames that no faggot feeds, nor steel has lit!"

"The Emperor's drunken soldiery are abed," I said.

Emily, quivering, bit my ear and said, "You will find
your heart's desire in Byzantium."

"Sam said the same thing to me."

"And lose it there. And you will suffer, and regret, and repent, and you will not be the same as you were before."

"That sounds serious," I said.

"Beware love in Byzantium!" the prophetess shrilled. "Beware! Beware!"

" . . . the jaws that bite, the claws that catch!" sang Shigemitsu.

I promised Emily that I would be careful.

But the light of prophecy was gone from her eyes. She sat up, blinked several times, smiled uncertainly, and said, "Who are you?" Her thighs were tightly clasped around my left hand.

"I'm the guest of honor. Jud Elliott."

"I don't know you. What do you do?"

"Time Courier. Will be. I'm leaving to start service tomorrow."

"I think I remember now. I'm Emily."

"Yes, I know. You're with a helix parlor?"

"Someone's been talking about me!"

"Not much. What do you do there?"

"I'm a splitter," she said. "I separate genes. You see, when somebody is carrying the gene for red hair, and wants to transmit that to his children, but the gene is linked to, let's say, the gene for hemophilia, I split off the unwanted gene and edit it out."

"It sounds like very difficult work," I ventured.

"Not if you know what you're doing. There's a six-month training course."

"I see."

"It's interesting work. It tells you a lot about human nature, seeing how people want their children to come out. You know, not everybody wants improvements edited in. We get some amazing requests."

"I guess it depends on what you mean by improvements," I said.

"Well, there *are* certain norms of appearance. We assume that it's better to have thick, lustrous hair than none at all. Better for a man to be two meters tall than one meter tall. Better to have straight teeth than crooked ones. But what would you say if a woman comes in and tells you to design a son with undescended testicles?"

"Why would anybody want a child like that?"

"She doesn't like the idea of his fooling around with girls," Emily said.

"Did you do it?"

"The request was two full points below the mark on the genetic deviation index. We have to refer all such requests to the Board of Genetic Review."

"Would they approve it?" I asked.

"Oh, no, never. They don't authorize counterproductive mutations of that sort."

"I guess the poor woman is just going to have a baby with balls, then."

Emily smiled. "She can go to bootleg helixers, if she likes. They'll do anything for anybody. Don't you know about them?"

"Not really."

"They produce the far-out mutations for the avantgarde set. The children with gills and scales, the children with twenty fingers, the ones with zebra-striped skin. The bootleggers will notch any gene at all—for the right price. They're terribly expensive. But they're the wave of the future."

"They are?"

"Cosmetic mutations are on the way in," Emily declared. "Don't misunderstand—*our* parlor won't touch the things. But this is the last generation of uniformity the human race is going to have. Variety of genotype and phenotype—that's what's ahead!" Her eyes sparkled with sudden lunacy, and I realized that a slow-acting floater must have exploded in her veins in the last few minutes. Drawing close to me, she whispered, "What do you think of this idea? Let's make a baby right now, and I'll redesign it after hours at the parlor! We'll keep up with the trends!"

"I'm sorry," I said. "I've had my pill this month."

"Let's try anyway," she said, and slipped her eager hand into my pants.

18.

I reached Istanbul on a murky summer afternoon and caught an express pod across the Bosphorus to the Time Service headquarters, on the Asian side. The city hadn't changed much since my last visit a year before. That was no surprise. Istanbul hasn't really changed since Kemal Ataturk's time, and that was 150 years ago. The same gray buildings, the same archaic clutter of unlabeled streets, the same overlay of grit and grime. And the same heavenly mosques floating above the dilapidation.

I admire the mosques tremendously. They show that the Turks were good for *something*. But to me, Istanbul is a black joke of a city that someone has painted over the wounded stump of my beloved Constantinople. The little pieces of the Byzantine city that remain hold more magic for me than Sultan Ahmed's mosque, the Suleimaniye, and the mosque of Beyazit, all taken together.

The thought that I would soon be seeing Constantinople as a living city, with all the Turkish excrescences swept away, almost made me stain my pants with glee.

The Time Service had set up shop in a squat, formidable building of the late twentieth century, far up the Bosphorus, practically facing the Turkish fortress of Rumeli

Hisari, from which the Conqueror strangled Byzantium in 1453. I was expected; even so, I had to spend fifteen minutes milling in an anteroom, surrounded by angry tourists complaining about some foulup in scheduling. One red-faced man kept shouting, "Where's the computer input? I want all this on record in the computer!" And a tired, angelic-looking secretary kept telling him wearily that everything he was saying *was* going on record, down to the ultimate bleat. Two swaggering giants in Time Patrol uniforms cut coolly through the mêlée, their faces grimly set, their minds no doubt riveted to duty. I could almost hear them thinking, "Aha! *Aha!*" A thin woman with a wedge-shaped face rushed up to them, waved papers at their deep-cleft chins, and yelled, "Seven months ago I confirmed these reservations, yet! Right after Christmas it was! And now they tell me—" The Time Patrolmen kept walking. A robot vendor entered the waiting room and started to sell lottery tickets. Behind it came a haggard, unshaven Turk in a rumpled black jacket, peddling honeycakes from a greasy tray.

I admired the quality of the confusion. It showed genius.

Still, I wasn't unhappy to be rescued. A Levantine type who might have been a cousin of my fondly remembered instructor Najeeb Dajani appeared, introduced himself to me as Spiros Protopopolos, and led me hastily through a sphincter door I had not noticed. "You should have come through the side way," he said. "I apologize for this delay. We didn't realize you were here."

He was about thirty, plump, sleek, with sunglasses and a great many white teeth. As we shot upshaft to the Couriers' lounge he said, "You have never worked as a Courier before, yes?"

"Yes," I said. "Never. My first time."

"You will love it! The Byzantium run especially. Byzantium, it is so—how shall I express it?" He pressed his pudgy palms rapturously together. "Surely you must feel some of it. But only a Greek like myself can respond fully. Byzantium! Ah, Byzantium!"

"I'm Greek also," I said.

He halted the shaft and raised his glasses. "You are not Judson Daniel Elliott III?"

"I am."

"This is Greek?"

"My mother's name was originally Passilidis. She was born in Athens. My maternal grandfather was mayor of Sparta. On his mother's side he was descended from the Markezinis family."

"You are my brother!" cried Spiros Protopopolos.

It turned out that six of the nine other Time Couriers assigned to the Byzantium run were Greeks by nationality or descent; there were two Germans, Herschel and Melamed, while the tenth man was a slick, dark-haired Spaniard named Capistrano who later on, when deep in his cups, confided to me that his great-grandmother had been a Turk. He may have invented that so I'd despise him; Capistrano had a distinct streak of masochism.

Five of my nine colleagues were currently up the line and four were here in now-time Istanbul, thanks to the scheduling mishap that was causing so much dismay in the anteroom. Protopopolos made the introductions: Melamed, Capistrano, Pappas, meet Elliott. Melamed was fair-haired and hid behind a dense sandy beard; Pappas had hollow cheeks, sad eyes, and a drooping mustache. They were both about forty. Capistrano looked a little younger.

An illuminated board monitored the doings of the other members of the team: Herschel, Kolettis, Plastiras, Metaxas, and Gompers. "Gompers?" I said. Protopopolos replied, "His grandmother was pure Hellene." The five of them were scattered over ten centuries, according to that board, with Kolettis in 1651 B.P., and Metaxas in 606 B.P.—that is, in A.D. 408 and 1453—and the others in between. As I stared at the board, Kolettis moved down the line by more than a century. "They have gone to see the riots," Melamed said softly, and Capistrano nodded, sighing.

Pappas brewed strong coffee for me. Capistrano uncorked a bottle of Turkish brandy, which I found a little hard to ingest. He prodded me encouragingly, saying, "Drink, drink, it's the best you'll taste in the last fifteen centuries!" I remembered Sam's advice that I should learn how to drink, and forced the stuff down, longing for a weed, a floater, a fume, anything decent.

While I relaxed with my new comrades, a Time Patrolman came into the room. He didn't use the scanner to get entry permission, or even knock; he just barged in. "Can't you ever be polite?" Pappas growled.

"Up yours," said the Time Patrolman. He sank down into a web and unbuttoned his uniform shirt. He was a chunky Aryan-looking sort with a hairy chest; what looked like golden wire curled toward his clavicles. "New man?" he said, jerking his head at me.

"Jud Elliott," I said. "Courier."

"Dave Van Dam," he said. "Patrol." His huge hand enfolded mine. "Don't let me catch you screwing around up the line. Nothing personal, but I'm a tough bastard. It's so easy to hate us: we're incorruptible. Try me and see."

"This is the lounge for Couriers," said Capistrano thinly.

"You don't need to tell me that," said Van Dam. "Believe it or not, I can read."

"Are you now a Courier, then?"

"Do you mind if I relax a little with the opposition?" The Patrolman grinned, scratched his chest, and put the brandy bottle to his lips. He drank copiously and belched resonantly. "Christ, what a killer of a day! You know where I was today?"

Nobody seemed to care.

He continued anyway, "I spent the whole day in 1962!"

Nineteen goddam sixty-two! Checking out every floor of the Istanbul Goddam Hilton for two alleged timecrimers running an alleged artifact siphon. What we heard was they were bringing gold coins and Roman glass down from 1400 B.P. and selling them to American tourists in the Hilton, then investing the proceeds on the stock market and hiding the stash in a Swiss bank for pickup in now-time. Christ! You know, you can make *billions* that way? You buy in a bear-market year and stick it away for a century and you end up owning the world. Well, maybe so, but we didn't see a thing in the whole goddam Hilton except plenty of legitimate free enterprise based in then-time. Crap on it!" He took another pull on the brandy bottle. "Let them run a recheck upstairs. Find their own goddam timecrimers."

"This is the lounge for Couriers," Capistrano said once more.

The Patrolman took no notice. When he finally left, five minutes later, I said, "Are they all like that?"

Protopopolos said, "This was one of the refined ones. Most of the others are boors."

19.

They put me to bed with a hypnosleep course in Byzantine Greek, and when I woke up I not only could order a meal, buy a tunic, and seduce a virgin in Byzantine argot, but I knew some phrases that could make the mosaics of Haghia Sophia peel from the walls in shame. I hadn't known about those phrases when I was a graduate student at Harvard, Yale, and Princeton. Good stuff, hypnosleep.

I still wasn't ready to go out solo as a Courier. Protopopolos, who was serving as staff router this month, arranged to team me with Capistrano for my first time out. If everything went smoothly, I'd be put on my own in a few weeks.

The Byzantium run, which is one of the most popular that the Time Service offers, is pretty standard stuff. Every tour is taken to see the coronation of an emperor, a chariot race in the Hippodrome, the dedication of Haghia Sophia, the sack of the city by the Fourth Crusade, and the Turkish conquest. A tour like that stays up the line for seven days. The fourteen-day tour covers all that plus the arrival of the First Crusade in Constantinople, the riots of 532, an imperial wedding, and a couple of lesser events. The Courier has his options about which coronations, emperors, or chariot races to go to; the idea is to avoid contributing to the Cumulative Paradox by cluttering any one event with too many tourists. Just about every major period between Justinian and the Turks gets visited, although we're cautioned to avoid the years of bad earthquakes, and absolutely prohibited, under penalty of obliteration by the Time Patrol, from entering the bubonic plague years of 745-47.

On my last night in now-time I was so excited I couldn't sleep. Partly I was keyed up over the fear of blundering somehow on my first assignment as a Courier; it's a big responsibility to be a Courier, even with a colleague along, and I was afraid of committing some terrible mistake. The thought of having to be rescued by the Time Patrol upset me. What a humiliation!

But mainly I was worried about Constantinople. Would it live up to my dream of it? Or *would it let me down?* All my life I had cherished an image of that golden, glittering city of the past; now, on the verge of going up the line to it, I trembled.

I got up and stumbled around the little room they had given me, feeling drawn and tense. I was off all drugs and wasn't allowed to smoke—Couriers have to taper off such things ahead of time, since it's obviously an illegal anachronism to light up a weed in a tenth-century street. Capistrano had given me the dregs of his brandy, but that was small consolation. He heard me walking into furniture, though, and came to see what the trouble was.

"Restless?" he asked.

"Very."

"I always am, before a jump. It never wears off."

He talked me into going out with him to soothe our nerves. We crossed to the European side and wandered at random through the silent streets of the new city, up from Dolmabahce Palace at the shore to the old Hilton, and down past Taksim to the Galata Bridge and into Istanbul proper. We walked tirelessly. We seemed to be the only ones awake in the city. Through the winding maze of a market we wound, emerging on one of those streets leading to Haghia Sophia, where we stood a while in front of the majestic old building. I imprinted its features on my brain—the extraneous minarets, the late buttresses —and tried to make myself believe that in the morning I'd see it in its true form, serene mistress of the city, no longer compelled to share its grand plaza with the alien loveliness of the Blue Mosque across the way.

On and on we went, scrambling over the fragments of the Hippodrome, circling Topkapi, making our way to the sea and the old sea wall. Dawn found us outside the Yedikule fortress, in the shadow of the crumbling Byzantine rampart. We were half asleep. A Turkish boy of about fifteen approached us politely and asked, first in French and then in English, if we were in the market for anything— old coins, his sister, hashish, Israeli currency, gold jewelry, his brother, a carpet. We thanked him and said we weren't. Undaunted, he summoned his sister, who may have been fourteen but looked four or five years older.

"Virgin," he said. "You like her? Nice figure, eh? What are you, American, English, German? Here, you look, eh?" She unsnapped her blouse at a harsh command from him, and displayed attractive taut round breasts. Dangling on a string between them was a heavy Byzantine bronze coin, possibly a *follis*. I peered close for a better look. The boy, breathing garlic at me, realized suddenly that it was the coin and not the breasts that I was studying, and made a smooth switch, saying, "You like old coins, eh? We find plenty under wall in a pot. You wait here, I show you, yes?" He ran off. The sister sullenly closed her blouse. Capistrano and I walked away. The girl followed us, calling out to us to stay, but by the time we had gone twenty meters she lost interest. We were back at the Time Service building in an hour, by pod.

After breakfast we got into costume: long silk tunics, Roman sandals, light cloaks. Capistrano solemnly handed me my timer. By now I had been well trained in its use. I slipped it in place against my skin and felt a dazzling surge of power, knowing that now I was free to transport myself to any era, and was accountable to no one so long as I kept in mind the preservation of the sanctity of now-time. Capistrano winked at me.

"Up the line," he said.

"Up the line," I said.

We went downstairs to meet our eight tourists.

20.

The jumping-off place for the Byzantium run is almost always the same: the plaza in front of Haghia Sophia. The ten of us, feeling faintly foolish in our robes, were taken there by bus, arriving about ten that morning. More conventional tourists, merely there to see Istanbul, flocked back and forth between the great cathedral and nearby Sultan Ahmed. Capistrano and I made sure that everybody's timer was in place and that the rules of time-travel had been thoroughly nagged into everyone's skull.

Our group included a pair of pretty young men from London, a couple of maidenly German schoolteachers, and two elderly American husband-and-wife outfits. Everybody had had the hypnocourse in Byzantine Greek, and for the next sixty days or so would be as fluent in that as in their native languages, but Capistrano and I had to keep reminding the Americans and one of the German girls to speak it.

We jumped.

I felt the momentary disorientation that always comes when you go up the line. Then I got my bearings and discovered that I had departed from Istanbul and had reached Constantinople.

Constantinople did not let me down.

The grime was gone. The minarets were gone. The mosques were gone. The Turks were gone.

The air was blue and sweet and clear. We stood in the great plaza, the Augusteum, in front of Haghia Sophia. To my right, where there should have been bleak gray office buildings, I saw open fields. Ahead of me, where the blue fantasy of Sultan Ahmed's mosque should have been, I saw a rambling conglomeration of low marble palaces. To the side rose the flank of the Hippodrome. Figures in colorful robes, looking like fugitives from Byzantine mosaics, sauntered through the spacious square.

I swung around for my first view of Haghia Sophia without her minarets.

Haghia Sophia was not there.

On the familiar site I saw the charred and tumbled ruins of an unfamiliar rectangular basilica. The stone walls stood but precariously; the roof was gone. Three soldiers drowsed in the shadow of its facade. I was lost.

Capistrano said droningly, "We have journeyed sixteen centuries up the line. The year is 408; we have come to behold the baptismal procession of Emperor Arcadius' son, who will one day rule as Theodosius II. To our rear, on the site of the well-known cathedral of Haghia Sophia, we may see the ruins of the original basilica, built during the reign of the Emperor Constantius, son of Constantine the Great, and opened for prayer on the 15th of December, 360. This building was burned on the 20th of June, 404, during a rebellion, and as you can see, reconstruction has not yet begun. The church will be rebuilt about thirty years down the line by Emperor Theodosius II, and you will view it on our next stop. Come this way."

As though in a dream I followed, as much a tourist as our eight charges. Capistrano did all the work. He lectured us in a perfunctory but comprehensive way about the marble buildings ahead, which were the beginning of the Great Palace. I couldn't reconcile what I saw with the ground plans I had memorized at Harvard; but of course the Constantinople I had studied was the later, greater, post-Justinian city, and now I stood in the city at its dawn. We turned inland, away from the palace district, into a residential district where the houses of the rich, blank-fronted and courtyarded, mixed helter-skelter with the rush-roofed hovels of the poor. And then we emerged on the Mese, the grand processional street, lined by arcaded shops, and on this day, in honor of the baptism of the prince, decked with silk hangings adorned with gold.

All the citizens of Byzantium were here, packing the street elbow to elbow in anticipation of the grand parade. Food shops were busy; we smelled grilled ham and baked lamb, and eyed stalls laden with cheeses, nuts, unfamiliar fruits. One of the German girls said she was hungry, and Capistrano laughed and bought spitted lamb for us all, paying for it with bright copper coins worth a fortune to a numismatist. A one-eyed man sold us wine out of a huge cool amphora, letting us drink right from the ladle. Once it became obvious to the other peddlers in the vicinity that we were susceptible customers, they crowded around by the dozens, offering us souvenirs, candied sweets, elderly-looking hard-boiled eggs, pans of salted nuts, trays of miscellaneous animal organs, eyeballs and other balls. This was the real thing, the genuinely archaic past; that array of vended oddities and the reek of sweat and garlic coming from the mob of vendors told us that we were a long way from 2059.

"Foreigners?" asked a bearded man who was selling little clay oil lamps. "Where from? Cyprus? Egypt?"

"Spain," said Capistrano.

The oil-lamp man eyed us in awe, as though we had claimed to come from Mars. "Spain," he repeated. "Spain! Wonderful! To travel so far, to see our city—" He gave our whole group a detailed survey, taking a quick inventory and fastening on blonde and breasty Clotilde, the more voluptuous of our two German schoolteachers. "Your slavegirl is a Saxon?" he asked me, feeling the merchandise through Clotilde's loose robes. "Ah, very nice! You are a man of taste!" Clotilde gasped and pried his fingers from her thigh. Coldly Capistrano seized the man, pushing him up against the wall of a shop so roughly that a dozen of his clay lamps tumbled to the pavement and shattered. The vendor winked, but Capistrano said something chilly under his breath and gave the man a terrible glare. "I meant no harm," the vendor protested. "I thought she was a slave!" He muttered a curt apology and limped away. Clotilde was trembling— whether from outrage or excitement, it was hard to tell. Her companion, Lise, looked a little envious. No Byzantine street peddler had ever fondled *her* bare flesh!

Capistrano spat. "That could have been troublesome. We must always be on our guard; innocent pinching can turn quickly to complications and catastrophe."

The peddlers edged away from us. We found places near the front of the mob, facing the street. It seemed to me that many of the faces in the crowd were un-Byzantine, and I wondered if they were the faces of time-travelers. A time is coming, I thought, when we from down the line will throng the past to the choking point. We will fill all our yesterdays with ourselves and crowd out our own ancestors.

"Here they come!" a thousand voices shouted.

Trumpets blared in several different keys. In the distance there appeared a procession of nobles, clean-cut and close-cropped in the Roman fashion, for this was still as much a Roman city as it was a Greek one. Everyone wore white silk—imported at great cost by caravan from China, Capistrano murmured; the Byzantines had not yet stolen the secret of silk manufacture—and the late afternoon sun, striking the splendid robes at a steep angle, gave the procession such a glow of beauty that even Capistrano, who had seen it all before, was moved. Slowly, slowly, the high dignitaries advanced.

"They look like snowflakes," whispered a man behind me. "Dancing snowflakes!"

It took nearly an hour for these high ones to pass us. Twilight came. Following the priests and dukes of Byzantium were the imperial troops, carrying lighted candles that flickered in the deepening dusk like an infinity of stars. Then came more priests, bearing medallions and icons; and then a prince of the royal blood, carrying the gurgling, plump infant who would be the mighty Emperor Theodosius II; and then the reigning emperor himself, Arcadius, clad in imperial purple. The Emperor of Byzantium! I repeated that to myself a thousand times. I, Judson Daniel Elliott III, stood bareheaded under the Byzantine sky, here in A.D. 408, while the Emperor of Byzantium, robes aswish, walked past me! Even though the monarch was merely the trifling Arcadius, the insignificant interpolation between the two Theodosii, I trembled.

I swayed. The pavement heaved and bucked beneath me. "Are you ill?" whispered Clotilde anxiously. I sucked breath and begged the universe to stand still. I was overwhelmed, and by Arcadius. What if this had been Justinian? Constantine? Alexius?

You know how it is. Eventually I got to see even those great ones. But by then I had seen too much up the line, and though I was impressed, I wasn't engulfed with awe. Of Justinian my clearest memory is that he sneezed; but when I think of Arcadius, I hear trumpets and see stars whirling in the sky.

21.

We stayed that night in an inn overlooking the Golden Horn; on the other side of the water, where Hiltons and countinghouses one day would rise, was only an impenetrable darkness. The inn was a substantial wooden building with a dining hall on the ground floor and huge, rough, dormitory-style rooms above. Somehow I expected to be asked to sleep on the floor in a strew of rushes, but no, there were beds of a recognizable sort, and mattresses stuffed with rags. Sanitary facilities were outside, behind the building. There were no baths; we were expected to use the public bathhouses if we craved cleanliness. The ten of us shared one room, but fortunately none of us minded that. Clotilde, when she undressed, indignantly went around showing us the purpling bruises left by the vendor's grip on her soft white thigh; her angular friend Lise looked gloomy again, for having nothing to show.

That night we did little sleeping. There was too much noise, for one thing, since the celebration of the imperial baptism went on raucously throughout the city until almost dawn. But who could sleep, anyway, knowing that the world of the early fifth century lay just beyond the door?

One night before and sixteen centuries down the line, Capistrano had kindly seen me through a siege of sleeplessness. Now he did it again. I rose and stood by the little slit of a window, peering at the bonfires in the city, and when he noticed me he came over and said, "I understand. Sleeping is hard at first."

"Yes."

"Shall I get a woman for you?"

"No."

"We'll take a walk, then?"

"Can we leave them?" I asked, looking at our eight tourists.

"We won't go far. We'll stay just outside, within reach if some trouble starts."

The air was heavy and mild. Snatches of obscene song floated up from the tavern district. We walked toward it; the taverns were still open and full of drunken soldiers. Swarthy prostitutes offered their wares. One girl, hardly sixteen, had a coin on a string between her bare breasts. Capistrano nudged me to notice it, and we laughed. "The same coin, maybe?" he asked. "But different breasts?" I shrugged. "Perhaps the same breasts, too," I said, thinking of the unborn girl who had been for sale at the Yedikule a night ago. Capistrano bought two flasks of oily Greek wine and we returned to the inn, to sit quietly downstairs and drink the darkness away.

He did most of the talking. Like many Time Couriers, his life had been a complex, jagged one full of detours, and he let his autobiography dribble out between gulps of wine. Noble Spanish ancestors, he said (he didn't tell me about the Turkish great-grandmother until months later, when he was far more thoroughly drunk); early marriage to a virgin of high family; education at the best universities of Europe. Then inexplicable decline, loss of ambition, loss of fortune, loss of wife. "My life," said Capistrano, "broke in half when I was twenty-seven years of age. I required total reintegration of personality. As you see, the effort was not a true success." He spoke of a series of temporary marriages, adventures in criminality, experiments with hallucinatory drugs that made weeds and floaters look innocent. When he enrolled as a Time Courier, it was only as an alternative to suicide. "I keyed to an output and asked for a bit at random," he said. "Positive, and I become a Courier. Negative, and I drink poison. The bit came up positive. Here I am." He drained his wine.

To me that night he seemed a wonderful mixture of the desperate, tragic romantic and the self-dramatizing charlatan. Of course, I was drunk myself, and very young. But I told him how much I admired his quest for identity, and secretly wished that I could learn the knack of seeming so appealingly destroyed, so interestingly lost.

"Come," he said, when the last of the wine was gone. "To dispose of the corpses."

We hurled our flasks into the Golden Horn. Streaks of dawn were emerging. As we walked slowly back to the inn, Capistrano said, "I have made a little hobby of tracing my ancestors, do you know? It is my own private research. Here—look at these names." He produced a small, thick notebook. "In each era I visit," he said, "I seek out my ancestors and list them here. Already I know several hundred of them, going back to the fourteenth century. Do you realize how immense the number of one's ancestors is? We have two parents, and each of them has two parents, and each of them two parents—go back only four generations and you have already thirty ancestors!"

"An interesting hobby," I said.

Capistrano's eyes blazed. "More than a hobby! More than a hobby! A matter of death and life! Look, my friend, whenever I grow more tired than usual of existence, all I must do is find one of these people, *one,* and destroy him! Take his life when he is still a child, perhaps. Then return to now-time. And in that moment, swiftly, without pain, my own tiresome life ceases ever to have been!"

"But the Time Patrol—"

"Helpless," said Capistrano. "What can the Patrol do? If my crime is discovered, I am seized and erased from history for timecrime, right? If my crime is not discovered —and why should it be?—then I have erased myself. Either way I am gone. Is this not the most charming way of suicide?"

"In eliminating your own ancestor," I said, "you might be changing now-time to a greater degree. You'd also eliminate your own brothers and sisters—uncles—grandparents and all of *their* brothers and sisters—all by removing one prop from the past!"

He nodded solemnly. "I am aware of this. And so I compile these genealogies, you see, in order to determine how best to effect my own erasure. I am not Samson; I have no wish to bring the temple crashing down with myself. I will look for the strategic person to eliminate—one who is himself sinful, incidentally, for I will not slay the truly innocent—and I will remove that person and thus myself, and perhaps the changes in now-time will not be terribly great. If they are, the Patrol will discover and undo them, and still give me the exit I crave."

I wondered if he was crazy or just drunk. A little of both, I decided.

I felt like telling him that if he really wanted to kill himself that badly, it would be a whole lot less trouble for everybody else if he'd just go jump in the Bosphorus.

I felt a twinge of terror at the thought that the whole Time Service might be permeated by Capistranos, all shopping around for the most interestingly self-destructive way of changing the past.

Upstairs, the early light revealed eight sleepers, huddled two by two. Our elderly married folks slept peacefully; the two pretty boys from London looked sweaty and tousled after some busy buggery; Clotilde, smiling, slept with her hand tucked between Lise's pale thighs, and Lise's left hand was cupped cozily about Clotilde's maidenly but firm right breast. I lay down on my lonely bed and slipped quickly into sleep. Soon Capistrano woke me, and we woke the others. I felt ten thousand years old.

We had a breakfast of cold lamb and went out for a quick daylight walking tour of the city. Most of the interesting things had not yet been built, or else were still in early forms; we didn't stay long. At noon we went to the Augusteum to shunt. "Our next stop," Capistrano announced, "will be A.D. 532, where we will see the city of Justinian's time and witness the riots which destroyed it, making possible the construction of the finer and more grand city that won such eternal fame." We backed into the shadows of the ruined original Haghia Sophia, so that no passersby would be startled by the sight of ten people vanishing. I set all the timers. Capistrano produced his pitchpipe and gave the master signal. We shunted.

22.

Two weeks later we all returned down the line to 2059. I was dizzied, intoxicated, my soul full of Byzantium.

I had seen the highlights of a thousand years of greatness. The city of my dreams had come to life for me. The meat and wine of Byzantium had passed through my bowels.

From a Courier's professional point of view, the trip had been a good one, that is, uneventful. Our tourists had not entangled themselves in trouble, nor had any paradoxes been created, as far as we could tell. There had been a little friction only one night, when Capistrano, very drunk, tried to seduce Clotilde; he wasn't subtle about it, letting seduction shade into rape when she resisted, but I managed to separate them before her nails got into his eyes. In the morning he wouldn't believe it. "The blonde lesbian?" he asked. "I would stoop so low? You must dream it!" And then he insisted on going eight hours up the line to see if it had really happened. I had visions of a sober Capistrano taking his earlier sozzled self to task, and it scared me. I had to argue him out of it in a blunt and direct way, reminding him of the Time Patrol's regulation prohibiting anyone from engaging in conversation with himself of a different now-time basis, and threatening to report him if he tried it. Capistrano looked wounded, but he let the matter drop. And when we came down the line and he filed a report of his own, upon request, concerning my behavior as a Courier, he gave me the highest rating. Protopopolos told me that afterward.

"Your next trip," said Protopopolos, "will be as assistant to Metaxas, on the one-week tour."

"When do I leave?"

"In two weeks," he said. "Your layoff comes first, remember? And after you return from the trip with Metaxas, you begin soloing. Where will you spend your layoff?"

"I think I'll go down to Crete or Mykonos," I said, "and get a little rest on the beach."

The Time Service insists that Couriers take two-week vacations between trips. The Time Service doesn't believe in pushing its Couriers too hard. During layoffs, Couriers are completely at liberty. They can spend the whole time relaxing in now-time, as I proposed to do, or they can sign up with a time tour, or they can simply go hopping by themselves to any era that may interest them.

There's no charge for timer use when a Courier makes jumps up the line in his layoff periods. The Time Service wants to encourage its employees to feel at home in all periods of the past, and what better way than to allow unlimited free shunting?

Protopopolos looked a little disappointed when I said I'd spend my vacation sunning myself in the islands. "Don't you want to do some jumping?" he asked.

The idea of making time-jumps on my own at this stage of my career scared me, frankly. But I couldn't tell Protopopolos that. I also considered the point that in another month he'd be handing me the responsibility for the lives of an entire tour group. Maybe this conversation was part of the test of my qualifications. Were they trying to see if I had the guts to go jumping on my own?

Protopopolos seemed to be fishing for an answer.

I said, "On second thought, why waste a chance to do some jumping? I'll have a peek at post-Byzantine Istanbul."

"With a tour group?"

"On my own," I said.

23.

So I went jumping, smack into the Paradox of Discontinuity.

My first stop was the wardrobe department. I needed

costumes suited for Istanbul of the sixteenth through nineteenth centuries. Instead of giving me a whole sequence
of clothes to fit the changing fashions, they decked me
out in an all-purpose Moslem rig, simple white robes of
no particular era, nondescript sandals, long hair, and a
straggly youthful beard. By way of pocket money they
supplied me with a nice assortment of gold and silver
pieces of the right eras, a little of everything that might
have been circulating in medieval Turkey, including some
bezants of Greek-ruled times, miscellaneous coinage of
the sultans, and a good deal of Venetian gold. All this
was installed in a currency belt that I wore just above my
timer, the coins segregated from left to right according to
centuries, so that I wouldn't get into trouble by offering
an eighteenth-century dinar in a sixteenth-century market
place. There was no charge for the money; the Time Service runs a continuous siphon of its own, circulating coinage between now-time and then-time for the benefit of its
personnel, and a Courier going on holiday can sign out
any reasonable amount to cover his expenses. To the Service it's only play money, anyway, infinitely replenishible
at will. I like the system.

I took hypnosleep courses in Turkish and Arabic before
I left. The Special Requests department fabricated a
quick cover identity for me that would work well in any
era of my intended visit: if questioned, I was supposed to
identify myself as a Portuguese national who had been
kidnapped on the high seas by Algerian pirates when ten
years old, and raised as a Moslem in Algiers. That would
account for flaws in my accent and for my vagueness
about my background; if I had the misfortune to be inter-
rogated by a real Portuguese, which wasn't likely, I could
simply say that I couldn't remember much about my life
in Lisbon and had forgotten the names of my forebears.
So long as I kept my mouth shut, prayed toward Mecca
five times a day, and watched my step, I wasn't likely to
get into trouble. (Of course, if I landed in a really serious

mess, I could escape by using my timer, but in the Time Service that's considered a coward's route, and also undesirable because of the implications of witchcraft that you leave behind when you vanish.)

All these preparations took a day and a half. Then they told me I was ready to jump. I set my timer for 500 B.P., picking the era at random, and jumped.

I arrived on August 14, 1559, at nine-thirty in the evening. The reigning sultan was the great Suleiman I, nearing the close of his epoch. Turkish armies threatened the peace of Europe; Istanbul was bursting with the wealth of conquest. I couldn't respond to this city as I had to the sparkling Constantinople of Justinian or Alexius, but that was a personal matter having to do with ancestry, chemistry, and historical affinity. Taken on its own merits, Suleiman's Istanbul was a city among cities.

I spent half the day roaming it. For an hour I watched a lovely mosque under construction, hoping it was the Suleimaniye, but later in the day I found the Suleimaniye, brand-new and glistening in the noon light. I made a special pilgrimage, covertly consulting a map I had smuggled with me, to find the mosque of Mehmet the Conqueror, which an earthquake would bring down in 1766. It was worth the walk. Toward midafternoon, after an inspection of the mosquified Haghia Sophia and the sad ruins of the Great Palace of Byzantium across the plaza (Sultan Ahmed's mosque would be rising there fifty years down the line), I made my way to the Covered Bazaar, thinking to buy a few small trinkets as souvenirs, and when I was no more than ten paces past the entrance I caught sight of my beloved guru Sam.

Consider the odds against that: with thousands of years in which to roam, the two of us coming on holiday to the same year and the same day and the same city, and meeting under the same roof!

He was clad in Moorish costume, straight out of *Othello*. There was no mistaking him; he was by far the tallest man in sight, and his coal-black skin glistened brilliantly against his white robes. I rushed up to him.

"Sam!" I cried. "Sam, you old black bastard, what luck to meet you *here.*"

He whirled in surprise, frowned at me, looked puzzled. "I know you not," he said coldly.

"Don't let the beard fool you. It's me, Sam. Jud Elliott."

He glared. He growled. A crowd began to gather. I wondered if I had been wrong. Maybe this wasn't Sam, but Sam's multi-great-grandfather, made to look like his twin by a genetic fluke. No, I told myself, this is the authentic Sambo.

But then why is he pulling out that scimitar?

We had been talking in Turkish. I switched to English and said, "Listen, Sam, I don't know what's going on, but I'm willing to ride along with your act. Suppose we meet in half an hour outside Haghia Sophia, and we can—"

"Infidel dog!" he roared. "Beggar's spawn! Masturbator of pigs! Away from me! Away, cutpurse!"

He swished the scimitar menacingly above my head and continued to rave in Turkish. Suddenly in a lower voice he muttered, "I don't know who the hell you are, pal, but if you don't clear out of here fast I'm going to have to slice you in half." That much was in English. In Turkish again he cried, "Molester of infants! Drinker of toad's milk! Devourer of cameldung!"

This was no act. He genuinely didn't recognize me, and he genuinely didn't want anything to do with me. Baffled, I backed away from him, hustled down one of the subsidiary corridors of the bazaar, stepped out into the open, and hastily shunted myself ten years down the line. A couple of people saw me go, but faex on them; to a Turk of 1559 the world must have been full of efreets and jinni, and I was just one more phantom.

I didn't stay in 1569 more than five minutes. Sam's wild reaction to my greeting had me so mystified that I couldn't relax and see the sights. I had to have an explanation. So I hurried on down the line to 2059, materializing a block from the Covered Bazaar and nearly getting smeared by a taxi. A few latter-day Turks grinned and pointed at my medieval Turkish robes. The unsophisticated apes hadn't yet learned to take returning time-travelers for granted, I guess.

I went quickly to the nearest public communications booth, thumbed the plate, and put through a call to Sam.

"He is not at his home number," the master information output told me. "Should we trace him?"

"Yes, please," I said automatically.

A moment later I slapped myself for stupidity. Of course he won't be home, you idiot! He's up the line in 1559!

But the master communications network had already begun tracing him. Instead of doing the sensible thing and hanging up, I stood there like a moron, waiting for the inevitable news that the master communications network couldn't find him anywhere.

About three minutes went by. Then the bland voice said, "We have traced your party to Nairobi and he is standing by for your call. Please notify if you wish to proceed."

"Go ahead," I said, and Sam's ebony features blossomed on the screen.

"Is there trouble, child?" he asked.

"What are you doing in Nairobi?" I screamed.

"A little holiday among my own people. Should I not be here?"

"Look," I said, "I'm on my layoff between Courier jobs, and I've just been up the line to 1559 Istanbul, and I met you there."

"So?"

"How can you be there if you're in Nairobi?"

"The same way that there can be twenty-two specimens of your Arab instructor back there watching the

Romans nail up Jesus," Sam said. "Sheet, man, when will you learn to think four-dimensionally?"

"So that's a different you up the line in 1559?"

"It better be, buster! He's there and I'm here!" Sam laughed. "A little thing like that shouldn't upset you, man. You're a Courier now, remember?"

"Wait. Wait. Here's what happened. I walked into the Covered Bazaar, see, and there you were in Moorish robes, and I let out this big whoop and ran up to you to say hello. And you didn't know me, Sam! You started waving your scimitar, and cursing me out, and you told me in English to get the hell away from you, and —"

"Well, hey, man, you know it's against regulations to talk to other time-travelers when you're up the line. Unless you set out from the same now-time as the other man, you're supposed to ignore him even if you see through his cover. Fraternization is prohibited because—"

"Yeah, sure, but it was *me,* Sam. I didn't think you'd pull rules on *me.* You didn't even know me, Sam!"

"That's obvious. But why are you so upset, kid?"

"It was like you had amnesia. It scared me."

"But I *couldn't* have known you."

"What are you talking about?"

Sam began to laugh. "The Paradox of Discontinuity! Don't tell me they never taught you that one!"

"They said something about it, but I never paid much attention to a lot of that stuff, Sam."

"Well, pay attention now. You know what year it was I took that Istanbul trip?"

"No."

"It was 2056, '55, someplace back there. And I didn't meet you until three or four years later—this spring, it was. So the Sam you found in 1559 never saw you before. Discontinuity, see? You were working from a now-time basis of 2059, and I was working from a basis of maybe '55, and so you were a stranger to me, but I wasn't a stranger to you. That's one reason why Couriers aren't supposed to talk to friends they run into by accident up the line."

I began to see.

"I begin to see," I said.

"To me," said Sam, "you were some dumb fresh kid trying to make trouble, maybe even a Time Patrol fink. I didn't know you and I didn't want anything to do with you. Now that I think about it a little, I remember something like that happening when I was there. Somebody from down the line bothering me in the bazaar. Funny that I never connected him with you, though!"

"I had a fake beard on, up the line."

"That must have been it. Well, listen, are you all straightened out now?"

"The Paradox of Discontinuity, Sam. Sure."

"You'll remember to keep clear of old friends when you're up the line?"

"You bet. Christ, Sam, you really terrified me with that scimitar!"

"Otherwise, how's it going?"

"Great," I said. "It's really great."

"Watch those paradoxes, kid," Sam said, and blew me a kiss.

Much relieved, I stepped out of the booth and went up the line to 1550 to watch them build the mosque of Suleiman the Magnificent.

24.

Themistoklis Metaxas was the chief Courier for my second time-tour of Byzantium. From the moment I met him I sensed that this man was going to play a major role in my destiny, and I was right.

Metaxas was bantam-sized, maybe 1.5 meters tall. His skull was triangular, flat on top and pointed at the chin. His hair, thick and curly, was going gray. I guess he was about fifty years old. He had small glossy dark eyes, heavy brows, and a big sharp slab of a nose. He kept his lips curled inward so that he didn't seem to have lips at all. There was no fat on him anywhere. He was unusually strong. His voice was low and compelling.

Metaxas had charisma. Or should I call it chutzpah?

A little of both, I think. For him the whole universe revolved around Themistoklis Metaxas; suns were born only that they might shed starlight on Themistoklis Metaxas; the Benchley Effect had been invented solely to enable Themistoklis Metaxas to walk through the ages. If he ever died, the cosmos would crumble.

He had been one of the first Time Couriers ever hired, more than fifteen years ago. If he had cared to have the job, he could have been the head of the entire Courier Service by now, with a platoon of wanton secretaries and no need to battle fleas in old Byzantium. By choice, though, Metaxas remained a Courier on active duty, doing nothing but the Byzantium run. He practically regarded himself as a Byzantine citizen, and even spent his layoffs there, in a villa he had acquired in the suburbs of the early twelfth century.

He was engaged on the side in a variety of small and large illegalities; they might be interrupted if he retired as a Courier, so he didn't retire. The Time Patrol was terrified of him and let him have his own way in everything. Of course, Metaxas had more sense than to meddle with the past in any way that might cause serious changes in now-time, but aside from that his plunderings up the line were totally uninhibited.

When I met him for the first time, he said to me, "You haven't lived until you've laid one of your own ancestors."

25.

It was a big group: twelve tourists, Metaxas, and me. They always loaded a few extras into his tours because he was such an unusually capable Courier and in such great demand. I tagged along as an assistant, soaking up experience against my first solo trip, which would be coming next time.

Our dozen included three young and pretty single girls, Princeton co-eds making the Byzantium trip on gifts from their parents, who wanted them to learn something; two of the customary well-to-do middle-aged couples, one from Indianapolis and one from Milan; two youngish interior decorators, male and queer, from Beirut; a recently divorced response manipulator from New York, around forty-five and hungry for women; a puffy-faced little high-school teacher from Milwaukee, trying to improve his mind, and his wife; in short, the customary sampling.

At the end of the first introductory session all three of the Princeton girls, both interior decorators, and the Indianapolis wife were visibly hungering to go to bed with Metaxas. Nobody paid much attention to me.

"It will be different after the tour starts," said Metaxas consolingly. "Several of the girls will become available to you. You *do* want the girls, don't you?"

He was right. On our first night up the line he picked one of the Princeton girls for himself, and the other two resigned themselves speedily to accepting the second best. For some reason, Metaxas chose a pugnosed redhead with splashy freckles and big feet. He left for me a long, cool, sleek brunette, so flawless in every way that she was obviously the product of one of the world's finest helix men, and a cute, cheerful honey-blonde with warm eyes, smooth flesh, and the breasts of a twelve-year-old. I picked the brunette and regretted it; she came on in bed like something made of plastic. Toward dawn I traded her for the blonde and had a better time.

Metaxas was a tremendous Courier. He knew everybody and everything, and maneuvered us into superb positions for the big events.

"We are now," he said, "in January, 532. The Emperor Justinian rules. His ambition is to conquer the world and govern it from Constantinople, but most of his great achievements lie ahead. The city, as you see, still looks much as it did in the last century. In front of you is the Great Palace; to the rear is the rebuilt Haghia Sophia of Theodosius II, following the old basilica plan, not yet reconstructed with the familiar domes. The city is tense; there will soon be civil disorder. Come this way."

Shivering in the cold, we followed Metaxas through the city, down byways and avenues I had not traveled when I came this way earlier with Capistrano. Never once on this trip did I catch sight of my other self or Capistrano or any of that group; one of Metaxas' legendary skills was his ability to find new approaches to the standard scenes.

Of course, he had to. At this moment there were fifty or a hundred Metaxases leading tours through Justinian's city. As a matter of professional pride he wouldn't want to intersect any of those other selves.

"There are two factions in Constantinople now," said Metaxas. "The Blues and the Greens, they are called. They consist of perhaps a thousand men on each side, all troublemakers, and far more influential than their numbers indicate. The factions are something less than political parties, something more than mere supporters of sports teams, but they have characteristics of both. The Blues are more aristocratic; the Greens have links to the lower classes and the commercial strata. Each faction backs a team in the Hippodrome games, and each backs a certain course of governmental policies. Justinian has long been sympathetic to the Blues, and the Greens mistrust him. But as emperor he has tried to appear neutral. He would actually like to suppress both factions as threats to his power. Each night now the factions run wild in the streets. Look: those are the Blues."

Metaxas nodded at a cluster of insolent-looking bravos across the way: eight or nine idling men with long tumbles of thick hair to their shoulders, and festoons of beards and mustaches. They had cut back only the hair on the front of their heads. Their tunics were drawn in tight at the wrists, but flared out enormously from there to the shoulders; they wore gaudy capes and breeches and carried short two-edged swords. They looked brutal and dangerous.

"Wait here," said Metaxas, and went over to them.

The Blues greeted him like an old friend. They clapped him on the back, laughed, shouted in glee. I couldn't hear the conversation, but I saw Metaxas grasping hands, talking quickly, articulately, confidently. One of the Blues offered him a flask of wine and he took a deep drink;

then, hugging the man in mock tipsiness, Metaxas cunningly whisked the Blue's sword from its sheath and pretended to run him through. The rowdies capered and applauded. Now Metaxas pointed at us; there were nods of agreement, oglings of the girls, winks, gestures. Finally we were summoned across the street.

"Our friends invite us to the Hippodrome as their guests," said Metaxas. "The races begin next week. Tonight we are permitted to join them in their revels."

I could hardly believe it. When I'd been here with Capistrano, we skulked about, keeping out of sight, for this was a time of rape and murder by night, and all laws ceased to function after dark. How did Metaxas dare to bring us so close to the criminals?

He dared. And that night we roamed Constantinople, watching the Blues rob, ravish, and kill. For other citizens, death lay just around any corner; we were immune, privileged witnesses to the reign of terror. Metaxas presided over the nightmare prowl like a sawed-off Satan, cavorting with his Blue friends and even fingering one or two victims for them.

In the morning it seemed like a dream. The phantoms of violence vanished with the night; by pale winter sunlight we inspected the city and listened to Metaxas' historical commentary.

"Justinian," he said, "was a great conqueror, a great lawgiver, a great diplomat, and a great builder. This is history's verdict. We also have the *Secret History* of Procopius, which says that Justinian was both a knave and a fool, and that his wife Theodora was a demonic whorish villainess. I know this Procopius: a good man, a clever writer, something of a puritan, a little too gullible. But he's right about Justinian and Theodora. Justinian is a great man in the great things and a terribly evil man in the petty things. Theodora"—he spat—"is a whore among whores. She dances naked at dinners of state; she exhibits her body in public; she sleeps with her servants. I've heard she gives herself to dogs and donkeys, too. She's every bit as depraved as Procopius claims."

Metaxas' eyes twinkled. I knew without being told that he must have shared Theodora's bed.

Later that day he whispered, "I can arrange it for you. The risks are slight. Did you ever dream you could sleep with the Empress of Byzantium?"

"The risks—"

"What risks? You have your timer! You can get free! Listen to me, boy, she's an acrobat! She wraps her heels around your ears. She *consumes* you. I can fix it up for you. The Empress of Byzantium! Justinian's wife!"

"Not this trip," I blurted. "Some other time. I'm still too new at this business."

"You're afraid of her."

"I'm not ready to fuck an empress just yet," I said solemnly.

"Everybody else does it!"

"Couriers?"

"Most of them."

"On my next trip," I promised. The idea appalled me. I had to turn it off somehow. Metaxas misunderstood; I wasn't shy, or afraid of being caught by Justinian, or anything like that; but I couldn't bring myself to intersect with history that way. Traveling up the line was still fantasy for me; humping the celebrated monstress Theodora would make the fantasy all too real. Metaxas laughed at me, and for a while I think he felt contempt for me. But afterward he said, "It's okay. Don't let me rush you into things. When you're ready for her, though, don't miss her. I recommend her personally."

26.

We stayed around for a couple of days to watch the early phases of the riots. The New Year's Games were about to begin, and the Blues and Greens were growing more unruly. Their roughnecking was verging on anarchy; no one was safe in the streets after dark. Justinian worriedly ordered the factions to halt their maraudings, and various ringleaders were arrested. Seven were condemned to death, four by decapitation because they were caught carrying weapons, three by hanging on grounds of conspiracy.

Metaxas took us to see the performance. One of the Blues survived his first hanging when the rope broke under his weight. The imperial guards put him up there again, and again the gallows couldn't finish him, though the rope left fiery marks on his throat. So they put him aside for a while and strung up a Green, and bungled that job twice too; they were about to put the battered victims through a third hanging apiece when some outraged monks came boiling out of their monastery, grabbed the men in the midst of the confusion, and spirited them across the Golden Horn by rowboat to sanctuary in some church. Metaxas, who had seen all this before, cackled wildly at the fun. It seemed to me that his face peered at me from a thousand places in the crowd that had turned out for the executions.

Then the racing season began at the Hippodrome, and we went as guests of Metaxas' friendly gang of Blues. We had plenty of company; 100,000 Byzantines were in the stands. The tiers of marble seats were crowded far past capacity, but space had been saved for us.

I hunted for myself in the stands, knowing that I sat somewhere else here with Capistrano and that tour; but in the crush I couldn't catch a glimpse of myself. I saw plenty of Metaxas, though.

The blonde Princetonian gasped when we got to our seats. "Look there!" she said. "The things from Istanbul!" Down the center of the arena was a row of familiar monuments, marking the boundary between the outward and inward courses of the track. The serpent column from Delphi, brought here by Constantine, was there, and the great obelisk of Thutmose III, stolen out of Egypt by the first Theodosius. The blonde remembered them from Istanbul down the line, where they still stand, though the Hippodrome itself is gone.

"But where's the third one?" she asked.

Metaxas said softly, "The other obelisk has not yet been erected. Best not to talk about it."

It was the third day of the races—the fatal day. An ugly mood gripped this arena where emperors had been made and unmade. Yesterday and the day before, I knew, there had been nasty outcries when Justinian appeared in the imperial box; the crowd had yelled to him to free the imprisoned ringleaders of the factions, but he had ignored the shouts and let the races proceed. Today, January 13, Constantinople would erupt. Time-tourists love catastrophes; this would be a good one. I knew. I had seen it already.

Below, officials were completing the preliminary rituals. Imperial guards, standards flying, paraded grandly. Those leaders of the Blues and Greens who were not in jail exchanged chilly ceremonial greetings. Now the mob stirred, and Justinian entered his box, a man of middle height, rather plump, with a round, florid face. Empress Theodora followed. She wore clinging, diaphanous silks, and she had rouged her nipples; they blazed through the fabric like beacons.

Justinian mounted the steps of his box. The cries began: "Free them! Let them out!" Serenely he lifted a fold of his purple robe and blessed the audience with the sign of the Cross, three times, once toward the center block of seats, then to the right, then to the left. The uproar grew. He threw a white kerchief down. Let the games begin! Theodora stretched and yawned and pulled up her robe to study the contours of her thighs. The stable doors burst open. Out came the first four chariots.

They were quadrigas, four-horse vehicles; the audience forgot about politics as, wheel to wheel, the chariots went into action. Metaxas said pleasantly, "Theodora has been to bed with each of the drivers. I wonder which one is her favorite." The empress looked profoundly bored. I had been surprised to find her here, the last time: I had thought that empresses were barred from the Hippodrome. As indeed they were, but Theodora made her own rules.

The charioteers hustled down to the spina, the row of monuments, and came round and back up the course. A race ran seven rounds; seven ostrich eggs were set out on a stand, and as each round was completed one egg was removed. We watched two races. Then Metaxas said, "Let us shunt forward by one hour and get to the climax of this." Only Metaxas would pull a bit like that: we adjusted all the timers and shunted, en masse, in casual disregard of the rules for public jumping. When we reappeared in the Hippodrome, the sixth race was about to begin.

"Now starts the trouble," said Metaxas happily.

The race was run. But as the victor came forth to receive his crown, a booming voice bellowed from out of a group of Blues, "Long live the Greens and Blues!"

An instant later, from the seats of the Greens, came the answering cry: "Long live the Blues and Greens!"

"The factions are uniting against Justinian," Metaxas said, quietly, schoolmasterishly. The chaos that was engulfing the stadium didn't ruffle him.

"Long live the Greens and Blues!"

"Long live the Blues and Greens!"

"Long live the Greens and Blues!"

"Victory!"

"Victory!"

"Victory!"

And the one word, "Victory!" became a mighty cry from thousands of throats. *"Nika! Nika!* Victory!"

Theodora laughed. Justinian, scowling, conferred with officers of his imperial guard. Greens and Blues marched from the Hippodrome, followed by a happy, screaming mob bent on destruction. We hung back, keeping a judicious distance; I caught sight of other equally cautious little groups of spectators, and knew they were no Byzantines.

Torches flared in the streets. The imperial prison was aflame. The prisoners were free, the jailers were burning. Justinian's own guard, afraid to interfere, looked on soberly. The rioters piled faggots against the gate of the Great Palace, across the plaza from the Hippodrome. Soon the palace was on fire. Theodosius' Haghia Sophia was aflame; bearded priests, waving precious icons, appeared on its blazing roof and toppled back into the inferno. The senate house caught fire. It was a glorious orgy of destruction. Whenever snarling rioters approached us, we adjusted timers and shunted down the line, taking care to jump no more than ten or fifteen minutes at a hop, so that we wouldn't reappear right inside some fire that hadn't been set when we shunted.

"Nika! Nika!"

Constantinople's sky was black with oily smoke, and flames danced on the horizon. Metaxas, his wedge-shaped face smudged and sooty, his eyes glinting with excitement, seemed constantly on the verge of breaking away from us and going to join the destroyers.

"The firemen themselves are looting," he called to us. "And look—the Blues burn the houses of the Greens, and the Greens burn the houses of the Blues!"

A tremendous exodus was under way, as terrified citizens streamed toward the docks and begged the boatmen to ferry them to the Asian side. Unharmed, invulnerable, we moved through the holocaust, witnessing the walls of the old Haghia Sophia collapse, watching flames sweep the Great Palace, observing the behavior of the looters and the arsonists and the rapists who paused in fire-spattered alleys to pump some screaming silk-clad noblewoman full of proletarian jissom.

Metaxas skillfully edited the riots for us; he had timed everything dozens of visits ago, and he knew exactly which highlights to hit.

"Now we shunt forward six hours and forty minutes," he said.

"Now we jump three hours and eight minutes."

"Now we jump an hour and a half."

"Now we jump two days."

We saw everything that mattered. With the city still aflame, Justinian sent bishops and priests forth bearing sacred relics, a piece of the True Cross, the rod of Moses, the horn of Abraham's ram, the bones of martyrs; the frightened clerics paraded bravely about, asking for a miracle, but no miracles came, only cascades of brickbats and stones. A general led forty guardsmen out to protect the holy men. "That is the famous Belisarius," said Metaxas. Messages came from the emperor, announcing the deposing of unpopular officials; but churches were sacked, the imperial library given the torch, the baths of Zeuxippus were destroyed.

On January 18, Justinian was bold enough to appear publicly in the Hippodrome to call for peace. He was hissed down by the Greens and fled as stone-throwing began. We saw a worthless prince named Hypatius proclaimed as emperor by the rebels in the Square of Constantine; we saw General Belisarius march through the smoldering city in defense of Justinian; we saw the butchery of the insurgents.

We saw everything. I understood why Metaxas was the most coveted of Couriers. Capistrano had done his best to give his people an exciting show, but he had wasted too much time in the early phases. Metaxas, leaping brilliantly over hours and days, unveiled the entire catastrophe for us, and brought us at last to the morning when order was restored and a shaken Justinian rode through the charred ruins of Constantinople. By a red dawn we saw the clouds of ash still dancing in the air. Justinian studied the blackened hull of Haghia Sophia, and we studied Justinian.

Metaxas said, "He is planning the new cathedral. He will make it the greatest shrine since Solomon's Temple in Jerusalem. Come: we have seen enough destruction. Now let us see the birth of beauty. Down the line, all of you! Five years and ten months down the line, and behold Haghia Sophia!"

27.

"On your next layoff," said Metaxas, "visit me at my villa. I live there now in 1105. It is a good time to be in Byzantium; Alexius Comnenus rules and rules wisely. I'll have a lusty wench ready for you, and plenty of wine. You'll come?"

I was lost in admiration for the sharp-faced little man. We were nearing the end of our tour, with only the Turkish Conquest yet to do, and he had revealed to me in a stunning way the difference between an inspired Courier and a merely competent one.

Only a lifetime of dedication to the task could achieve such results, could provide such a show.

Metaxas hadn't just taken us to the standard highlights. He had shown us any number of minor events, splicing us in for an hour here, two hours there, creating for us a glorious mosaic of Byzantine history that dimmed the luster of the mosaics of Haghia Sophia. Other Couriers made a dozen stops, perhaps; Metaxas made more than fifty.

He had a special fondness for the foolish emperors. We had listened to a speech of Michael II, the Stammerer, and we had watched the antics of Michael III, the Drunkard, and we had attended the baptism of the fifth Constantine, who had the misfortune to soil the font and was known for the rest of his life as Constantine Copronymus, Constantine the Pisser. Metaxas was completely at home in Byzantium in any one of a thousand years. Coolly, easily, confidently, he ranged through the eras.

The villa he maintained was a mark of his confidence and his audacity. No other Courier had ever dared to create a second identity for himself up the line, spending all his holidays as a citizen of the past. Metaxas ran his villa on a now-time basis; when he had to leave it for two weeks to run a tour, he took care to return to it two weeks after his departure. He never overlapped himself, never let himself go to it at a time when he was already in residence; there was only one Metaxas permitted to use it, and that was the now-time Metaxas. He had bought the villa ten years ago in his double now-time: 2049 down the line, 1095 in Byzantium. And he had maintained his basis with precision; it was ten years later for him in both places. I promised to visit him in 1105. It would be an honor, I said.

He grinned and said, "I'll introduce you to my great-great-multi-great-grandmother when you come, too. She's a terrific lay. You remember what I told you about screwing your own ancestors? There's nothing finer!"

I was stunned. "Does she know who you are?"

"Don't talk nonsense," said Metaxas. "Would I break the first rule of the Time Service? Would I even hint to anyone up the line that I came from the future? *Would I?* Even Themistoklis Metaxas abides by *that* rule!"

Like the moody Capistrano, Metaxas had devoted much effort to hunting out his ancestors. His motives were altogether different, though. Capistrano was plotting an elaborate suicide, but Metaxas was obsessed with transtemporal incest.

"Isn't it risky?" I asked.

"Just take your pills and you're safe, and so is she."

"I mean the Time Patrol—"

"You make sure they don't find out," said Metaxas. "That way it isn't risky."

"If you happen to get her pregnant, you might become your own ancestor."

"Groovy," said Metaxas.

"But—"

"People don't get people pregnant by accident any more, boy. Of course," he added, "some day I might want to knock her up on purpose."

I felt the time-winds blowing up a gale.

I said, "You're talking anarchy!"

"Nihilism, to be more accurate. Look here, Jud, look at this book. I've got all my female ancestors listed, hundreds of them, from the nineteenth century back to the tenth. Nobody else in the world has a book like this except maybe some snotty ex-kings and queens, and even they don't have it this complete."

"There's Capistrano," I said.

"He goes back only to the fourteenth century! Anyway, he's sick in the head. You know why he does his genealogies?"

"Yes."

"He's pretty sick, isn't he?"

"Yes," I said. "But tell me, why are you so eager to sleep with your own ancestors?"

"Do you really want to know?"

"Really."

Metaxas said, "My father was a cold, hateful man. He beat his children every morning before breakfast for exercise. *His* father was a cold, hateful man. He forced his children to live like slaves. *His* father—I come from a long line of tyrannical authoritarian dictatorial males. I despise them all. It is my form of rebellion against the father-image. I go on and on through the past, seducing the wives and sisters and daughters of these men whom I loathe. Thus I puncture their icy smugness."

"In that case, then, to be perfectly consistent, you must have—your own mother—begun with—"

"I draw the line at abominations," said Metaxas.

"I see."

"But my grandmother, yes! And several great-grandmothers! And on and on and on!" His eyes glowed. It was a divine mission with him. "I have ploughed through twenty, thirty generations already, and I will keep on for thirty more!" Metaxas laughed his shrill, satanic laugh. "Besides," he said, "I enjoy a good lay as much as the next man. Others seduce at random; Metaxas seduces *systematically!* It gives meaning and structure to my life. This interests you, eh?"

"Well—"

"It is life's most intense joy, what I do."

I pictured a row of naked women lying side by side, reaching off to infinity. Every one of them had the wedge-shaped head and sharp features of Themistoklis Metaxas. And Metaxas was moving patiently up the line, pausing to stick it into this one, and the one next to her, and the next, and the next, and in his tireless fashion he balled right up the line until the spread-legged women grew hairy and chinless, the womenfolk of Pithecanthropus erectus, and there was Metaxas erectus still jazzing his way back to the beginning of time. Bravo, Metaxas! Bravo!

"Why don't you try it sometime?" he asked.

"Well—"

"They tell me you are of Greek descent."

"On my mother's side, yes."

"Then probably your ancestors lived right here in Constantinople. No Greek worth anything would have lived in Greece itself at this time. At this very moment a luscious ancestress of yours is in this very city!"

"Well—"

"Find her!" cried Metaxas. "Fuck her! It is joy! It is ecstasy! Defy space and time! Stick your finger in God's eye!"

"I'm not sure I really want to," I said. But I did.

28.

As I say, Metaxas transformed my life. He changed my destinies in many ways, not all of them good. But one good thing he did for me was to give me confidence. His charisma and his chutzpah both rubbed off on me. I learned arrogance from Metaxas.

Up until this point I had been a modest and self-effacing young man, at least while I was around my elders.

Especially in my Time Service aspect I had been unpushy and callow. I did a lot of forelock-tugging and no doubt came across even more naive than I really was. I acted this way because I was young and had a lot to learn, not only about myself, which everybody does, but also about the workings of the Time Service. So far I had met a lot of men who were older, smarter, slicker, and more corrupt than myself, and I had treated them with deference: Sam, Dajani, Jeff Monroe, Sid Buonocore, Capistrano. But now I was with Metaxas, who was the oldest, smartest, slickest and most corrupt of them all, and he imparted momentum to me, so that I stopped orbiting other men and took up a trajectory of my own.

Later I found out that this is one of Metaxas' functions in the Time Service. He takes moist-eyed young Couriers-in-training and fills them full of the swagger they need to be successful operators in their own right.

When I got back from my tour with Metaxas I no longer feared my first solo as a Courier. I was ready to go. Metaxas had showed me how a Courier can be a kind of artist, assembling a portrait of the past for his clients, and that was what I wanted to be. The risks and responsibilities didn't trouble me now.

Protopopolos said, "When you come back from your layoff, you'll take six people out on the one-week tour."

"I'll skip the layoff. I'm ready to leave right now!"

"Well, your tourists aren't. Anyway, the law says you've got to rest between trips. So rest. I'll see you back here in two weeks, Jud."

So I had a holiday against my will. I was tempted to accept Metaxas' invitation to his villa in 1105, but it occurred to me that maybe Metaxas had had enough of my company for a while. Then I toyed with the idea of signing up with a time-tour to Hastings or Waterloo or even back to the Crucifixion to count the Dajanis. But I passed that up, too. Now that I was on the threshold of leading a tour myself, I didn't want to have to be led by somebody else, not just at the moment. I needed to be more secure in my new-found confidence before I dropped down under some other Courier's leadership again.

I dithered around in now-time Istanbul for three days, doing nothing special. Mainly I hung around the Time Service headquarters, playing stochastic chess with Kolettis and Melamed, who also happened to be off duty at this time. On the fourth day I hopped a shortshot for Athens. I didn't know why I was going there until I got there.

I was up on the Acropolis when I realized what my mission was. I was wandering around the ruins, fending off the peddlers of hologram slides and the guided-tour hucksters, when an advert globe came drifting toward me. It hovered about four feet away from me at eye level, radiating a flickering green glow designed to compel my attention, and said, "Good afternoon. We hope you're enjoying your visit to twenty-first-century Athens. Now that you've seen the picturesque ruins, how would you like to see the Parthenon as it *really* looked? See the Greece of Socrates and Aristophanes? Your local Time Service office is on Aeolou Street, just opposite the Central Post Office, and—"

Half an hour later I checked in at the Aeolou Street headquarters, identified myself as a Courier on vacation, and outfitted myself for a shunt up the line.

Not to the Greece of Socrates and Aristophanes, though.

I was heading for the Greece of the prosaic year 1997, when Konstantin Passalidis was elected mayor of Sparta.

Konstantin Passalidis was my mother's father. I was about to start tracing my ancestral seed back to its sprouting place.

Dressed in the stark, itchy clothes of the late twentieth century, and carrying crisp and colorful obsolete banknotes, I shunted back sixty years and caught the first pod from Athens to Sparta. Pod service was brand new in

Greece in 1997, and I was in mortal terror of a phaseout all the way down, but the alignment held true and I got to Sparta in one piece.

Sparta was remarkably hideous.

The present Sparta is not, of course, a linear descendant of the old militaristic place that caused so much trouble for Athens. That Sparta faded away gradually, and vanished altogether in medieval times. The new Sparta was founded in the early nineteenth century on the old site. In Grandfather Passilidis' heyday it was a city of about 80,000 people, having grown rapidly after the installation of Greece's first fusion-power plant there in the 1980's.

It consisted of hundreds of identical apartment houses of gray brick, arranged in perfectly straight rows. Every one of them was ten stories high, decked with lemon-colored balconies on every floor, and about as appealing as a jail. At one end of this barracks-like city was the shining dome of the power plant; at the other was a downtown section of taverns, banks, and municipal offices. It was quite charming, if you find brutality charming.

I got off the pod and walked downtown. There weren't any master information outputs to be seen on the streets —I guess the network hadn't yet gone into operation here —but I had no trouble finding Mayor Passilidis. I stopped at a tavern for a quick *ouzo* and said, "Where can I find Mayor Passilidis?" and a dozen friendly Spartans escorted me to City Hall.

His receptionist was a dark-haired girl of about twenty with big breasts and a faint mustache. Her Minoan Revival bodice was neatly calculated to distract a man's attention from the shortcomings of her face. Wiggling those pink-tipped meaty globes at me, she said huskily, "Can I help you?"

"I'd like to see Mayor Passilidis. I'm from an American newspaper. We're doing an article on Greece's ten most dynamic young men, and we feel that Mr. Passilidis—"

It didn't sound convincing even to me. I stood there studying the beads of sweat on the white mounds of her bosom, waiting for her to turn me away. But she bought the story unhesitatingly, and with a minimum of delay I was escorted into His Honor's office.

"A pleasure to have you here," my grandfather said in perfect English. "Won't you sit down? Can I get you a martini, maybe? Or if you'd prefer a weed—"

I froze. I panicked. I didn't even take his hand when he offered it to me.

The sight of Konstantin Passilidis terrified me.

I had never seen my grandfather before, of course. He was gunned down by an Abolitionist hoodlum in 2010, long before I was born—one of the many victims of the Year of Assassins.

Time-travel had never seemed so frighteningly real to me as it did right now. Justinian in the imperial box at the Hippodrome was nothing at all compared to Konstantin Passilidis greeting me in his office in Sparta.

He was in his early thirties, a boy wonder of his time. His hair was dark and curly, just beginning to gray at the fringes, and he wore a little clipped mustache and a ring in his left ear. What terrified me so much was our physical resemblance. He could have been my older brother.

After an endless moment I snapped out of my freeze. He was a little puzzled, I guess, but he courteously offered me refreshment again, and I declined, telling him I didn't indulge, and somehow I found enough poise to launch my "interview" of him.

We talked about his political career and all the wonderful things he planned to do for Sparta and for Greece. Just as I was starting to work the conversation around to the personal side, to his family background, he looked at his watch and said, "It's time for lunch. Will you be my guest?"

What he had in mind was a typical Mediterranean siesta, closing the office down for three hours and going home. We drove there in his little electric runabout, with the mayor himself at the steering rod. He lived in one of the gray apartment houses, like any ordinary citizen: four humble rooms on the fifth floor.

"I'd like you to meet my wife," Mayor Passilidis said. "Katina, this is an American newspaperman, Jud Elliott. He wants to write about my career."

I stared at my grandmother.

My grandmother stared at me.

We both gasped. We were both amazed.

29.

She was beautiful, the way the girls on the Minoan murals are beautiful. Dark, very dark, with black hair, olive skin, dark eyes. Peasant strength to her. She didn't expose her breasts the way the fashionable mustachioed receptionist had done, but her thin blouse wasn't very concealing. They were high and round. Her hips were broad. She was lush, fertile, abundant. I suppose she was about twenty-three years old, perhaps twenty-four.

It was lust at first sight. Her beauty, her simplicity, her warmth, captivated me instantly. I felt a familiar tickling in the scrotum and a familiar tightening of the glutei. I longed to rip away her clothing and sink myself deep into her hot tangled black shrubbery.

This was not a Metaxian incestuous wish. It was an innocent and purely animal reaction.

In that onrushing tide of yearning I didn't even think of her as my grandmother. I thought of her only as a young and fantastically desirable woman. A couple of ticks later I realized on an emotional level who she was, and I went limp at once.

She was Grandma Passilidis. And I remembered Grandma Passilidis.

I used to visit her at the senior citizens' camp near Tampa. She died when I was fourteen, in '49, and though she was only in her seventies then, she had always seemed terribly old and decrepit to me, a withered, shrunken, palsied little woman who wore black clothing all the time. Only her eyes—my God, her dark, liquid, warm, shining eyes!—had ever given any hint that she might once have been a healthy and vital human being.

Grandma Passilidis had had all kinds of diseases, feminine things first—prolapses of the uterus or whatever it is they get—and then kidney breakdowns and the rest. She had been through a dozen or more organ transplants, but nothing had helped, and all through my childhood she had inexorably declined. I was always hearing of some new crisis on her road to the grave, the poor old lady!

Here was the same poor old lady, miraculously relieved of her burden of years. And here was I, mentally snuggling between the thighs of my mother's mother. O vile impiety, that man should travel backward through time and think such thoughts!

Young Mrs. Passilidis' reaction to me was equally potent, although not at all lustful. For her, sex began and ended with the mayoral pecker. She stared at me not in desire but in astonishment and blurted finally, "Konstantin, he looks just like you!"

"Indeed?" said Mayor Passilidis. He hadn't noticed it before.

His wife propelled us both toward the living-room mirror, giggling and excited. The soft masses of her bosom jostled up against me and I began to sweat. "Look!" she cried. "Look there? Like brothers you are!"

"Amazing," said Mayor Passilidis.

"An incredible coincidence," I said. "Your hair is thicker, and I'm a little taller, but—"

"Yes! Yes!" The mayor clapped his hands. "Can it be that we are related?"

"Impossible," I said solemnly. "My family's from Boston. Old New England stock. Nevertheless it *is* amazing. You're sure you didn't have ancestors on the Mayflower, Mr. Passilidis?"

"Not unless there was a Greek steward on board."

"I doubt that."

"So do I. I am pure Greek on both sides for many generations," he said.

"I'd like to talk about that with you a little if I could," I said casually. "For example, I'd like to know—"

Just then a sleepy and completely naked five-year-old girl came out of one of the bedrooms. She planted herself shamelessly before me and asked me who I was. How sweet, I thought. That saucy little rump, that pink little slit—how *clean* little girls always look when they're naked. Before puberty messes them up.

Passilidis said proudly, "This is my daughter Diana."

A voice of thunder said in my brain, "THE NAKEDNESS OF THY MOTHER SHALT THOU NOT UNCOVER."

I looked away, shattered, and covered my confusion with a coughing fit. Little Diana's fleeceless labia blazed in my soul. As though sensing that I saw something improper about the child's bareness, Katina Passilidis hustled a pair of panties onto her.

I was still shaking. Passilidis, puzzled, uncorked some retsina. We sat on the balcony in the bright midday light. Below, some schoolchildren waved and shouted greetings to the mayor. Little Diana toddled out to be played with, and I tousled her fluffy hair and pressed the tip of her nose and felt very, very strange about all of this.

My grandmother provided a handsome lunch of boiled lamb and pastitsio. We went through a bottle and a half of retsina. I finished pumping the mayor about politics and shifted to the topic of his ancestors. "Have your people always lived in Sparta?" I asked.

"Oh, no," he said. "My grandfather's people came here a century ago from Cyprus. That is, on my father's side. On my mother's side I am Athenian, for many generations back."

"That's the Markezinis family?" I said.

He gave me a queer look. "Why, yes! How did you—"

"Something I came across while I was reading up on you," I said hurriedly.

Passilidis let the point pass. Now that he was on the subject of his family he grew expansive—maybe it was the wine—and favored me with the genealogical details. "My father's people were on Cyprus for at least a thousand years," he said. "There was a Passilidis there when the Crusaders came. On the other hand, my mother's ancestors came to Athens only in the nineteenth century, after the defeat of the Turks. Before that they lived in Shqiperi."

"Shqiperi?"

"Albania. They settled there in the thirteenth century when the Latins seized Constantinople. And then they remained, through the Serbians, through the Turks, through the time of Skanderbeg the rebel, always retaining their Greek heritage against all difficulties."

My ears prickled. "You mentioned Constantinople? You can trace your ancestry there?"

Passilidis smiled. "Do you know Byzantine history?"

"Slightly," I said.

"Perhaps you know that in the year 1204 the Crusaders seized Constantinople and ruled it for a while as a Latin kingdom. The Byzantine nobility fled, and several new Byzantine splinter states formed—one in Asia Minor, one on the Black Sea, and one in the west, in Albania. My ancestors followed Michael Angelus Comnenus into Albania, rather than submit to the rule of the Crusaders."

"I see." I was trembling again. "And the family name? It was Markezinis even back then?"

"Oh, no, Markezinis is a late Greek name! In Byzantium we were of the Ducas family."

"You *were?*" I gasped. It was as if he had been a German claiming Hohenzollern blood, or an Englishman laying claim to Plantagenet genes. "Ducas! Really?"

I had seen the gleaming palaces of the Ducas family. I had watched forty proud Ducases march clad in cloth of gold through the streets of Constantinople, to celebrate the rise of their cousin Constantine to the imperial throne. If Passilidis was a Ducas, *I* was a Ducas.

"Of course," he said, "the family was very large, and I believe we were of a minor branch. Still, it is something to take pride in, descent from such a family."

"It certainly is. Could you give me the names of any of your Byzantine ancestors, maybe? The first names?"

I must have sounded as though I planned to look them up the next time I was in Byzantium. Which I did, but Passilidis wasn't supposed to suspect that, because time-travel hadn't been invented yet.

He frowned and said, "Do you need this for the article you are writing?"

"No, not really. I'm just curious."

"You seem to know more than a little about Byzantium." It worried him that an American barbarian would recognize the name of a famous Byzantine family.

I said, "Just casual knowledge. I studied it in school."

"Sadly, I can give you no names. This information has not come down to us. But perhaps some day, when I have retired from politics, I will search the old records—"

My grandmother poured us more wine, and I stole a

quick, guilty peek at her full, swaying breasts. My mother climbed on my knee and made little trilling noises. My grandfather shook his head and said, "It is very surprising, the way you resemble me. Can I take your photograph?"

I wondered if it went against Time Patrol regulations. I decided that it probably did. But also I saw no polite way to refuse such a trifling request.

My grandmother produced a camera. Passilidis and I stood side by side and she took a picture of us for him, and then one for me. She pulled them from the camera when they were developed and we studied them intently.

"Like brothers," she said over and over. "Like brothers!"

I destroyed my print as soon as I was out of the apartment. But I suppose that somewhere in my mother's papers there is an old and faded flattie photograph showing her father as a young man, standing beside a somewhat younger man who looks very much like him, and whom my mother probably assumed was some forgotten uncle of hers. Perhaps the photograph still exists. I'd be afraid to look.

30.

Grandfather Passilidis had saved me a great deal of trouble. He had lopped almost eight centuries off what I was already starting to think of as my quest.

I jumped down the line to now-time, did some research in the Time Service headquarters at Athens, and had myself outfitted as a Byzantine noble of the late twelfth century, with a sumptuous silk tunic, black cloak, and white bonnet. Then I podded up north to Albania, getting off at the town of Gjinokaster. In the old days this town was known as Argyrokastro, in the district of Epirus.

From Gjinokaster I went up the line to the year 1205.

The peasant folk of Argyrokastro were awed by my princely garb. I told them I was seeking the court of Michael Angelus Comnenus, and they told me the way and sold me a donkey to help me get there. I found Michael and the rest of the exiled Byzantines holding a chariot race in an improvised Hippodrome at the foot of a range of jagged hills. Quietly I affiliated myself with the crowd.

"I'm looking for Ducas," I told a harmless-looking old man who was passing around some wine.

"Ducas? Which one?"

"Are there many here? I bear a message from Constantinople for a Ducas, but they did not tell me there was more than one."

The old man laughed. "Just before me," he said, "I see Nicephorus Ducas, John Ducas, Leo Ducas, George Ducas, Nicephorus Ducas the Younger, Michael Ducas, Simeon Ducas, and Dimitrios Ducas. I am unable to find at the moment Eftimios Ducas, Leontios Ducas, Simeon Ducas the Tall, Constantine Ducas, and—let me think—Andronicus Ducas. Which member of the family, pray, do you seek?"

I thanked him and moved down the line.

In sixteenth century Gjinokaster I asked about the Markezinis family. My Byzantine garb earned me some strange glances, but the Byzantine gold pieces I carried got me all the information I needed. One bezant and I was given the location of the Markezinis estate. Two bezants more and I had an introduction to the foreman of the Markezinis vineyard. Five bezants—a steep price—and I found myself nibbling grapes in the guest-hall of Gregory Markezinis, the head of the clan. He was a distinguished man of middle years with a flowing gray beard and burning eyes; he was stern but hospitable. As we talked, his daughters moved serenely about us, refilling our cups, bringing more grapes, cold legs of lamb, mounds of rice. There were three girls, possibly thirteen, fifteen, and seventeen years old. I took good care not to look too closely at them, knowing the jealous temperament of mountain chieftains.

They were beauties: olive skin, dark eyes, high breasts, full lips. They might have been sisters of my radiant grandmother Katina Passilidis. My mother Diana, I believe, looked this way in girlhood. The family genes are powerful ones.

Unless I happened to be climbing on the wrong branch of the tree, one of these girls was my great-great-multi-great-grandmother. And Gregory Markezinis was my great-great-great-multi-great-grandfather.

I introduced myself as a wealthy young Cypriote of Byzantine descent who was traveling the world in search of pleasure and adventure. Gregory, whose Greek was slightly contaminated by Albanian words (did his serfs speak Gheg or Tosk? I forget) had evidently never met a Cypriote before, since he accepted my accent as authentic. "Where have you been?" he asked.

Oh, I said, Syria and Libya and Egypt, and Rome and Paris and Lisbon, and to London to attend the coronation of Henry VIII, and Prague, and Vienna. And now I was working my way eastward again, into the Turkish domain, determined despite all risks to visit the graves of my ancestors in Constantinople.

He raised an eyebrow at the mention of ancestors. Energetically hacking off a slice of lamb with his dagger, he said, "Was your family a high one in the old days?"

"I am of the Ducas line."

"Ducas?"

"Ducas," I said blandly.

"I am of the Ducas line as well."

"Indeed!"

"Beyond doubt!"

"A Ducas in Epirus!" I cried. "How did it happen?"

"We came here with the Comneni, after the Latin pigs took Constantinople."

"Indeed!"

"Beyond doubt!"

He called for more wine, the best in the house. When his daughters appeared, he did a little dance, crying, "A kinsman! A kinsman! The stranger is a kinsman! Give him proper greeting!"

I found myself engulfed in Markezinis daughters, overwhelmed by taut youthful breasts and sweet musky bodies. Chastely I embraced them, as a long-lost cousin would.

Over thick, elderly wine we talked genealogy. I went first, picking a Ducas at random—Theodoros—and claiming that he had escaped to Cyprus after the debacle in Constantinople in 1204, to found my line. Markezinis had no way of disproving that, and in fact he accepted it at face value. I unreeled a long list of Ducas forebears up the line between myself and distant Theodoros, using customary Byzantine names. When I concluded I said, "And you, Gregory?"

Using his knife to scratch family trees into the table top at some of the difficult points, Markezinis traced his line back to a Nicholas Markezinis of the late fourteenth century who had married the eldest daughter of Manuel Ducas of Argyrokastro, that Ducas having had only daughters and therefore bringing his immediate line to an end. From Manuel, then, Markezinis took things back in a leisurely way to the expulsion of the Byzantines from Constantinople by the Fourth Crusade. The particular Ducas of his direct line who had fled to Albania was, he said, Simeon.

My gonads plunged in despair.

"Simeon?" I said. "Do you mean Simeon Ducas the Tall, or the other one?"

"Were there two? How could you know?"

Cheeks flaming, I improvised, "I have to confess that I am something of a student of the family. Two Simeon Ducases followed the Comneni to this land, Simeon the Tall and a man of shorter stature."

"Of this I know nothing," said Markezinis. "I have been taught that my ancestor's name was Simeon. And his father was Nicephorus, whose palace was close to the church of St. Theodosia, by the Golden Horn. The Venetians burned the palace of Nicephorus when they took the city in 1204. And the father of Nicephorus—" He hesitated, shaking his head slowly and sadly from side to side like an aging buffalo. "I do not remember the name of the father of Nicephorus. I have forgotten the name of the father of Nicephorus. Was it Leo? Michael? Basil? I forget. My head is full of wine."

"It does not matter that much," I said. With the ancestry traced into Constantinople, there would be no further difficulties.

"Romanos? John? Isaac? It is right here, inside my head, but there are so many names—so many names—"

Still muttering names, he fell asleep at the table.

A dark-eyed daughter showed me to a drafty bedroom. I could have shunted instead, having learned all here that I had come to know; but it seemed civil to spend the night under my multi-great-grandfather's roof, rather than vanishing like a thief. I stripped, snuffed the candle, got into bed.

In the darkness a soft-bodied wench joined me under the blankets.

Her breasts nicely filled my hands and her fragrance was sweetly musky. I couldn't see her, but I assumed she must be one of the Markezinis' three daughters, coming to show how hospitable the family could be.

My palm slid down her smoothly rounded belly to its

base, and when I reached the junction of her thighs, her legs opened to me, and I found her ready for love.

I felt obscurely disappointed at the thought that Markezinis' daughters would give themselves so freely to strangers—even a noble stranger claiming to be a cousin. After all, these were my *ancestors*. Was my line of descent muddied by the sperm of casual wayfarers?

That thought led logically to the really troublesome one, which was, if this girl is really my great-great-multigreat-grandmother, what am *I* doing in bed with her? To hell with sleeping with strangers—should she sleep with descendants? When I began this quest at Metaxas' prodding, it wasn't really with the intent of committing transtemporal incest—but yet here I was doing it, it seemed.

Guilt blossomed in me and I became so nervous that it made me momentarily impotent.

But my bedmate slithered down to my waist and restored my virility with busy lips. A fine old Byzantine trick, I thought, and, rigid again, I slipped into her and pronged her with gusto. I soothed my conscience by telling myself that the chances were two out of three that this girl was merely my great-great-multi-great-*aunt,* in which case the incest must surely be far less serious. So far as bloodlines went, the connection between myself and any sixteenth-century aunt must be exceedingly cloudy.

My conscience let me alone after that, and the girl and I gasped our way to completion. And then she rose, and went from the room, and as she passed the window a sliver of moonlight illuminated her white buttocks and her pale thighs and her long blonde hair, and I realized what I should have known all along, which is that the Markezinis girls would not come like Eskimo wenches to sleep with guests, but that someone had thoughtfully sent in a slave-girl for my amusement. So much for the prickings of conscience. Absolved even of the most tenuous incest, I slept soundly.

In the morning, over a breakfast of cold lamb and rice,

Gregory Markezinis said, "Word reaches me that the Spaniards have found a new world beyond the Ocean Sea. Do you think there's truth in it?"

This was the year A.D. 1556.

I said, "Beyond all doubt it's true. I saw the proof in Spain, at the court of King Charles. It's a world of gold and jade and spices—of red-skinned men—"

"*Red*-skinned men? Oh, no, cousin Ducas, no, no, I can never believe that!" Markezinis roared in delight, and summoned his daughters. "The new world of the Spaniards—its men have red skins! Cousin Ducas tells us so!"

"Well, copper-colored, really," I murmured, but Markezinis scarcely heard.

"Red skins! Red skins! And no heads, but eyes and mouths in their chests! And men with a single leg, which they raise above their heads at midday to shield themselves from the sun! Yes! Yes! Oh, wonderful new world! Cousin, you amuse me!"

I told him I was glad to bring him such pleasure. I thanked him for his gracious hospitality, and chastely embraced each of his daughters, and prepared to take my leave. And suddenly it struck me that if my ancestors' name had been Markezinis from the fourteenth century through the twentieth, then none of these girls could possibly be ancestral to me. My priggish pangs of conscience had been pointless, except insofar as they taught me where my inhibitions lay. "Do you have sons?" I asked my host.

"Oh, yes," he said, "six sons!"

"May your line increase and prosper," I said, and departed, and rode my donkey a dozen kilometers out into the countryside, and tethered it to an olive tree, and shunted down the line.

31.

At the end of my layoff I reported for duty, and set out for the first time solo as a Time Courier.

I had six people to take on the one-week tour. They didn't know it was my first solo. Protopopolos didn't see any point in telling them, and I agreed. But I didn't *feel* as though it were my first solo. I was full of Metaxian chutzpah. I emanated charisma. I feared nothing except fear itself.

At the preliminary meeting I told my six the rules of time-touring in crisp, staccato phrases. I invoked the dread menace of the Time Patrol as I warned against changing the past either carelessly or by design. I explained how they could best keep out of trouble. Then I handed out timers and set them.

"Here we go," I said. "Up the line."

Charisma. Chutzpah.

Jud Elliott, Time Courier, on his own!

Up the line!

"We have arrived," I said, "in 1659 B.P., better known to you as the year 400. I've picked it as a typical early Byzantine time. The ruling emperor is Arcadius. You remember from now-time Istanbul that Haghia Sophia should be back there, and the mosque of Sultan Ahmed should be there. Well, of course, Sultan Ahmed and his mosque are currently a dozen centuries in the future, and the church behind us is the original Haghia Sophia, constructed forty years ago when the city was still very

young. Four years from now it'll burn down during a rebellion caused by the exiling of Bishop John Chrysosto-
mos by Emperor Arcadius after he had criticized Arcadius' wife Eudoxia. Let's go inside. You see that the walls
are of stone but the roof is wooden—"

My six tourists included a real-estate developer from
Ohio, his wife, their gawky daughter and her husband,
plus a Sicilian shrink and his bowlegged temporary wife:
a typical assortment of prosperous citizens. They didn't
know a nave from a narthex, but I gave them a good look
at the church, and then marched them through Arcadius'
Constantinople to set the background for what they'd see
later. After two hours of this I jumped down the line to
408 to watch the baptism of little Theodosius again.

I caught sight of myself on the far side of the street,
standing close to Capistrano. I didn't wave. My other self
did not appear to see me. I wondered if this present self of
mine had been standing here that other time, when I was
here with Capistrano. The intricacies of the Cumulative
Paradox oppressed me. I banished them from mind.

"You see the ruins of the old Haghia Sophia," I said.
"It will be rebuilt under the auspices of this infant, the
future Theodosius II, and opened to prayer on October,
10, 445—"

We shunted down the line to 445 and watched the ceremony of dedication.

There are two schools of thought about the proper way
to conduct a time-tour. The Capistrano method is to take
the tourists to four or five high spots a week, letting them
spend plenty of time in taverns, inns, back alleys, and
marketplaces, and moving in such a leisurely way that
the flavor of each period soaks in deeply. The Metaxas
method is to construct an elaborate mosaic of events, hit-
ting the same high spots but also twenty or thirty or forty
lesser events, spending half an hour here and two hours
there. I had experienced both methods and I preferred
Metaxas' approach. The serious student of Byzantium

wants depth, not breadth; but these folk were not serious students. Better to make a pageant of Byzantium for them, hurry them breathless through the eras, show them riots and coronations, chariot races, the rise and fall of monuments and kings.

And so I took my people from time to time in imitation of my idol Metaxas. I gave them a full day in early Byzantium, as Capistrano would have done, but I split it into six shunts. We ended our day's work in 537, in the city Justinian had built on the charred ruin of the one destroyed by the rioting Blues and Greens.

"We've come to December 27," I said. "Justinian will inaugurate the new Haghia Sophia today. You see how much larger the cathedral is than the ones that preceded it—a gigantic building, one of the wonders of the world. Justinian has poured the equivalent of hundreds of millions of dollars into it."

"Is this the one they have in Istanbul now?" asked Mr. Real Estate's son-in-law doubtfully.

"Basically, yes. Except that you don't see any minarets here—the Moslems tacked those on, of course, after they turned the place into a mosque—and the gothic buttresses haven't been built yet, either. Also the great dome here is not the one you're familiar with. This one is slightly flatter and wider than the present one. It turned out that the architect's calculations of thrust were wrong, and half the dome will collapse in 558 after weakening of the arches by earthquakes. You'll see that tomorrow. Look, here comes Justinian."

A little earlier that day I had shown them the harried Justinian of 532 attempting to cope with the Nika riots. The emperor who now appeared, riding in a chariot drawn by four immense black horses, looked a good deal more than five years older, far more plump and florid of face, but he also seemed vastly more sure of himself, a figure of total command. As well he should be, having surmounted the tremendous challenge to his power that the riots presented, and having rebuilt the city into something uniquely glorious.

Senators and dukes lined the approach; we remained respectfully to one side, amid the commoners. Priests, deacons, deaconesses, subdeacons, and cantors awaited the imperial procession, all in costly robes. Hymns in the ancient mode rose to heaven. The Patriarch Menos appeared at the colossal imperial door of the cathedral; Justinian dismounted; the patriarch and the emperor, hand in hand, entered the building, followed by the high officials of state.

"According to a tenth-century chronicle," I said, "Justinian was overcome by emotion when he entered his new Haghia Sophia. Rushing to the apse, he gave thanks to God who had allowed him to achieve such a building, and cried out, 'O Solomon, I have surpassed thee.' The Time Service thought it might be interesting for visitors to this era to hear this famous line, and so some years back we planted an Ear just beside the altar." I reached into my robes. "I've brought along a pickup speaker which will transmit Justinian's words to us as he nears the apse. Listen."

I switched on the speaker. At this moment, any number of other Couriers in the crowd were doing the same thing. A time will come when so many of us are clustered in this moment that Justinian's voice, amplified by a thousand tiny speakers, will boom majestically across the whole city.

From the speaker in my palm came the sound of footsteps.

"The emperor is walking down the aisle," I said.

The footsteps halted abruptly. Justinian's words came to us—his first exclamation upon entering the architectural masterpiece of the ages.

Thick-voiced with rage, the emperor bellowed, "Look up there, you sodomitic simpleton! Find me the motherhumper who left that scaffold hanging in the dome! I

want his balls in an alabaster vase before mass begins!"
Then he sneezed in imperial wrath.

I said to my six tourists, "The development of time-travel has made it necessary for us to revise many of our most inspiring anecdotes in the light of new evidence."

32.

That night as my tired tourists slept, I slipped away from them to carry out some private research.

This was strictly against regulations. A Courier is supposed to remain with the clients at all times, in case an emergency occurs. The clients, after all, don't know how to operate their timers, so only the Courier can help them make a quick escape from trouble.

Despite this I jumped six centuries down the line, while my tourists slept, and I visited the era of my prosperous ancestor Nicephorus Ducas.

Which took chutzpah, of course, considering that this was my first solo trip. But actually I wasn't running any serious risks.

The safe way to carry out such side trips, as Metaxas had explained to me, is to set your timer carefully and make sure that your net absence from your tourists is one minute or less. I was departing from December 27, 537, at 2345 hours. I could go up or down the line from there and spend hours, days, weeks, or months elsewhere. When I had finished with my business, all I had to do was set my timer to bring me back to December 27, 537, at 2346 hours. From the point of view of my sleeping tourists I'd have been gone only sixty seconds.

Of course, it wouldn't be proper to land at 2344 hours on the return trip, which is to say to come back a minute before I had left. There would then be two of me in the same room, which produces the Paradox of Duplication, a subspecies of the Cumulative Paradox, and is certain to bring a reprimand or worse if the Time Patrol hears of it. No: precise coordination is necessary.

Another problem is the difficulty of making an exact point-to-point shunt. The inn where my group was lodged in 537 would almost certainly no longer exist by 1175, the year of my immediate destination. I couldn't blindly shunt forward from the room, because I might find myself materializing in some awkward place later constructed on the site—a dungeon, say.

The only safe way would be to go out in the street and shunt from there, both coming and going. This, though, requires you to be away from your tourists more than sixty seconds, just figuring the time necessary to go downstairs, find a safe and quiet place for your shunt, etc. And if a Time Patrolman comes along on a routine checkup and recognizes you in the street and asks you why the hell you aren't with the clients, you're in trouble.

Nevertheless I shunted down the line and got away with it.

I hadn't been in 1175 before. It was probably the last really good year Byzantium had.

It seemed to me that an atmosphere of gathering trouble hung over Constantinople. Even the clouds looked ominous. The air had the tang of impending calamity.

Subjective garbage. Being able to move freely along the line distorts your perspective and colors your interpretation. I knew what lay ahead for these people; they didn't. Byzantium in 1175 was cocky and optimistic; I was imagining all the omens.

Manuel I Comnenus was on the throne, a good man,

coming to the end of a·long, brilliant career. Disaster was closing in on him. The Comnenus emperors had spent the whole twelfth century recapturing Asia·Minor from the Turks, who had grabbed it the century before. I knew that one year down the line, in 1176, Manuel was going to lose his entire Asian empire in a single day, at the battle of Myriocephalon. After that it would be downhill all the way for Byzantium. But Manuel didn't know that yet. Nobody here did. Except me.

I headed up toward the Golden Horn. The upper end of town was the most important in this period; the center of things had shifted from the Haghia Sophia/Hippodrome/Augusteum section to the Blachernae quarter, in the northernmost corner of the city at the angle where the city walls met. Here, for some reason, Emperor Alexius I had moved the court at the end of the eleventh century, abandoning the jumbled old Great Palace. Now his grandson Manuel reigned here in splendor, and the big feudal families had built new palaces nearby, all along the Golden Horn.

One of the finest of these marble edifices belonged to Nicephorus Ducas, my many-times-removed-great-grand-father.

I spent half the morning prowling around the palace grounds, getting drunk on the magnificence of it all. Toward midday the palace gate opened and I saw Nicephorus himself emerge in his chariot for his noontime drive: a stately figure with a long, ornately braided black beard and elaborate gold-trimmed robes. On his breast he wore a pendant cross, gilded and studded with huge jewels; his fingers glistened with rings. A crowd had gathered to watch the noble Nicephorus leave his palace.

Gracefully he scattered coins to the multitude as he rode forth. I caught one: a thin, shabby bezant of Alexius I, nicked and filed at the edges. The Comnenus family had debased the currency badly. Still, it's no small thing to be able to toss even debased gold coins to a mob of miscellaneous onlookers.

I have that worn and oily-looking bezant to this day. I think of it as my inheritance from my Byzantine multi-great-grandfather.

Nicephorus' chariot vanished in the direction of the imperial palace. A filthy old man standing beside me sighed, crossed himself many times, and murmured, "May the Savior bless the blessed Nicephorus! Such a wonderful person!"

The old man's nose had been lopped off at the base. He had also lost his left hand. The kindly Byzantines of this latter-day era had made mutilation the penalty for many minor crimes. A step forward; the Code of Justinian called for death in such cases. Better to lose eye or tongue or nose than life.

"Twenty years I spent in the service of Nicephorus Ducas!" the old man went on. "The finest years of my life, they were."

"Why did you leave?" I asked.

He held forth the stump of his arm. "They caught me stealing books. I was a scribe, and I hungered to keep some of the books I copied. Nicephorus has so many! He would not have missed five or six! But they caught me and I lost my hand and also my employment, ten years ago."

"And your nose?"

"In that very harsh winter six years back I stole a barrel of fish. I am a very poor thief, always getting caught."

"How do you support yourself?"

He smiled. "By public charity. And by begging. Can you spare a silver nomisma for an unhappy old man?"

I inspected the coins I carried. By ill luck all my silver pieces were early ones, of the fifth and sixth centuries, long out of circulation; if the old man tried to pass one, he'd be arrested on charges of robbing some aristocratic collector, and probably would lose his other hand. So I

pressed a fine gold bezant of the early eleventh century
into his palm. He stared at it in amazement. "I am yours,
noble sir!" he cried. "I am wholly yours!

"Come with me to the nearest tavern, then, and answer
a few questions," I said.

"Gladly! Gladly!"

I bought us wine and pumped him on the Ducas genealogy. It was hard for me to look at his mutilated face,
and so as we talked I kept my eyes trained on his shoulder; but he seemed accustomed to that. He had all the information I was seeking, for one of his duties while in the
service of the Ducases had been to copy out the family
records.

Nicephorus, he said, was then forty-five years old, having been born in 1130. The wife of Nicephorus was the
former Zoe Catacalon, and they had seven children: Simeon, John, Leo, Basil, Helena, Theodosia, and Zoe. Nicephorus was the eldest son of Nicetas Ducas, born in
1106; the wife of Nicetas was the former Irene Cerular-
ius, whom he had married in 1129. Nicetas and Irene had
had five other children: Michael, Isaac, John, Romanos,
and Anna. Nicetas' father had been Leo Ducas, born in
1070; Leo had married the former Pulcheria Botaniates
in 1100, and their children, other than Nicetas, included
Simeon, John, Alexander—

The recitation went on and on, carrying the Ducases
back through the generations of Byzantium, into the tenth
century, the ninth, the eighth, names growing cloudy now,
gaps appearing in the record, the old man frowning, fum-
bling, apologizing for scanty data. I tried a couple of
times to stop him, but he would not be stopped, until
finally he sputtered out with a Tiberius Ducas of the seventh century whose existence, he said, was possibly apoc-
ryphal.

"This, you understand, is merely the lineage of Nicephorus Ducas," he said. "The imperial family is a distinct
branch, which I can trace back for you through the

Comneni to Emperor Constantine X and his ancestors,
who—"

Those Ducases didn't interest me, even though they
were distantly related to me in some way. If I wanted to
know the lineage of the imperial Ducases, I could find it
in Gibbon. I cared only for my own humbler branch of
the family, the collateral offshoot from the imperial line.
Thanks to this hideous outcast scribe I was able to secure
the path of those Ducases through three Byzantine centuries, down to Nicephorus. And I already knew the rest of
the line, from Nicephorus's son Simeon of Albania to Simeon's several-times-grandson Manuel Ducas of Argyrokastro, whose eldest daughter married Nicholas Markezinis, and through the Markezinis line until a Markezinis daughter married a Passilidis son and produced my
estimable grandfather Konstantin, whose daughter Diana
wed Judson Daniel Elliott II and brought forth into the
world my own ultimate self.

"For your trouble," I said, and gave the filthy scribe
another gold piece, and fled from the tavern while he still
was muttering dazed thanks.

I knew Metaxas would be proud of me. A little jealous,
even—for in short order I had put together a lengthier
family tree than his own. *His* went back to the tenth century, mine (a little shakily) to the seventh. Of course, he
had an annotated list of hundreds of ancestors, and I
knew details of only a few dozen, but he had started
years ahead of me.

I set my timer carefully and shunted back to December
27, 537. The street was dark and silent. I hurried into the
inn. Less than three minutes had elapsed since my departure, even though I had spent eight hours down the line
in 1175. My tourists slept soundly. All was well.

I was pleased with myself. By candlelight I sketched
the details of the Ducas line on a scrap of old vellum. I
wasn't really planning to *do* anything with the genealogy.
I wasn't looking for ancestors to kill, like Capistrano, or

ancestors to seduce, like Metaxas. I just wanted to gloat a little over the fact that my ancestors were Ducases. Some people don't have ancestors at all.

33.

I don't think I was quite the equal of Metaxas as a Courier, but I gave my people a respectable view of Byzantium. I did a damned good job, especially for a first try.

We shunted through all the highlights and some of the lowlights. I showed them the baptism of Constantine the Pisser; the smashing of the icons under Leo III; the invasion by the Bulgars in 813; the trees of gilded bronze in the Magnaura Hall of Theophilus; the debaucheries of Michael the Drunkard; the arrival of the First Crusade in 1096 and 1097; the much more disastrous arrival of the Fourth Crusade in 1204; the reconquest of Constantinople by the Byzantines in 1261, and the coronation of Michael VIII; in short, all that counted.

My people loved it. Like most time-tourists, they particularly loved the riots, insurrections, rebellions, sieges, massacres, invasions, and fires.

"When do you show us the Turks come bustin' in?" the Ohio real-estate-man kept asking. "I want to see those goddam Turks wreck the place!"

"We're moving toward it," I told him.

First I gave them a look at Byzantium in the sunset years, under the dynasty of the Palaeologi. "Most of the empire is gone," I said, as we dropped down the line into 1275. "The Byzantines think and build on a small scale now. Intimacy is the key word. This is the little Church of St. Mary of the Mongols, built for a bastard daughter of Michael VIII who for a short while was married to a Mongol khan. See the charm? The simplicity?"

We glided on down the line to 1330 to look in on the Church of Our Savior in Chora. The tourists had already seen it down the line in Istanbul under its Turkish name, Kariye Camii; now they saw it in its pre-mosquified condition, with all its stunning mosaics intact and new. "See, there," I said. "There's the Mary who married the Mongol. She's still there down the line. And this—the early life and miracles of Christ—that one's gone from our time, but you can see how superb it was here."

The Sicilian shrink holographed the whole church; he was carrying a palm camera that the Time Service regards as permissible, since nobody up the line is likely to notice it or comprehend its function. His bowlegged tempie waddled around oohing at everything. The Ohio people looked bored, as I knew they would. No matter. I'd give them culture if I had to shove it up them.

"When do we see the Turks?" the Ohioans asked restlessly.

We skipped lithely over the Black Death years of 1347 and 1348. "I can't take you there," I said, when the protests came. "You've got to sign up for a special plague tour if you want to see any of the great epidemics."

Mr. Ohio's son-in-law grumbled, "We've had all our vaccinations."

"But five billion people down the line in now-time are unprotected," I explained. "You might pick up some contamination and bring it back with you, and start a worldwide epidemic. And then we'd have to edit your whole time-trip out of the flow of history to keep the disaster from happening. You wouldn't want that, would you?"

Bafflement.

"Look, I'd take you there if I could," I said. "But I

can't. It's the law. Nobody can enter a plague era except under special supervision, which I'm not licensed to give."

I brought them down in 1385 and showed them the withering of Constantinople, a shrunken population within the great walls, whole districts deserted, churches falling into ruins. The Turks were devouring the surrounding countryside. I took my people up on the walls back of the Blachernae quarter and showed them the horsemen of the Turkish sultan prowling in the countryside beyond the city limits. My Ohio friend shook his fist at them. "Barbarian bastards!" he cried. "Scum of the earth!"

Down the line to 1398 we came. I showed them Anadolu Hisari, Sultan Beyazit's fortress on the Asiatic side of the Bosphorus. A summer haze made it a trifle hard to see, so we shunted a few months into autumn and looked again. Surreptitiously we passed around a little pair of field glasses. Two elderly Byzantine monks appeared, saw the field glasses before I could get hold of them and hide them, and wanted to know what we were looking through.

"It helps the eyes," I said, and we got out of there fast.

In the summer of 1422 we watched Sultan Murat II's army bashing at the city walls. About 20,000 Turks had burned the villages and fields around Constantinople, massacred the inhabitants, uprooted the vines and olive trees, and now we saw them trying to get into the city. They moved siege machines up to the walls, went to work with battering rams, giant catapults, all the heavy artillery of the time. I got my people right up close to the battle line to see the fun.

The standard technique for doing this is to masquerade as holy pilgrims. Pilgrims can go anywhere, even into the front lines. I distributed crosses and icons, taught everybody how to look devout, and led them forward, chanting and intoning. There was no hope of getting them to chant genuine Byzantine hymns, of course, and so I told them to chant anything they liked, just making sure it sounded somber and pious. The Ohio people did *The Star Spangled Banner* over and over, and the shrink and his friend sang arias from Verdi and Puccini. The Byzantine defenders paused in their work to wave to us. We waved back and made the sign of the Cross.

"What if we get killed?" asked the son-in-law.

"No chance of it. Not permanently, anyway. If a stray shot gets you, I'll summon the Time Patrol, and they'll pull you out of here five minutes ago."

The son-in-law looked puzzled.

"Celeste Aida, forma divina—"

". . . so proudly we hailed—"

The Byzantines fought like hell to keep the Turks out. They dumped Greek fire and boiling oil on them, hacked off every head that peered over the wall, withstood the fury of the artillery. Nevertheless it seemed certain that the city would fall by sunset. The evening shadows gathered.

"Watch this," I said.

Flames burst forth at several points along the wall. The Turks were burning their own siege machines and pulling back!

"Why?" I was asked. "Another hour and they'll have the city."

"Byzantine historians," I said, "later wrote that a miracle had taken place. The Virgin Mary had appeared, clad in a violet mantle, dazzlingly bright, and had walked along the walls. The Turks, in terror, withdrew."

"Where?" the son-in-law demanded. "I didn't see any miracle! I didn't see any Virgin Mary!"

"Maybe we ought to go back half an hour and look again," said his wife vaguely.

I explained that the Virgin Mary had not in fact been seen on the battlements; rather, messengers had brought word to Sultan Murad of an uprising against him in Asia

Minor, and, fearing he might be cut off and besieged in Constantinople if he succeeded in taking it, the sultan had halted operations at once to deal with the rebels in the east. The Ohioans looked disappointed. I think they genuinely had wanted to see the Virgin Mary. "We saw her on last year's trip," the son-in-law muttered.

"That was different," said his wife. "That was the *real* one, not a miracle!"

I adjusted timers and we shunted down the line.

Dawn, April 5, 1453. We waited for sunrise on the rampart of Byzantium. "The city is isolated now," I said. "Sultan Mehmet the Conqueror has built the fortress of Rumeli Hisari up along the European side of the Bosphorus. The Turks are moving in. Come, look, listen to this."

Sunrise broke. We peered over the top of the wall. A deafening shout went up. "Across the Golden Horn are the tents of the Turks—200,000 of them. In the Bosphorus are 493 Turkish ships. There are 8,000 Byzantine defenders, 15 ships. No help has come from Christian Europe for Christian Byzantium, except 700 Genoese soldiers and sailors under the command of Giovanni Giustiniani." I lingered on the name of Byzantium's last bulwark, stressing the rich echoes of the past: "Giustiniani. . . . Justinian—" No one noticed. "Byzantium is to be thrown to the wolves," I went on. "Listen to the Turks roar!"

The famous Byzantine chain-boom was stretched across the Golden Horn and anchored at each bank: great rounded logs joined by iron hooks, designed to close the harbor to invaders. It had failed once before, in 1204; now it was stronger.

We jumped down the line to April 9, and watched the Turks creep closer to the walls. We skipped to April 12, and saw the great Turkish cannon, the Royal One, go into action. A turncoat Christian named Urban of Hungary had built it for the Turks; 100 pair of oxen had dragged it to the city; its barrel, three feet across, fired

1,500-pound granite projectiles. We saw a burst of flame, a puff of smoke, and then a monstrous ball of stone rise sleepily, slowly, and slam with earthshaking force against the wall, sending up a cloud of dust. The thud jarred the whole city; the explosion lingered in our ears. "They can fire the Royal One only seven times a day," I said. "It takes a while to load it. And now see this." We shunted forward by a week. The invaders were clustered about the giant cannon, readying it to fire. They touched it off; it exploded with a frightful blare of flame, sending huge chunks of its barrel slewing through the Turks. Bodies lay everywhere. The Byzantines cheered from the walls. "Among the dead," I said, "is Urban of Hungary. But soon the Turks will build a new cannon."

That evening the Turks rushed the walls, and we watched, singing *America the Beautiful* and arias from *Otello,* as the brave Genoese of Giovanni Giustiniani drove them off. Arrows whistled overhead; a few of the Byzantines fired clumsy, inaccurate rifles.

I did the final siege so brilliantly that I wept at my own virtuosity. I gave my people naval battles, hand-to-hand encounters at the walls, ceremonies of prayer in Haghia Sophia. I showed them the Turks slyly hauling their ships overland on wooden rollers from the Bosphorus to the Golden Horn, in order to get around the famous chain-boom, and I showed them the terror of the Byzantines when dawn on April 23 revealed 72 Turkish warships at anchor inside the harbor, and I showed them the gallant defeat of those ships by the Genoese.

We skipped forward through the days of the siege, watching the walls diminishing but remaining unbreached, watching the fortitude of the defenders grow and the determination of the attackers lessen. On May 28 we went by night to Haghia Sophia, to attend the last Christian service ever to be held there. It seemed that all the city was in the cathedral: Emperor Constantine XI and his court, beggars and thieves, merchants, pimps, Roman

Catholics from Genoa and Venice, soldiers and sailors, dukes and prelates, and also a good many disguised visitors from the future, more, perhaps, than all the rest combined. We listened to the bells tolling, and to the melancholy *Kyrie,* and we dropped to our knees, and many, even some of the time-travelers, wept for Byzantium, and when the service ended the lights were dimmed, veiling the glittering mosaics and frescoes.

And then it was May 29, and we saw a world on its last day.

At two in the morning the Turks rushed St. Romanus Gate. Giustiniani was wounded; the fighting was terrible, and I had to keep my people back from it; the rhythmic *"Allah! Allah!"* grew until it filled the universe with noise, and the defenders panicked and fled, and the Turks burst into the city.

"All is over," I said. "Emperor Constantine perishes in battle. Thousands flee the city; thousands take refuge behind the barred doors of Haghia Sophia. Look now: the pillaging, the slaughter!" We jumped frantically, vanishing and reappearing, so that we would not be run down by the horsemen galloping joyously through the streets. Probably we startled a good many Turks, but in all that frenzy the miraculous vanishing of a few pilgrims would attract no excitement. For a climax I swept them into May 30, and we watched Sultan Mehmet ride in triumph into Byzantium, flanked by viziers and pashas and janissaries.

"He halts outside Haghia Sophia," I whispered. "He scoops up dirt, drops it on his turban; it is his act of contrition before Allah, who has given him such a glorious victory. Now he goes in. It would not be safe for us to follow him there. Inside he finds a Turk hacking up the mosaic floor, which he regards as impious; the sultan will strike the man and forbid him to harm the cathedral, and then he will go to the altar and climb upon it and make his Salaam. Haghia Sophia becomes Ayasofya, the mosque. There is no more Byzantium. Come. Now we go down the line."

Dazed by what they had seen, my six tourists let me adjust their timers. I sounded the note on my pitchpipe, and down the line we went to 2059.

In the Time Service office afterward, the Ohio real-estate man approached me. He stuck out his thumb in the vulgar way that vulgar people do, when they're offering a tip. "Son," he said, "I just want to tell you, that was one hell of a job you did! Come on over with me and let me stick this thumb on the input plate and give you a little bit of appreciation, okay?"

"I'm sorry," I said. "We're not permitted to accept gratuities."

"Crap on that, son. Suppose you don't pay any attention, and I just get some stash thumbed into your account, okay? Let's say you don't know a thing about it."

"I can't prevent a transfer of funds that I don't know about," I said.

"Good deal. By damn, when those Turks came into the city, what a show! What a show!"

When I got next month's account statement I found he had thumbed a cool thousand into my credit. I didn't report myself to my superiors. I figured I had earned it, rules or not.

34.

I figured I had also earned the right to spend my layoff at Metaxas' villa in 1105. No longer a pest, a driveling apprentice, I was a full member of the brotherhood of Time

Couriers. And one of the best in the business, in my opinion. I didn't have to fear that I'd be unwelcome at Metaxas' place.

Checking the assignment board, I found that Metaxas, like myself, had just finished a tour. That meant he'd be at his villa. I picked up a fresh outfit of Byzantine clothes, requisitioned a pouch of gold bezants, and got ready to jump to 1105.

Then I remembered the Paradox of Discontinuity.

I didn't know *when* in 1105 I was supposed to arrive. And I had to allow for Metaxas' now-time basis up there. In now-time for me it was currently November, 2059. Metaxas had just jumped up the line to some point in 1105 that corresponded, for him, to November of 2059. Suppose that point was in July, 1105. If, not knowing that, I shunted back to—say—March, 1105, the Metaxas I'd find wouldn't know me at all. I'd be just some uninvited snot barging in on the party. If I jumped to—say—June, 1105, I'd be the young newcomer, not yet a proven quantity, whom Metaxas had just taken out on a training trip. And if I jumped to—say—October, 1105, I'd meet a Metaxas who was three months ahead of me on a now-time basis, and who therefore knew details of my own future. That would be the Paradox of Discontinuity in the other direction, and I wasn't eager to experience it; it's dangerous and a little frightening to run into someone who has lived through a period that you haven't reached yet, and no Time Serviceman enjoys it.

I needed help.

I went to Spiros Protopopolos and said, "Metaxas invited me to visit him during my layoff, but I don't know when he is."

Cautiously Protopopolos said, "Why do you think I know? He doesn't confide in me."

"I thought he might have left some record with you of his now-time basis."

"What the hell are you talking about?"

I wondered if I had made some hideous blunder. Bull-ing ahead, I winked and said, "*You* know where Metaxas is now. And maybe you know when, too. Come on, Proto. I'm in on the story. You don't need to be cagey with me."

He went into the next room and consulted Plastiras and Herschel. They must have vouched for me. Protopopolos, returning, whispered in my ear, "August 17, 1105. Say hello for me."

I thanked him and got on my way.

Metaxas lived in the suburbs, outside the walls of Con-tantinople. Land was cheap out there in the early twelfth century, thanks to such disturbances as the invasion of the marauding Patzinak barbarians in 1090 and the ar-rival of the disorderly rabble of Crusaders six years later. The settlers outside the walls had suffered badly then. Many fine estates had gone on the market. Metaxas had bought in 1095, when the landowners were still in shock over their injuries at the hands of the Patzinaks and were starting to worry about the next set of invaders.

He had one advantage denied to the sellers: he had al-ready looked down the line and seen how stable things would be in the years just ahead, under Alexius I Com-nenus. He knew that the countryside in which his villa was set would be spared from harm all during the twelfth century.

I crossed into Old Istanbul and cabbed out to the ruins of the city wall, and beyond it for about five kilometers. Naturally, this wasn't any suburban countryside in now-time, but just a gray sprawling extension of the modern city.

When I figured I was the proper distance out of town, I thumbed the plate and dismissed my cab. Then I took up a position on the sidewalk, checking things out for my jump. Some kids saw me in my Byzantine costume and came over to watch, knowing that I must be going to go back in time. They called gaily to me in Turkish, maybe asking me to take them along.

One angelically grimy little boy said in recognizable French, "I hope they cut your head off."

Children are so sweetly frank, aren't they? And so charmingly hostile, in all eras.

I set my timer, gestured obscenely at my well-wisher, and went up the line.

The gray buildings vanished. The November bleakness gave way to the sunny glow of August. The air I breathed was suddenly fresh and fragrant. I stood beside a broad cobbled road running between two green meadows. A modest chariot drawn by two horses came clopping up and halted before me.

A lean young man in simple country clothes leaned out and said, "Sir, Metaxas has sent me to fetch you to him."

"But—he wasn't expecting—"

I shut up fast, before I said something out of line. Obviously Metaxas *was* expecting me. Had I hit the Paradox of Discontinuity, somehow?

Shrugging, I climbed up into the chariot.

As we rode into the west, my driver nodded to the acres of grapevines to the left of the road and the groves of fig trees to the right. "All this," he said proudly, "belongs to Metaxas. Have you ever been here before?"

"No, never," I said.

"He is a great man, my master. He is a friend to the poor and an ally to the mighty. Everyone respects him. Emperor Alexius himself was here last month."

I felt queasy about that. Bad enough that Metaxas had carved out a now-time identity for himself ten centuries up the line; what would the Time Patrol say about his hobnobbing with emperors? Giving advice, no doubt; altering the future by his foreknowledge of events; cementing himself into the historical matrix of this era as a valued adviser to royalty! Could anyone match him for gall?

Figs and grapes gave way to fields of wheat. "This, too, belongs to Metaxas," said the driver.

I had pictured Metaxas living in some comfortable little villa on a hectare or two of land, with a garden in front and perhaps a vegetable plot in the rear. I hadn't realized that he was a major landowner on such a scale.

We passed grazing cattle, and a mill worked by plodding oxen, and a pond no doubt well stocked with fish, and then we came to a double row of cypress trees that guarded a side road branching from the main highway, and took that road, and a splendid villa appeared, and at its entrance waited Metaxas, garbed in raiment suitable for the companion of an emperor.

"Jud!" he cried, and we embraced. "My friend! My brother! Jud, they tell me about the tour you led! Magnificent! Your tourists, they never stopped praising you?"

"Who told you?"

"Kolettis and Pappas. They're here. Come in, come in, come in! Wine for my guest! A change of robes for him! Come in, Jud, come in!"

35.

The villa was classical in style, atrium-and-peristyle, with a huge central courtyard, colonnaded walkways, mosaic floors, frescoed walls, a great apsed reception room, a pond in the courtyard, a library bulging with scrolls, a dining room whose round gold-inlaid ivory table could have seated three dozen, a statuary hall, and a marble bathroom. Metaxas' slaves hustled me toward the bathroom, and Metaxas called out that he'd see me later.

I got the royal treatment.

Three dark-haired slave wenches—Persians, Metaxas said later—ministered to me in the bath. All they wore were loinstrings, and in a moment I was wearing less than that, for in a giggling jiggle of breasts they stripped me and went to work buffing and soaping me until I gleamed. Steam bath, hot bath, cold bath—my pores got the full workout. When I emerged they dried me *most* detailedly and robed me in the most elegant tunic I ever expect to wear. Then they vanished, with a saucy wigwag of bare bottoms as they disappeared through some subterranean passageway. A middle-aged butler appeared and conveyed me to the atrium, where Metaxas awaited me with beakers of wine.

"You like it?" he asked.

"I feel I'm in a dream."

"You are. And I'm the dreamer. You saw the farms? Wheat, olives, cattle, figs, everything. I own. My tenants farm. Each year I acquire new land on the profits of last year's work."

"It's incredible," I said. "And what's even more incredible is that you get away with it."

"I have earned my invulnerability," said Metaxas simply. "The Time Patrol knows I must not be persecuted."

"They realize you're here?"

"I believe they do," he said. "They stay away, though. I take care to make no significant changes in the fabric of history. I'm no villain. I'm merely self-indulgent."

"But you *are* changing history just by being here! Some other landowner must have held these lands in the real 1105."

"This is the real 1105."

"I mean the original, before Benchley Effect visitors began coming here. You've interpolated yourself into the landowner rolls, and—my God, the chariot driver spoke of you as Metaxas! Is that the name you use here?"

"Themistoklis Metaxas. Why not? It is a good Greek name."

"Yes, but—look, it must be in all the documents, the tax records, everything! You've certainly changed the Byzantine archives that have come down to us, putting yourself in where you weren't in before. What—"

"There is no danger," Metaxas said. "So long as I take no life and create no life here, so long as I cause no one to change a previously decided course of action, all is well. You know, making a real alteration in the time flow is a difficult thing. You have to do something big, like killing a monarch. Simply being here, I introduce tiny changes, but they are damped out by ten centuries of time, and no real change results down the line. Do you follow?"

I shrugged. "Just tell me one thing, at least. How did you know I was coming?"

Laughing, he said, "I looked two days down the line and you were here. Therefore I checked for your time of arrival and arranged to have Nicholas meet you. It saved you a long walk, yes?"

Of course. I just hadn't been thinking four-dimensionally. It stood to reason that Metaxas would habitually scan his immediate future here, so he'd never be the victim of some unpleasant surprise in this sometimes unpredictable era.

"Come," Metaxas said. "Join the others."

They were lounging on divans by the courtyard pool, nibbling bits of roasted meat that slavegirls in diaphanous robes popped into their mouths. Two of my fellow Couriers were there, Kolettis and Pappas, both enjoying layoffs. Pappas, of the drooping mustache, managed to look sad even while pinching a firm Persian buttock, but Kolettis, plump and boisterous, was in high form, singing and laughing. A third man, whom I didn't know, was peering at the fish in the pool. Though dressed in twelfth-century robes, he had a face that was instantly recognizable as modern, I thought. And I was right.

"This is Scholar Magistrate Paul Speer," said Metaxas to me in English. "A visiting academic. Meet Time Courier Jud Elliott, Dr. Speer."

We touched hands formally. Speer was about fifty, somewhat desiccated, a pale little man with an angular face and quick, nervous eyes. "Pleased," he said.

"And this," said Metaxas, "is Eudocia."

I had noticed her the instant I entered the courtyard, of course. She was a slim, auburn-haired girl, fair-skinned but with dark eyes, nineteen or twenty years old. She was heavily laden with jewelry, and so obviously was not just one of the slavegirls; yet her costume was daring by Byzantine standards, consisting only of a light double winding of translucent silk. As the fabric pulled taut against her, it displayed small high breasts, boyish buttocks, a shallow navel, even a hint of the triangular tuft at her loins. I prefer my women dark of hair and complexion and voluptuous of figure, but even so this Eudocia was enormously attractive to me. She seemed tense, coiled, full of pent-up fury and fervor.

She studied me in cool boldness and indicated her approval by placing her hands at her thighs and arching her back. The movement pulled her robes closer and showed me her nakedness in greater detail. She smiled. Her eyes sparkled wantonly.

In English, Metaxas said to me, "I've told you of her. She's my great-great-multi-great-grandmother. Try her in your bed tonight. The hip action is incredible!"

Eudocia smiled more warmly. She didn't know what Metaxas was saying, but she must have known he was talking about her. I tried not to stare too intently at the exposed beauties of the fair Eudocia. Is a man supposed to ogle his host's great-great-multi-great-grandmother?

A bare and beautiful slave offered me lamb and olives

en brochette. I swallowed without tasting. My nostrils were filled with the perfume of Eudocia.

Metaxas gave me wine and led me away from her. "Dr. Speer," he said, "is here on a collecting trip. He's a student of classical Greek drama, in search of lost plays."

Dr. Speer clicked his heels. He was the sort of Teutonic pedant who, you automatically know, would use his full academic title on all occasions. *Achtung! Herr Scholar Magistrate Speer!* Scholar Magistrate Speer said, "It has been most successful for me so far. Of course, my search is just beginning, yet already from Byzantine libraries I have obtained the *Nausicaa* and *Triptolemus* of Sophocles, and of Euripides the *Andromeda,* the *Peliades,* the *Phaethon,* and the *Oedipus,* and also of Aeschylus a nearly complete manuscript of *The Women of Aetna.* So you see I have done well." He clicked heels again.

I knew better than to remind him that the Time Patrol frowns on the recovery of lost masterpieces. Here in Metaxas' villa we were all ipso facto breakers of Patrol regulations, and accessories before and after the fact to any number of timecrimes.

I said, "Do you plan to bring these manuscripts down to now-time?"

"Yes, of course."

"But you can't publish them! What will you do with them?"

"Study them," said Scholar Magistrate Speer. "Increase the depth of my understanding of the Greek drama. And in time I will plant each manuscript in some place where archaeologists are likely to discover it, and so these plays will be restored to the world. It is a minor crime, is it not? Can I be called evil for wishing to enlarge our scanty stock of Sophocles?"

It seemed quite all right to me.

To me it has always seemed like numbnoggin uptightness to have made it illegal to go up the line to discover lost manuscripts or paintings. I can see where it wouldn't be desirable to let somebody go back to 1600 and make off with Michelangelo's *Pietá* or Leonardo's *Leda*. That would be timechange and timecrime, since the *Pietá* and the *Leda* must make their way year by year toward our now-time, and not leapfrog over four and a half centuries. But why not allow us to obtain works of art that we don't already have? Who's injured by it?

Kolettis said, "Doc Speer, you're absolutely right! Hell, they let historians inspect the past to make corrections in the historical record, don't they? And when they bring out their revisionist books, it goddam well alters the state of knowledge!"

"Yes," said Pappas. "As for example when it was noticed that Lady Macbeth was in fact a tender woman who struggled in vain to limit the insane ambitions of her bloodthirsty husband. Or we could consider the case of the Moses story. Or what we know now about Richard III. Or the truth about Joan of Arc. We've patched up standard history in a million places since Benchley Effect travel began, and—"

"—and so why not patch up some of the holes in literary history?" Kolettis asked. "Here's to Doc Speer! Steal every goddam play there is, Doc!"

"The risks are great," said Speer. "If I am caught I will be severely punished, perhaps stripped of my academic standing." He said it as though he'd prefer to be parted from his genitals. "The law is so foolish—they are such frightened men, these Time Patrol, worried about changes even that are virtuous."

To the Time Patrol no change is virtuous. They accept historical revisions because they can't help themselves; the enabling legislation specifically permits that kind of research. But the same law prohibits the transportation of any tangible object from up the line, except as required for the functions of the Time Service itself, and the Patrol sticks to the letter of it.

I said, "If you're looking for Greek plays, why don't

you check out the Alexandria Library? You're bound to find a dozen there for every one that's survived into the Byzantine period."

Scholar Magistrate Speer gave me the smile one gives to clever but naive children.

"The Library of Alexandria," he explained ponderously, "is of course a prime target for scholars such as myself. Therefore it is guarded perpetually by a man of the Time Patrol in the guise of a scribe. He makes several arrests a month, I hear. I take no risk such as that. Here in Byzantium my goal is more hard but my exposure is not so much. I will look more. I still hope to find some ninety plays of Sophocles, and at least so many of Aeschylus, and—"

36.

Dinner that night was a gaudy feast. We gorged on soups, stews, grilled duck, fish, pork, lamb, asparagus, mushrooms, apples, figs, artichokes, hard-boiled eggs served in blue enamel egg cups, cheese, salads, and wine. Out of courtesy to Eudocia, who was at table with us, we conversed in Greek and therefore spoke not at all of time-travel or the iniquities of the Time Patrol.

After dinner, while dwarf jesters performed, I called Metaxas aside. "I have something to show you," I said, and handed him the roll of vellum on which I had inscribed my genealogy. He glanced at it and frowned.

"What is it?"

"My ancestry. Back to the seventh century."

"When did you do all this?" he asked, laughing.

"On my last layoff." I told him of my visits to Grandfather Passilidis, to Gregory Markezinis, to the time of Nicephorus Ducas.

Metaxas studied the list more carefully.

"*Ducas?* What is this, Ducas?"

"That's me. I'm a Ducas. The scribe gave me the details right back to the seventh century."

"Impossible. Nobody knows who the Ducases were, that early! It's false!"

"Maybe that part is. But from 950 on, it's legitimate. Those are my people. I followed them right out of Byzantium into Albania and on to twentieth-century Greece."

"This is the truth?"

"I swear it!"

"You clever little cockeater," Metaxas said fondly. "All in one layoff, you learned this. And a Ducas, no less! A Ducas!" He consulted the list again. "Nicephorus Ducas, son of Nicetas Ducas, son of—hmm—Leo Ducas! Pulcheria Botaniates!"

"What's wrong?"

"I know them," Metaxas cried. "They've been my guests here, and I've stayed with them. He's one of the richest men in Byzantium, do you know that? And his wife Pulcheria—such a beautiful girl—" He gripped my arm fiercely. "You'd swear? These are your ancestors?"

"I'm positive."

"Wonderful," Metaxas said. "Let me tell you about Pulcheria, now. She's—oh, seventeen years old. Leo married her when she was just a child; they do a lot of that here. She's got a waist like *this,* but breasts out to *here,* and a flat belly and eyes that turn you afire, and—"

I shook free of his grasp and jammed my face close to his.

"Metaxas, have you—"

I couldn't say it.

"—slept with Pulcheria? No, no, I haven't. God's truth,

Jud! I've got enough women here. But look, boy, here's *your* opportunity! I can help you to meet her. She's ripe for seduction. Young, childless, beautiful, bored, her husband so busy with business matters that he hardly notices her—and she's your own great-great-multi-grandmother besides!"

"That part is your clutchup, not mine," I reminded him. "For me it might be a reason to stay away from her, in fact."

"Don't be an idiot. I'll fix it all up for you in two, three days. An introduction to the Ducases, a night as a guest in their palace in town, a word to Pulcheria's lady in waiting—"

"No," I said.

"No?"

"No. I don't want to get mixed up in any of this."

"You're a hard man to make happy, Jud. You don't want to fuck Empress Theodora, you don't want to lay Pulcheria Ducas, you—say, next thing you'll tell me you don't want Eudocia either."

"I don't mind screwing one of *your* ancestors," I said. I grinned. "I wouldn't even mind putting a baby in Eudocia's belly. How would you feel if I turned out to be your multi-great-grandfather?"

"You can't," said Metaxas.

"Why not?"

"Because Eudocia remains unmarried and childless until 1109. Then she weds Basil Stratiocus and has seven sons and three daughters in the following fifteen years, including one who is ancestral to me. Christ, does she get fat!"

"All of that can be changed," I reminded him.

"Like holy crap it can," said Metaxas. "Don't you think I guard my own line of descent? Don't you think I'd obliterate you from history if I caught you making a timechange on Eudocia's marriage? She'll stay childless until Basil Stratiocus fills her up, and that's that. But she's yours for tonight."

And she was. Giving me the highest degree of hospitality in his lexicon, Metaxas sent his ancestress Eudocia into my bedroom. Her lean, supple body was a trifle meager for me; her hard little breasts barely filled my hands. But she was a tigress. She was all energy and all passion, and she clambered on top of me and rocked herself to ecstasy in twenty quick rotations, and that was only the beginning. It was dawn before she let me sleep.

And in my dreams I saw Metaxas escort me to the palace of the Ducases, and introduce me to my multi-great-grandfather Leo, who said serenely, "This is my wife Pulcheria," and in my dream it seemed to me that she was the loveliest woman I had ever seen.

37.

I had my first troublesome moment as a Courier on my next tour. Because I was too proud to call in the Time Patrol for help, I got myself involved in the Paradox of Duplication and also caught a taste of the Paradox of Transit Displacement. But I think I came out of it looking pretty good.

I was escorting nine tourists through the arrival of the First Crusade in Byzantium when the mess happened.

"In 1095," I told my people, "Pope Urban II called for the liberation of the Holy Land from the Saracens. Very shortly, the knights of Europe began to enroll in the Crusade. Among those who welcomed such a war of liberation was Emperor Alexius of Byzantium, who saw in it a way of regaining the territories in the Near East that Byzantium had lost to the Turks and the Arabs. Alexius sent word that he wouldn't mind getting a few hundred experienced knights to help him clean the infidels out. But he got a good deal more than that, as we'll see in a moment, down the line in 1096."

We shunted to August 1, 1096.

Ascending the walls of Constantinople, we peered out into the countryside and saw it full of troops: not mailed knights but a raggle-taggle band of tattered peasants.

"This," I said, "is the People's Crusade. While the professional soldiers were working out the logistics of their march, a scrawny, foul-smelling little charismatic named Peter the Hermit rounded up thousands of paupers and farmers and led them across Europe to Byzantium. They looted and pillaged along the way, cleaned out the harvest of half of Europe, and burned Belgrade in a dispute with the Byzantine administrators. But finally they got here, 30,000 of them."

"Which one is Peter the Hermit?" asked the most obstreperous member of the group, a full-blown, fortyish bachelor lady from Des Moines named Marge Hefferin.

I checked the time. "You'll see him in another minute and a half. Alexius has sent a couple of officials to invite Peter to court. He wants Peter and his rabble to wait in Constantinople until the knights and barons get here, since these people will get slaughtered by the Turks if they go over into Asia Minor without a military escort. Look: there's Peter now."

Two dandified Byzantine grandees emerged from the mob, obviously holding their breath and looking as though they'd like to hold their noses too. Between them marched a scruffy, barefoot, rag-clad, filthy, long-chinned, gnomish man with blazing eyes and a pock-marked face.

"Peter the Hermit," I said, "on his way to see the emperor."

We shunted forward three days. The People's Crusade was inside Constantinople and playing hell with Alexius' city. A good many buildings were aflame. Ten Crusaders were atop one of the churches, stripping the lead from its roof for resale. A highborn-looking Byzantine woman emerged from Haghia Sophia and was stripped bare and raped by a pack of Peter's pious pilgrims before our eyes.

I said, "Alexius has miscalculated by letting this riffraff into the city. Now he's making arrangements to get them out the other side, by offering free ferry service across the Bosphorus to Asia. On August 6 they'll start on their way. The Crusaders will begin by massacring the Byzantine settlements in western Asia Minor; then they'll attack the Turks and be wiped out almost completely. If we had time, I'd take you down to 1097 and across to see the mountain of bones along the road. That's what happened to the People's Crusade. However, the pros are on their way, so let's watch them."

I explained about the four armies of Crusaders: the army of Raymond of Toulouse, the army of Duke Robert of Normandy, the army of Bohemond and Tancred, and the army of Godfrey of Bouillon, Eustace of Boulogne, and Baldwin of Lorraine. Some of my people had read up on their Crusader history and nodded in recognition of the names.

We shunted to the final week of 1096. "Alexius," I said, "has learned his lesson from the People's Crusade. He doesn't plan to let the real Crusaders linger long in Constantinople. They all have to pass through Byzantium on their way to the Holy Land, but he's going to hustle them through in a hurry, and he'll make their leaders swear allegiance to him before he admits them."

We watched the army of Godfrey of Bouillon pitch camp outside the walls of Constantinople. We observed the envoys going back and forth, Alexius requesting the oath of allegiance, Godfrey refusing. With careful editing I covered four months in less than an hour, showing how mistrust and enmity were building up between the Christian Crusaders and the Christian Byzantines who were supposed to collaborate in the liberation of the Holy Land. Godfrey still refused to swear allegiance; Alexius not only kept the Crusaders sealed out of Constantinople, but now was blockading their camp, hoping to starve them into going away. Baldwin of Lorraine began to raid the suburbs; Godfrey captured a platoon of Byzantine soldiers and put them to death in view of the city walls. And on April 2 the Crusaders began to lay siege to the city.

"Observe how easily the Byzantines drive them off," I said. "Alexius, losing patience, has sent his best troops into battle. The Crusaders, not yet accustomed to fighting together, flee. On Easter Sunday, Godfrey and Baldwin submit, and swear allegiance to Alexius. All now is well. The emperor will give a banquet for the Crusaders in Constantinople, and then swiftly will ship them across the Bosphorus. More Crusaders, he knows, will arrive in a few days—the army of Bohemond and Tancred."

Marge Hefferin emitted a little gasping squeak at the sound of those names. I should have been warned.

We skipped forward to April 10 for a look at the next batch of Crusaders. Thousands of soldiers again camped outside Constantinople. They strolled around arrogantly in chain mail and surcoats, and playfully swatted each other with swords or maces when things got dull.

"Which one is Bohemond?" asked Marge Hefferin.

I scanned the field. "There," I said.

"Ooooh."

He *was* impressive. About two meters tall, a giant for his times, head and shoulders above everyone else around him. Broad shoulders, deep chest, close-cropped hair. Strangely white of skin. Swaggering posture. A grim customer, tough and savage.

He was cleverer than the other leaders, too. Instead of quarreling with Alexius over the business of swearing allegiance, Bohemond gave in immediately. Oaths, to him, were only words, and it was foolish to waste time bickering with the Byzantines when there were empires to be won in Asia. So Bohemond got quick entry to Constantinople. I took my people to the gate where he'd be passing into the city, so they could have a close look at him. A mistake.

The Crusaders came striding grandly in on foot, six abreast.

When Bohemond appeared, Marge Hefferin broke from the group. She ripped open her tunic and let her big pale breasts bobble into the open. An advertisement, I suppose.

She rushed toward Bohemond, squealing, "Bohemond, Bohemond, I love you, I've always loved you, Bohemond! Take me! Make me your slave, beloved!" And other words to that effect.

Bohemond turned and peered at her in bewilderment. I guess the sight of a hefty, shrieking, half-naked female running wildly in his direction must have puzzled him. But Marge didn't get within five meters of him.

A knight just in front of Bohemond, deciding that an assassination plot was unfolding, pulled out his dagger and jammed it right between Marge's big breasts. The impact halted her mad charge, and she staggered back, frowning. Blood burbled from her lips. As she toppled, another knight swung at her with a broadsword and just about cut her in half at the waist. Entrails went spilling all over the pavement.

The whole thing took about fifteen seconds. I had no chance to move. I stood aghast, realizing that my career as a Time Courier might just have come to an end. Losing a tourist is about the worst thing a Courier can do, short of committing timecrime itself.

I had to act quickly.

I said to my tourists, "Don't any of you move from the spot! That's an order!"

It wasn't likely that they'd disobey. They were huddled together in hysteria, sobbing and puking and shivering. The shock alone would hold them in place for a few minutes—more time than I'd need.

I set my timer for a two-minute jump up the line and shunted fast.

Instantly I found myself standing right behind myself. There I was, big ears and all, watching Bohemond saunter up the street. My tourists were standing on both sides of me. Marge Hefferin, breathing hard, rearing up on tiptoes for a better view of her idol, was already starting to undo her tunic.

I moved into position in back of her.

Just as she made the first movement toward the street, my hands shot out. I clamped my left hand on her ass and got the right hand on her breast and hissed in her ear, "Stay where you are or you'll be sorriest."

She squirmed and twisted. I dug my fingertips deep into the meat of her quivering rump and hung on. She writhed around to see who her attacker was, saw it was me, and stared in amazement at the other me a few paces to her left. All the fight went out of her. She sagged, and I whispered another reminder for her to stay put, and then Bohemond was past us and well up the street.

I released her, set my timer, and shunted down the line by sixty seconds.

My net absence from my tourists had been less than a minute. I half expected to find them still gagging and retching over the bloody smiting of Marge Hefferin. But the editing had succeeded. There was no corpse in the street now. No intestines were spilled beneath the boots of the marching Crusaders. Marge stood with the group, shaking her head in confusion and rubbing her backside. Her tunic still hung open and I could see the red imprints of my fingers on the soft globe of her right breast.

Did any of them suspect what had happened? No. No. Not even a phantom memory. My tourists did not experience the Paradox of Transit Displacement, for they had not made the jump-within-a-jump that I had; and so only I remembered what now was gone from their minds, could recall clearly the bloody event that I had transformed into a nonevent.

"Down the line!" I yelled, and shunted them all into 1098.

The street was quiet. The Crusaders were long since gone, and at the moment were hung up in Syria at the siege of Antioch. It was dusk on a sticky summer day and there were no witnesses to our sudden arrival.

Marge was the only one who realized that something funny had gone on; the others had not seen anything unusual occurring, but she clearly knew that an extra Jud Elliott had materialized behind her and prevented her from rushing out into the street.

"What the hell do you think you were doing?" I asked her. "You were about to run out into the street and throw yourself at Bohemond, weren't you?"

"I couldn't help it. It was a sudden compulsion. I've always loved Bohemond, don't you see? He's been my hero, my god—I've read every word anyone's written about him—and then there he was, right in front of me—"

"Let me tell you how events really unfolded," I said, and described the way she had been killed. Then I told her how I had edited the past, how I had pinched the episode of her death into a parallel line. I said, "I want you to know that the only reason I got you unkilled was to save my own job. It looks bad for a Courier if he can't keep control of his people. Otherwise I'd have been happy to leave you disemboweled. Didn't I tell you a million times *never* to break from cover?"

I warned her to forget every shred of my admission that I had changed events to save her life.

"The next time you disobey me in any way, though," I told her, "I'll—"

I was going to say that I'd ram her head up her tail and make a Moebius strip out of her. Then I realized that a Courier can't talk to a client that way, no matter what the provocation.

"—cancel your tour and send you down the line to now-time immediately, you hear me?"

"I won't ever try that again," she murmured. "I swear it. You know, now that you've told me about it, I can almost feel it happening. That dagger going into me—"

"It never happened."

"It never happened," she said doubtfully.

"Put some conviction into it. *It never happened.*"

"*It never happened,*" she repeated. "But I can almost feel it!"

38.

We all spent the night in an inn in 1098. Feeling tense and stale after so much delicate work, I decided to jump down to 1105, while my people slept, and drop in on Metaxas. I didn't even know if he'd be at his villa, but it was worth the try. I needed desperately to unwind.

I calibrated the timing with care.

Metaxas' last layoff had begun in early November, 2059, and he had jumped to mid-August, 1105. I figured he had spent ten or twelve days there. That schedule would have returned him to 2059 toward the end of November; and then, assuming he had taken out a group on a two-week tour, he'd have been able to get back to his villa by September 15 or so, 1105.

I played it safe and shunted down to September 20.

Now I had to find a way to get to his villa.

It is one of the oddities of the era of the Benchley Effect that I would find it easier to jump across seven years of time than to get myself a few dozen kilometers into the Byzantine countryside. But I did have that problem. I had no access to a chariot, and there aren't any cabs for hire in the twelfth century.

Walk? Ridiculous idea!

I contemplated heading for the nearest inn and dangling bezants in front of freelance charioteers until I found one willing to make the trip to Metaxas' place. As I considered this I heard a familiar voice yelling, "Herr Courier Elliott! Herr Courier Elliott!"

I turned. Scholar Magistrate Speer.

"Guten Tag, Herr Courier Elliott!" said Scholar Magistrate Speer.

"Guten—" I scowled, cut myself short, greeted him in a more Byzantine way. He smiled indulgently at my observance of the rules.

"I have a very successful visit been having," he said. "Since last I enjoyed with you company, have I found the *Thamyras* of Sophocles and also the *Melanippe* of Euripides, and further a partial text of what I believe is the *Archelaus* of Euripides. And then there is besides the text of a play that is claiming to be of Aeschylus the *Helios,* of which there is in the records no reference for. So perhaps is a forgery or otherwise is maybe a new discovery, I will see which only upon reading. Eh? A good visit, eh, Herr Courier!"

"Splendid," I said.

"And now I am returning to the villa of our friend Metaxas, just as soon as I complete a small purchase in this shop of spices. Would you accompany me?"

"You have wheels?" I asked.

"Was meinen Sie mit 'wheels'?"

"Transportation. A chariot."

"Naturlich! Over there. It waits for me, a chariot *mit* driver, from Metaxas."

"Swell," I said. "Take care of your business in the spice shop and then we can ride out to Metaxas' place together, okay?"

The shop was dark and fragrant. In barrels, jugs, flasks, and baskets it displayed its wares: olives, nuts, dates, figs, raisins, pistachios, cheeses, and spices both ground and whole of many different sorts. Speer, apparently running some errand for Metaxas' chef, selected a few items and pulled forth a purse of bezants to pay for them. While this was going on, an ornate chariot pulled up outside the shop and three figures dismounted and entered. One was a slavegirl—to carry the merchandise to the chariot, evidently. The second was a woman of mature years and simple dress—a duenna, I supposed, just the right kind of dragon to escort a Byzantine wife on a shopping expedition. The third person was the wife herself, obviously a woman of the very highest class making a tour of the town.

She was fantastically beautiful.

I knew at once that she was no more than seventeen. She had a supple, liquid Mediterranean beauty; her eyes were dark and large and glossy, with long lashes, and her skin was light olive in hue, and her lips were full and her nose aquiline, and her bearing was elegant and aristocratic. Her robes of white silk revealed the outlines of high, sumptuous breasts, curving flanks, voluptuous buttocks. She was all the women I had ever desired, united into one ideal form.

I stared at her without shame.

She stared back. Without shame.

Our eyes met and held, and a current of pure force passed between us, and I quivered as the full surge hit me. She smiled only on the left side of her mouth, quirking the lips in, revealing two glistening teeth. It was a smile of invitation, a smile of lust.

She nodded almost imperceptibly to me.

Then she turned away, and pointed to the bins, ordering this and this and this, and I continued to stare, until the duenna, noticing it, shot me a furious look of warning.

"Come," Speer said impatiently. "The chariot is waiting—"

"Let it wait a little longer."

I made him stay in the store with me until the three women had completed their transaction. I watched them leave, my eyes riveted to the subtle sway of my beloved's silk-sheathed tail. Then I whirled and pounced on the proprietor of the shop, seizing his wrist and barking, "That woman! What's her name?"

"Milord, I—that is—"

I flipped a gold piece to the counter. "Her name!"

"That is Pulcheria Ducas," he gasped. "The wife of the well-known Leo Ducas, who—"

I groaned and rushed out of the store.

Her chariot clattered off toward the Golden Horn.

Speer emerged. "Are you in good health, Herr Courier Elliott?"

"I'm sick as a pig," I muttered. "Pulcheria Ducas—that was Pulcheria Ducas—"

"And so?"

"I love her, Speer, can you understand that?"

Looking blankfaced, he said, "The chariot is ready."

"Never mind. I'm not going with you. Give Metaxas my best regards."

In anguish I ran down the street, aimlessly, my mind and my crotch inflamed with the vision of Pulcheria. I trembled. I streamed with sweat. I sobbed. Finally I came up against the wall of some church, and pressed my cheek to the cold stone, and touched my timer and shunted back to the tourists I had left sleeping in 1098.

39.

I was a lousy Courier for the rest of that trip.

Moody, withdrawn, lovesick, confused, I shuttled my people through the standard events, the Venetian invasion of 1204 and the Turkish conquest of 1453, in a routine, mechanical way. Maybe they didn't realize they were getting a minimum job, or didn't care. Maybe they blamed it on the trouble Marge Hefferin had caused. For better or for worse I gave them their tour and delivered them safely down the line in now-time and was rid of them.

I was on layoff again, and my soul was infected by desire.

Go to 1105? Accept Metaxas' offer, let him introduce me to Pulcheria?

I recoiled at the idea.

Time Patrol rules specifically forbid any kind of fraternization between Couriers (or other time-travelers) and people who live up the line. The only contact we are supposed to have with the residents of the past is casual and incidental—buying a bag of olives, asking how to get to Haghia Sophia from here, like that. We are not permitted to strike up friendships, get into long philosophical discussions, or have sexual intercourse with inhabitants of previous eras.

Especially with our own ancestors.

The incest taboo per se didn't scare me much; like all taboos, it isn't worth a whole lot any more, and while I'd hesitate at bedding my sister or my mother, I couldn't see any very convincing reason to abstain from bedding Pulcheria. I felt a little lingering puritanism, maybe, but I knew it would fade in a minute if Pulcheria became available.

What held me back, though, was the universal deterrent, fear of retribution. If the Time Patrol caught me sexing around with my multi-great-grandmother, they'd certainly fire me from the Time Service, might imprison me, might even try to invoke the death penalty for first-degree timecrime on the grounds that I had tried to become my own ancestor. I was terrified of the possibilities.

How could they catch me?

Plenty of scenarios presented themselves. For example:

I wangle introduction to Pulcheria. Somehow get into situation of privacy with her. Reach for her fair flesh; she screams; family bodyguards seize me and put me to death. Time Patrol, when I don't check in after my layoff, traces me, finds out what has happened, rescues me, then brings charges of timecrime.

Or:

I wangle introduction, etc., and seduce Pulcheria. Just at moment of mutual climax husband bursts into bedroom and impales me. Rest of scenario follows.

Or:

I fall so desperately in love with Pulcheria that I abscond with her to some distant point in time, say 400 B.C. or A.D. 1600, and we live happily ever after until Time Patrol catches us, returns her to proper moment of 1105, brings charges of timecrime against me.

Or:

A dozen other possibilities, all of them ending in the same melancholy way. So I resisted all temptation to spend my layoff in 1105 sniffing after Pulcheria. Instead, to suit the darkness of my mood in this time of unrequited lust, I signed up to do the Black Death tour.

Only the weirds, the freaks, the sickos, and the pervos

would take a tour like that, which is to say the demand is always pretty heavy. But as a vacationing Courier, I was able to bump a paying customer and get into the next group leaving.

There are four regular Black Death outings. One sets out from the Crimea for 1347 and shows you the plague as it spills out of Asia. The highlight of that tour is the siege of Kaffa, a Genoese trading port on the Black Sea, by Khan Janibeg of the Kipchak Mongols. Janibeg's men were rotten with plague, and he catapulted their corpses into the town to infect the Genoese. You have to book a reservation a year in advance for that one.

The Genoese carried the Black Death westward into the Mediterranean, and the second tour takes you to Italy, autumn of 1347, to watch it spread inland. You see a mass burning of Jews, who were thought to have caused the epidemic by poisoning the wells. The third tour brings you to France in 1348, and the fourth to England in the late spring of 1349.

The booking office got me on the England trip. I made a noon hop to London and joined the group two hours before it was about to leave. Our Courier was a tall, cadaverous man named Riley, with bushy eyebrows and bad teeth. He was a little strange, as you have to be to specialize in this particular tour. He welcomed me in friendly if moody fashion and got me fitted for a plague suit.

A plague suit is more or less a spacesuit, done up in black trim. You carry a standard fourteen-day rebreathing unit, you eat via an intake pipe, and you eliminate wastes with difficulty and complexity. The idea, naturally, is to keep you totally sealed off from the infectious environment. Tourists are told that if they open their suits even for ten seconds, they'll be marooned permanently in the plague era; and although this is not true at all, there hasn't been a case yet of a tourist calling the Time Service's bluff.

This is one of the few tours that operates to and from fixed points. We don't want returning groups materializing all over the place, carrying plague on their spacesuits, and so the Service has marked off jumping areas in red paint at the medieval end of each of the four plague tours. When your group is ready to come back, you go to a jumping area and shunt down the line from there. This materializes you within a sealed sterile dome; your suit is taken from you and you are thoroughly fumigated before you're allowed to rejoin the twenty-first century.

"What you are about to see," said Riley portentously, "is neither a reconstruction nor a simulation nor an approximation. It is the real thing, exaggerated in no way."

We shunted up the line.

40.

Clad in our black plastic suits, we marched single file through a land of the dead.

Nobody paid any attention to us. At such a time as this our costume didn't even seem outlandish; the black was logical, the airtight sealing of our suits even more logical. And though the fabric was a little on the anachronistic side for the fourteenth century, no one was curious. At this time, wise men stayed indoors and kept their curiosities on tight leashes.

Those who saw us must have assumed that we were priests going on a pilgrimage of prayer. Our somber suits, our single-file array, the fearlessness with which we paraded through the worst areas of infestation, all marked us as God's men, or else Satan's, and, either way, who would dare to interfere with us?

Bells tolled a leaden dirge, donging all day and half the night. The world was a perpetual funeral. A grim haze hung over London; the sky was never anything but gray and ashen all the time we were there. Not that nature was reinforcing the dolefulness, that old pathetic fallacy; no, the haze was man-made, for thousands of small fires were burning in England, consuming the clothes and the homes and the bodies of the stricken.

We saw plague victims in all stages, from the early staggering to the later trembling and sweating and falling and convulsing. "The onset of the disease," said Riley calmly, dispassionately, "is marked by hardenings and swellings of the glands in the armpits and the groin. The swellings rapidly grow to the size of eggs or apples. See, this woman here—" She was young, haggard, terror-stricken. She clutched desperately at the sprouting buboes and lurched past us through the smoky streets.

"Next," he said, "come the black blotches, first on the arms and thighs, then all over the body. And the carbuncles which, when lanced, give no relief. And then delirium, insanity, death always on the third day after the swellings appear. Observe here—" A victim in the late stages, groaning in the street, abandoned. "And here—" Pale faces looking down from a window. "Over here—" Heaped corpses at the door of a stable.

Houses were locked. Shops were barred. The only people in the streets were those already infected, roaming desperately about searching for a doctor, a priest, a miracle-worker.

Fractured, tormented music came to us from the distance: pipes, drums, viols, lutes, sackbuts, shawms, clarions, krummhorns, all the medieval instruments at once but giving forth not the pretty buzz and tootle of the middle ages, rather a harsh, discordant, keyless whine and screech. Riley looked pleased. "A procession of flagellants is coming!" he cried, elated. "Follow me! By all means, let's not miss it!"

And through the winding streets the flagellants came, men and women, naked to the waist, grimy, bloody, some playing on instruments, most wielding knotted whips, lashing, lashing, tirelessly bringing down the lash across bare backs, breasts, cheeks, arms, foreheads. They droned toneless hymns; they groaned in agony; they stumbled forward, a few of the whippers and some of the whipped already showing the buboes of the plague, and without looking at us they went by, down some dismal alley leading to a deserted church.

And we happy time-tourists picked our way over the dead and the dying and marched on, for our Courier wished us to drink this experience to the deepest.

We saw the bonfired bodies of the dead blackening and splitting open.

We saw other heaps of the unburied left in fields to rot.

We saw ghouls searching cadavers for items of value.

We saw a plague-smitten man fall upon a half-conscious plague-smitten woman in the streets, and part her thighs for one last desperate act of lust.

We saw priests on horseback fleeing from parishioners begging for Heaven's mercy.

We entered an unguarded palace to watch terrified surgeons letting blood from some dying duke.

We saw another procession of strange black-clad beings cross our street at an angle, their faces hidden behind mirrorlike plates, and we shivered at the grotesque sight of these nightmare marchers, these demons without faces, and we realized only slowly that we had intersected some other party of tourists.

Riley was ready with cool statistics. "The mortality rate of the Black Death," he announced, "was anywhere from one-eighth to two-thirds of the population in a given area. In Europe it is estimated that twenty-five per cent of the entire population perished; worldwide, the mortality was about thirty-three per cent. That is to say, a similar plague today would take the lives of more than two billion people."

We watched a woman emerge from a thatched house and, one by one, arrange the bodies of five children in the street so that they might be taken away by the department of sanitation.

Riley said, "The aristocracy was annihilated, causing great shifts in patterns of inheritance. There were permanent cultural effects as a result of the wholesale death of painters of a single school, of poets, of learned monks. The psychological impact was long-lasting; for generations it was thought that the mid-fourteenth century had done something to earn the wrath of God, and a return of His wrath was momentarily expected."

We formed the audience for a mass funeral at which two young and frightened priests muttered words over a hundred blotched and swollen corpses, tolled their little bells, sprinkled holy water, and signaled to the sextons to start the bonfire.

"Not until the early sixteenth century," said Riley, "will the population reach its pre-1348 level."

It was impossible for me to tell how the others were affected by these horrors, since we all were hidden in our suits. Probably most of my companions were fascinated and thrilled. I'm told that it's customary for a dedicated plague aficionado to take all four Black Death tours in succession, starting in the Crimea; many have gone through the set five or six times. My own reaction was one of diminishing shock. You accommodate to monstrous horror. I think that by the tenth time through I'd have been as cool and dispassionate as Courier Riley, that brimming fount of statistics.

At the end of our journey through hell we made our way to Westminster. On the pavement outside the palace, Time Service personnel had painted a red circle five meters in diameter. This was our jumping point. We gathered close in the middle. I helped Riley make the timer adjustments—on this tour, the timers are mounted on the outside of the suits. He gave the signal and we shunted.

A couple of plague victims, shambling past the palace, were witnesses to our departure. I doubt that it troubled them much. In a time when all the world is perishing, who can get excited over the sight of ten black demons vanishing?

41.

We emerged under a shimmering dome, yielded up our polluted suits, and came forth purged and purified and ennobled by what we had seen. But images of Pulcheria still obsessed me. Restless, tormented, I fought with temptation.

Go back to 1105? Let Metaxas insinuate me into the Ducas household? Bed Pulcheria and ease my yearnings?

No. No. No. No.

Fight temptation. Sublimate. Fuck an empress instead.

I hurried back to Istanbul and shunted up the line to 537. I went over to Haghia Sophia to look for Metaxas at the dedication ceremony.

Metaxas was there, in many parts of the throng. I spotted at least ten of him. (I also saw two Jud Elliotts, and I wasn't half trying.) On my first two approaches, though, I ran into the Paradox of Discontinuity; neither Metaxas knew me. One shook me off with a scowl of irritation, and the other simply said, "Whoever you are, we haven't met yet. Beat it." On the third try I found a Metaxas who recognized me, and we arranged to meet that evening at the inn where he was lodging his tour. He was staying down the line in 610 to show his people the coronation of Emperor Heraclius.

"Well?" he said. "What's your now-time basis, anyway?"

"Early December, 2059."

"I'm ahead of you," said Metaxas. "I'm out of the middle of February, 2060. We're discontinuous."

That scared me. This man knew two and a half months of my future. Etiquette required him to keep his knowledge to himself; it was quite possible that I would be/had been killed in January, 2060, and that this Metaxas knew all the details, but he couldn't drop a hint of that to this me. Still, the gap frightened me.

He saw it. "Do you want to go back and find a different one?" he asked.

"No. That's all right. I think we can manage."

His face was a frozen mask. He played by the rules; neither by inflection nor expression was he going to react to anything I said in a way that might reveal my own future to me.

"You once said you'd help me get into Empress Theodora."

"I remember that, yes."

"I turned you down then. Now I'd like to try her."

"No problem," said Metaxas. "Let's jump up to 535. Justinian will be preoccupied with building Haghia Sophia. Theodora's available."

"How easily?"

"Nothing to it," he said.

We shunted. On a cool spring day in 535 I went with Metaxas to the Great Palace, where he sought and found a plump, eunuchoid individual named Anastasius and had a long, animated discussion with him. Evidently Anastasius was chief procurer to the empress this year, and had the responsibility of finding her anywhere from one to ten young men a night. The conversation was carried on in low muttered tones, punctuated by angry outbursts, but from what I could hear of it I gathered that Anastasius was offering me an hour with Theodora, and that Metaxas was holding out for a whole night. I felt edgy about that. Virile I am, yes, but would I be able to entertain one of history's most celebrated nymphomaniacs from darkness to dawn? I signaled to Metaxas to accept something less grandiose, but he persisted, and in the end Anastasius agreed to let me have four hours with the empress.

"If he qualifies," the plump one said.

The test for qualification was administered by a ferocious little wench named Photia, one of the imperial ladies in waiting. Anastasius complacently watched us in action; Metaxas at least had the good taste to leave the room. Watching, I guess, was how Anastasius got his kickies.

Photia was black-haired, thin-lipped, busty, voracious. Have you ever seen a starfish devour an oyster? No? Well, imagine it, anyway. Photia was a starfish of sex. The suction was fantastic. I stayed with her, wrestled her into submission, pronged her off to ecstasy. And—I suppose—I passed my test with something to spare, because Anastasius gave me his seal of approval and set up my assignation with Theodora. Four hours.

I thanked Metaxas and he left, jumping down to his tour in 610.

Anastasius took charge of me. I was bathed, groomed, curried, required to swallow an oily, bitter potion that he claimed was an aphrodisiac. And an hour before midnight I was ushered into the bedchambers of the Empress Theodora.

Cleopatra. . . . Delilah. . . Harlow . . . Lucrezia Borgia. . . . Theodora. .

Had any of them ever existed? Was their legendary wantonness real? Could this truly be Judson Daniel Elliott III standing before the bed of the depraved Empress of Byzantium?

I knew the tales Procopius told of her. The orgies at dinners of state. The exhibitionist performances in the theater. The repeated illegitimate pregnancies and the annual abortions. The friends and lovers betrayed and tortured. The severed ears, noses, testicles, penes, limbs, and lips of those who displeased her. The offerings on the altar of Aphrodite of every orifice she owned. If only one story out of ten were true, her vileness was unequaled.

She was pale, fair-skinned, big-breasted, narrow-waisted, and surprisingly short, the top of her head barely reaching my chest. Perfumes drenched her skin, yet unmistakable fleshy reeks came through. Her eyes were fierce, cold, hard, slightly hyperthyroid: nymphomaniacal eyes.

She didn't ask my name. She ordered me to strip, and inspected me, and nodded. A wench brought us thick greasy wine in an enormous amphora. We drank a good deal of it, and then Theodora anointed herself with the rest, coating her skin with it from forehead to toes.

"Lick it off," she said.

I obeyed. I obeyed other commands too. Her tastes were remarkably various, and in my four hours I satisfied most of them. It may not have been the kinkiest four hours I ever spent, but came close. And yet her pyrotechnics chilled me. There was something mechanical and empty about the way Theodora presented now this, now that, now the other thing, for me to deal with. It was as if she were running through a script that she had played out a million times.

It was interesting in a strenuous way. But it wasn't overwhelming. I mean, I expected more, somehow, from being in bed with one of history's most famous sinners.

When I was fourteen years old, an old man who taught me a great deal about the way of the world said to me,

"Son, when you've jazzed one snatch you've jazzed them all."

I was barely out of my virginity then, but I dared to disagree with him. I still do, in a way, but less and less each year. Women do vary—in figure, in passion, in technique, in approach. But I've had the Empress of Byzantium, mind you, Theodora herself. I'm beginning to think, after Theodora, that that old man was right. When you've jazzed one snatch you've jazzed them all.

42.

I went back down to Istanbul and reported for duty, and took a party of eight out on the two-week tour.

Neither the Black Death nor Theodora had burned away my passion for Pulcheria Ducas. I hoped now that I'd shake free of that dangerous obsession by getting back to work.

My tour group included the following people:

J. Frederick Gostaman of Biloxi, Mississippi, a retail dealer in pharmaceuticals and transplant organs, along with his wife, Louise, his sixteen-year-old daughter Palmyra, and his fourteen-year-old son Bilbo.

Conrad Sauerabend of St. Louis, Missouri, a stockbroker, traveling alone.

Miss Hester Pistil of Brooklyn, New York, a young schoolteacher.

Leopold Haggins of St. Petersburg, Florida, a retired manufacturer of power cores, and his wife Chrystal.

In short, the usual batch of overcapitalized and undereducated idlers. Sauerabend, who was fat and jowly and sullen, took an immediate dislike to Gostaman, who was fat and jowly and jovial, because Gostaman made a joking remark about the way Sauerabend was peering down the neckline of Gostaman's daughter at one of our orientation sessions. I think Gostaman was joking, anyway, but Sauerabend got red-faced and furious, and Palmyra, who though sixteen was underdeveloped enough to pass for a skinny thirteen, ran out of the room in tears. I patched things up, but Sauerabend continued to glare at Gostaman. Miss Pistil, the schoolteacher, who was a vacant-eyed blonde with an augmented bosom and an expression that managed to be both tense and languid, established at our first meeting that she is the sort of girl who takes these trips in order to get laid by Couriers; even if I hadn't been preoccupied with Pulcheria, I don't think I'd have taken advantage of her availability, but as things stood I felt very little urge to explore Miss Pistil's pelvis. This was not the case with young Bilbo Gostaman, who was such a fashion-plate that he was wearing knickers with padded groin (if they can revive Cretan bodices, why not the codpiece?) and who got his hand under Miss Pistil's skirt during our second orientation session. He thought he was being surreptitious about it, but I saw him, and so did old man Gostaman, who beamed in paternal pride, and so did Mrs. Chrystal Haggins, who was shocked into catalepsy. Miss Pistil looked thrilled, and squirmed a little to afford Bilbo a better angle for groping. Mr. Leopold Haggins, who was eighty-five and pretty leathery, meanwhile winked hopefully at Mrs. Louise Gostaman, a placid and matronly sort of woman who was destined to spend most of our tour fighting off the old scoundrel's quivering advances. You can see how it was.

Off we went for two happy weeks together.

I was, again, a second-rate Courier. I couldn't summon up the divine spark. I showed them everything I was supposed to show them, but I wasn't able to do the extra things, the leaping, cavorting, charismatic, Metaxian things, that I had vowed I would do on every trip.

Part of the trouble was my edginess over the Pulcheria situation. She danced in and out of my mind a thousand times a day. I pictured myself dropping down to 1105 or thereabouts and getting to work with her; surely she'd remember me from the spice shop, and surely that was an open invitation she had given me then.

Part of the trouble was the ebbing of my own sense of wonder. I had been on the Byzantium run for almost half a year, and the thrill was gone. A gifted Courier—a Metaxas—could derive as much excitement from his thousandth imperial coronation as from his third. And transmit that excitement to his people. Maybe I just wasn't a naturally gifted Courier. I was becoming bored with the dedication of Haghia Sophia and the baptism of Theodosius II, the way an usher in a stimmo house gets weary of watching orgies.

Part of the trouble was the presence of Conrad Sauerabend in the group. That fat, sweaty, untidy man was an instant turnoff for me every time he opened his mouth.

He wasn't stupid. But he was gross and coarse and crude. He was a leerer, a gaper, a gawker. I could count on him to make some blunt and inappropriate remark anywhere.

At the Augusteum he whistled and said, "What a parking lot this would make!"

Inside Haghia Sophia he clapped a white-bearded priest on the back and said, "I just got to tell you what a swell church you got here, priesto."

During a visit to the icon-smashings of Leo the Isaurian, when Byzantium's finest works of art were being destroyed as idols, he interrupted an earnest iconoclastic fanatic and said, "Don't be such a dumb prick. You know that you're hurting this city's tourist trade?"

Sauerabend was also a molester of little girls, and proud of it. "I can't help it," he explained. "It's my particular personal clutchup. The shrink calls it the Lolita complex. I like 'em twelve, thirteen years old. You know, old enough to bleed, maybe to have a little hair on it, but still kind of unripe. Get 'em before the tits grow, that's my ideal. I can't stand all that swinging meat on a woman. Pretty sick, huh?"

Pretty sick, yes. And also pretty annoying, because we had Palmyra Gostaman with us; Sauerabend couldn't stop staring at her. The lodgings provided on a time-tour don't always give the tourists much privacy, and Sauerabend ogled the poor girl into despair. He drooled over her constantly, forcing her to dress and undress under a blanket as if this was the nineteenth or twentieth century; and when her father wasn't looking, he'd get his fat paws on her behind or the little bumps of her breasts and whisper lewd propositions in her ear. Finally I had to tell him that if he didn't stop bothering her, I'd bounce him from the tour. That settled him down for a few days. The girl's father, incidentally, thought the whole incident was very funny. "Maybe what that girl needs is a good banging," he said to me. "Get the body juices flowing, huh?" Papa Gostaman also approved of his son Bilbo's affair with Miss Pistil, which also became a nuisance, since we wasted a terrific amount of time waiting for them to finish their current copulations. I'd be giving a preliminary talk on what we were to see this morning, get me, and Bilbo would be standing behind Miss Pistil, and suddenly she'd get this transfigured look on her face and I'd know he'd done it again, up with her skirt in back, *wham!* Bilbo looked pleased as hell all the time, which I suppose was reasonable enough for a fourteen-year-old boy having an affair with a woman ten years his senior. Miss Pistil looked guilty. Her sore conscience, though, didn't keep her from opening the gate for Bilbo three or four times a day.

I didn't find all this conducive to creative Couriering.

Then there were minor annoyances, such as the

ineffectual lecheries of old Mr. Haggins, who persecuted the dim Mrs. Gostaman mercilessly. Or the insistence of Sauerabend on fiddling around with his timer. "You know," he said several times, "I bet I could ungimmick this thing so I could run it myself. Used to be an engineer, you know, before I took up stockbroking." I told him to leave his timer alone. Behind my back, he went on tinkering with it.

Still another headache was Capistrano, whom I met by chance in 1097 while Bohemond's Crusaders were entering Constantinople. He showed up while I was concentrating on the replay of the Marge Hefferin scene. I wanted to see how permanent my correction of the past had been.

This time I lined my people up on the opposite side of the street. Yes, there I was; and there was Marge, eager and impatient and hot for Bohemond; and there was the rest of the group. As the Crusaders paraded toward us, I felt almost dizzy with suspense. Would I see myself save Marge? Or would I see Marge leap toward Bohemond and be cut down? Or would some third alternative unreel? The fluidity, the mutability, of the time stream, that was what terrified me now.

Bohemond neared. Marge was undoing her tunic. Heavy creamy breasts were visible. She tensed and readied herself for the dash into the street. And a second Jud Elliott materialized out of nowhere across the way, right behind her. I saw the look of shock on Marge's face as my alter ego's steely fingers clamped tight to her ass. I saw his hand splay wide to seize her breast. I saw her whirl, struggle, sag; and as Bohemond went by, I saw myself vanish, leaving only the two of me, one on each side of the processional avenue.

I was awash with relief. Yet I was also troubled, because I knew now that my editing of this scene was embedded in the time-flow for anyone to see. Including some passing Time Patrolman, perhaps, who might happen to observe the brief presence of a doubled Courier and wonder what was going on. At any time in the next million millennia the Patrol might monitor that scene— and then, no matter if it went undiscovered until the year 8,000,000,000,008, I would be called to account for my unauthorized correction of the record. I could expect to feel the hand on my shoulder, the voice calling my name—

I felt a hand on my shoulder. A voice called my name. I spun around. *"Capistrano!"*

"Sure, Capistrano. Did you expect someone else?"

"I—I—you surprised me, that's all." I was shaking. My knees were watery.

I was so upset that it took me a few seconds to realize how awful Capistrano looked.

He was frayed and haggard; his glossy dark hair was graying and stringy; he had lost weight and looked twenty years older than the Capistrano I knew. I sensed discontinuity and felt the fear that I always felt when confronted with someone out of my own future.

"What's the trouble?" I asked.

"I'm coming apart. Breaking up. Look, there's my tour over there." He indicated a clump of time-travelers who peered intently at the Crusaders. "I can't stay with them any more. They sicken me. Everything sickens me. It's the end for me, Elliott, absolutely the end."

"Why? What's wrong?"

"I can't talk about it here. When are you staying tonight?"

"Right here in 1097. The inn by the Golden Horn."

"I'll see you at midnight," Capistrano said. He clutched my arm for a moment. "It's the end, Elliott. Really the end. God have mercy on my soul!"

43.

Capistrano appeared at the inn just before midnight. Under his cloak he carried a lopsided bottle, which he uncorked and handed to me. "Cognac," he said. "From 1825, bottled in 1775. I just brought it up the line."

I tasted it. He slumped down in front of me. He looked worse than ever: old, drained, hollow. He took the cognac from me and gulped it greedily.

"Before you say anything," I told him, "I want to know what your now-time basis is. Discontinuities scare me."

"There's no discontinuity."

"There isn't?"

"My basis is December, 2059. The same as yours."

"Impossible!"

"Impossible?" he repeated. "How can you say that?"

"Last time I saw you, you weren't even forty. Now you're easily past fifty. Don't fool me, Capistrano. Your basis is somewhere in 2070, isn't it? And if it is, for God's sake don't tell me anything about the years still ahead for me!"

"My basis is 2059," said Capistrano in a ragged voice. I realized from the thickness of his tone that this bottle of cognac was not the first for him tonight. "I am no older now than I ought to be, for you," he said. "The trouble is that I'm a dead man."

"I don't understand."

"Last month I told you of my great-grandmother, the Turk?"

"Yes."

"This morning I went down the line to Istanbul of 1955. My great-grandmother was then seventeen years old and unmarried. In a moment of wild despair I choked her and threw her into the Bosphorus. It was at night, in the rain; no one saw us. I am dead, Elliott. Dead."

"No, Capistrano!"

"I told you, long ago, that when the time came, I would make my exit that way. A Turkish slut—she who beguiled my great-grandfather into a shameful marriage —gone now. And so am I. Once I return to now-time, I have never existed. What shall I do, Elliott? You decide. Shall I jump down the line now and end the comedy?"

Sweating, I said, after a deep pull of the cognac, "Give me the exact date of your stopoff in 1955. I'll go down the line right now and keep you from harming her."

"You will not."

"Then you do it. Arrive in the nick of time and save her, Capistrano!"

He looked at me sadly. "What's the point? Sooner or later I'll kill her again. I have to. It's my destiny. I'm going to shunt down now. Will you look after my people?"

"I've got a tour of my own," I reminded him.

"Of course. Of course. You can't handle more. Just see that mine aren't stranded. I have to go—have to—"

His hand was on his timer.

"*Capis*—"

He took the cognac with him when he jumped.

Gone. Extinct. A victim of suicide by timecrime. Blotted out of history's pages. I didn't know how to handle the situation. Suppose I went down to 1955 and prevented him from murdering his great-grandmother. He was already a nonperson in now-time; could I retroactively restore him to existence? How did the Paradox of Transit

Displacement function in reverse? This was a case I had not studied. I wanted to do whatever was best for Capistrano; I also had his stranded tourists to think about.

I brooded over it for an hour. Finally I came to a sane if not romantic conclusion: this is none of my business, I decided, and I'd better call in the Time Patrol. Reluctantly I touched the alarm stud on my timer, the signal which is supposed to summon a Patrolman at once.

Instantly a Patrolman materialized. Dave Van Dam, the belching blond boor I had met on my first day in Istanbul.

"So?" he said.

"Timecrime suicide," I told him. "Capistrano just murdered his great-grandmother and jumped back to now-time."

"Son of a goddam bitch. Why do we have to put up with these unstable motherfuckers?"

I didn't bother to tell him that his choice of obscenity was inappropriate. I said, "He also left a party of tourists marooned here. That's why I called you in."

Van Dam spat elaborately. "Son of a goddam bitch," he said again. "Okay, I'm with it." He timed out of my room.

I was sick with grief over the stupid waste of a valuable life. I thought of Capistrano's charm, his grace, his sensitivity, all squandered because in a drunken moment of misery he had to timecrime himself. I didn't weep, but I felt like kicking furniture around, and I did. The noise woke up Miss Pistil, who gasped and murmured, "Are we being attacked?"

"You are," I said, and to ease my rage and anguish I dropped down on her bed and rammed myself into her. She was a little startled, but began to cooperate once she realized what was up. I came in half a minute and left her, throbbing, to be finished off by Bilbo Gostaman. Still in a black mood, I awakened the innkeeper and demanded his best wine, and drank myself into a foggy stupor.

Much later I learned that my dramatics had all been pointless. That slippery bastard Capistrano had had a change of heart at the last minute. Instead of shunting to 2059 and obliterating himself, he clung to his Transit Displacement invulnerability and stayed up the line in 1600, marrying a Turkish pasha's daughter and fathering three kids on her. The Time Patrol didn't succeed in tracing him until 1607, at which point they picked him up for multiple timecrime, hoisted him down to 2060, and sentenced him to obliteration. So he got his exit anyway, but not in a very heroic way. The Patrol also had to unmurder Capistrano's great-grandmother, unmarry him from the pasha's daughter in 1600, and uncreate those three kids, as well as find and rescue his stranded tourists, so all in all he was a great deal of trouble for everybody. "If a man wants to commit suicide," said Dave Van Dam, "why in hell can't he just drink carniphage in nowtime and make it easier on the rest of us?" I had to agree. It was the only time in my life when the Time Patrol and I saw things the same way.

44.

The mess over Capistrano and the general unsavoriness of this batch of tourists combined to push me into abysses of gloom.

I moved grimly along from epoch to epoch, but my heart wasn't in it. And by the time, midway through the second week, that we reached 1204, I knew I was going to do something disastrous.

Doggedly I delivered the usual orientation lecture.

"The old spirit of the Crusaders is reviving," I said, scowling at Bilbo, who was fondling Miss Pistil again, and scowling at Sauerabend, who was visibly dreaming of Palmyra Gostaman's meager breasts. "Jerusalem, which the Crusaders conquered a century ago, has been recaptured by the Saracens, but various Crusader dynasties still control most of the Mediterranean coast of the Holy Land. The Arabs now are feuding among themselves, and since 1199, Pope Innocent III has been calling for a new Crusade."

I explained how various barons answered the Pope's call.

I told how the Crusaders were unwilling to make the traditional land journey across all of Europe and down through Asia Minor into Syria. I told how they preferred to go by sea, landing at one of the Palestinian ports.

I discussed how in 1202 they applied to Venice, Europe's leading naval power of the time, for transportaton.

I described the terms by which the ancient and crafty Doge Enrico Dandolo of Venice agreed to provide ships.

"Dandolo," I said, "contracted to transport 4,500 knights with their horses, 9,000 squires, and 20,000 infantrymen, along with nine months' provisions. He offered to throw in fifty armed galleys to escort the convoy. For these services he asked 85,000 silver marks, or about $20,000,000 in our money. Plus half of all the territory or treasure that the Crusaders won in battle."

I told how the Crusaders agreed to this stiff price, planning to cheat the blind old Doge.

I told how the blind old Doge, once he had the Crusaders hung up in Venice, gripped them by the throats until they paid him every mark due him.

I told how the venerable monster seized control of the Crusade and set off in command of the fleet on Easter

Monday, 1203—heading not for the Holy Land but for Constantinople.

"Byzantium," I said, "is Venice's great maritime rival. Dandolo doesn't care warm spit for Jerusalem, but wants very badly to get control of Constantinople."

I explicated the dynastic situation. The Comnenus dynasty had come to a bad end. When Manuel II died in 1180, his successor was his young son Alexius II, who shortly was murdered by his father's amoral cousin, Andronicus. The elegantly depraved Andronicus was himself destroyed in a particularly ghastly way by an enraged mob, after he had ruled harshly for a few years, and in 1185 there came to the throne Isaac Angelus, an elderly and bumbling grandson of Alexius I, by the female line. Isaac ruled for ten haphazard years, until he was dethroned, blinded, and imprisoned by his brother, who became Emperor Alexius III.

"Alexius III still rules," I said, "and Isaac Angelus is still in prison. But Isaac's son, also Alexius, has escaped and is in Venice. He has promised Dandolo huge sums of money if Dandolo will restore his father to the throne. And so Dandolo is coming to Constantinople to overthrow Alexius III and make Isaac into an imperial puppet."

They didn't follow the intricacy of it. I didn't care. They'd figure it out as they saw things taking place.

I showed them the Fourth Crusade arriving at Constaninople at the end of June, 1203. I let them see Dandolo directing the capture of Scutari, Constantinople's suburb on the Asian side of the Bosphorus. I pointed out how the entrance to the port of Constantinople was guarded by a great tower and twenty Byzantine galleys, and blocked by a huge iron chain. I called their attention to the scene in which Venetian sailors boarded and took the Byzantine galleys while one of Dandolo's ships, equipped with monstrous steel shears, cut through the chain and opened the Golden Horn to the invaders. I allowed them to watch the superhuman Dandolo, ninety years old, lead the attackers over the ramparts of Constantinople. "Never before," I said, "have invaders broken into this city."

From a distance, part of a cheering mob, we watched Dandolo bring Isaac Angelus forth from his dungeon and name him Emperor of Byzantium, with his son crowned as co-emperor, by the style of Alexius IV.

"Alexius IV," I said, "now invites the Crusaders to spend the winter in Constantinople at his expense, preparing for their attack on the Holy Land. It is a rash offer. It dooms him."

We shunted down the line to the spring of 1204.

"Alexius IV," I said, "has discovered that housing thousands of Crusaders is bankrupting Byzantium. He tells Dandolo that he is out of money and will no longer underwrite their expenses. A furious dispute begins. While it proceeds, a fire starts in the city. No one knows who caused it, but Alexius suspects the Venetians. He sets seven decrepit ships on fire and lets them drift into the Venetian fleet. Look."

We saw the fire. We saw the Venetians using boathooks to drag the blazing hulks away from their own ships. We saw sudden revolution break out in Constantinople, the Byzantines denouncing Alexius IV as the tool of Venice, and putting him to death. "Old Isaac Angelus dies a few days later," I said. "The Byzantines find the son-in-law of the expelled Emperor Alexius III, and put him on the throne as Alexius V. This son-in-law is a member of the famous Ducas family. Dandolo has lost both his puppet emperors, and he is furious. The Venetians and the Crusaders decide now to conquer Constantinople and rule it themselves."

Once again I took a pack of tourists through scenes of battle as, on April 8, the struggle began. Fire, slaughter, rape, Alexius V in flight, the invaders plundering the city. April 13, in Haghia Sophia: Crusaders demolish the choir stalls with their twelve columns of silver, and pull apart the altar, and seize forty chalices and scores of silver candelabra. They take the Gospel, and the Crosses, and the altar cloth, and forty incense burners of pure gold. Boniface of Montferrat, the leader of the Crusade, seizes the imperial palace. Dandolo takes the four great bronze horses that the Emperor Constantine had brought from Egypt 900 years before; he will carry them to Venice and place them over the entrance to St. Mark's Cathedral, where they still are. The priests of the Crusaders scurry after relics: two chunks of the True Cross, the head of the Holy Lance, the nails that had held Christ on the Cross, and many similar objects, long revered by the Byzantines.

From the scenes of plunder we jumped to mid-May.

"A new Emperor of Byzantium is to be elected," I said. "He will not be a Byzantine. He will be a westerner, a Frank, a Latin. The conquerors choose Count Baldwin of Flanders. We can see his coronation procession."

We waited outside Haghia Sophia. Within, Baldwin of Flanders is donning a mantle covered with jewels and embroidered with eagle figures; he is handed a scepter and a golden orb; he kneels before the altar and is anointed; he is crowned; he mounts the throne.

"Here he comes," I said.

On a white horse, clad in glittering clothes that blaze as if on fire, Emperor Baldwin of Byzantium rides forth from the cathedral to the palace. Unwillingly, sullenly, the people of Byzantium pay homage to their alien master.

"Most of the Byzantine nobility has fled," I told my tourists, who were yearning for more battles, more fires. "The aristocracy has scattered to Asia Minor, to Albania, to Bulgaria, to Greece. For fifty-seven years the Latins will rule here, though Emperor Baldwin's reign will be brief. In ten months he will lead an army against Byzantine rebels and will be captured by them, never to return."

Chrystal Haggins said, "When do the Crusaders go to Jerusalem?"

"Not these. They never bother to go. Some of them stay here, ruling pieces of the former Byzantine Empire. The rest go home stuffed with Byzantine loot."

"How fascinating," said Mrs. Haggins.

We went to our lodgings. A terrible weariness had me in its grip. I had done my job; I had shown them the Latin conquest of Byzantium, as advertised in the brochures. Suddenly I couldn't stand their faces any longer. We dined, and they went to sleep, or at least to bed. I stood a while, listening to the passionate groans of Miss Pistil and the eager snorts of Bilbo Gostaman, listening to the protests of Palmyra as Conrad Sauerabend sneakily stroked her thighs in the dark, and then I choked back tears of fury and surrendered to my temptations, and touched my timer, and shunted up the line. To 1105. To Pulcheria Ducas.

45.

Metaxas, as always, was glad to help.

"It'll take a few days," he said. "Communications are slow here. Messengers going back and forth."

"Should I wait here?"

"Why bother?" Metaxas asked. "You've got a timer. Jump down three days, and maybe by then everything will be arranged."

I jumped down three days. Metaxas said, "Everything is arranged."

He had managed to get me invited to a soiree at the Ducas palace. Just about everyone of importance would be there, from Emperor Alexius Comnenus down. As my cover identity, I was to claim that I was Metaxas' cousin from the provinces, from Epirus. "Speak with a backwoods accent," Metaxas instructed me. "Dribble wine on your chin and make noises when you chew. Your name will be—ah—Nicetas Hyrtacenus."

I shook my head. "Too fancy. It isn't *me*."

"Well, then, George Hyrtacenus?"

"George Markezinis," I said.

"It sounds too twentieth century."

"To them it'll sound provincial," I said, and as George Markezinis I went to the Ducas soiree.

Outside the gleaming marble walls of the Ducas palace I saw two dozen Varangian guards stationed. The presence of these yellow-bearded Norse barbarians, the core of the imperial bodyguard, told me that Alexius was already within. We entered. Metaxas had brought his fair and wanton ancestress Eudocia to the party.

Within, a dazzling scene. Musicians. Slaves. Tables heaped with food. Wine. Gorgeously dressed men and women. Superb mosaic floors; tapestried walls, heavy with cloth of gold. The tinkle of sophisticated laughter; the shimmer of female flesh beneath nearly transparent silks.

I saw Pulcheria at once.

Pulcheria saw me.

Our eyes met, as they had met in the shop of sweets and spices, and she recognized me, and smiled enigmatically, and again the current surged between us. In a later era she would have fluttered her fan at me. Here, she withdrew her jeweled gloves and slapped them lightly across her left wrist. Some token of encouragement? She wore a golden circlet on her high, smooth forehead. Her lips were rouged.

"That's her husband to her left," Metaxas whispered. "Come. I'll introduce you."

I stared at Leo Ducas, my great-great-great-multi-great-grandfather, and my pride in having so distinguished an ancestor was tinged by the envy I felt for this man, who each night caressed the breasts of Pulcheria.

He was, I knew from my genealogical studies, thirty-five years old, twice the age of his wife. A tall man, graying at the temples, with unByzantine blue eyes, a neatly clipped little beard, a high-bridged, narrow nose, and thin, tightly compressed lips, he seemed austere, remote, unutterably dignified. I suspected that he might be boringly noble. He did make an impressive sight, and there was no austerity about his tunic of fine cut, nor about his jewelry, his rings and pendants and pins.

Leo presided over the gathering in serene style, befitting a man who was one of the premier nobles of the realm, and who headed his branch of the great house of Ducas. Of course, Leo's house was empty, and perhaps that accounted for the faint trace of despair that I imagined I saw on his handsome face. As Metaxas and I approached him, I picked up a stray exchange of conversation from two court ladies to my left:

". . . no children, and such a pity, when all of Leo's brothers have so many. And he the eldest!"

"Pulcheria's still young, though. She looks as if she'll be a good breeder."

"If she ever gets started. Why, she's close to eighteen!"

I wanted to reassure Leo, to tell him that his seed would descend even unto the twenty-first century, to let him know that in only a year's time Pulcheria would give him a son, Nicetas, and then Simeon, John, Alexander, and more, and that Nicetas would sire six children, among them the princely Nicephorus whom I had seen seventy years down the line, and the son of Nicephorus would follow an exiled leader into Albania, and then, and then, and then—

Metaxas said, "Your grace, this is my mother's sister's third son, George Markezinis, of Epirus, now a guest at my villa during the harvest season."

"You've come a long way," said Leo Ducas. "Have you been to Constantinople before?"

"Never," I said. "A wonderful city! The churches! The palaces! The bathhouses! The food, the wine, the clothes! The women, the beautiful women!"

Pulcheria glowed. She gave me that sidewise smile of hers again, on the side away from her husband. I knew she was mine. The sweet fragrance of her drifted toward me. I began to ache and throb.

Leo said, "You know the emperor, of course?"

With a grand sweep of his arm he indicated Alexius, holding court at the far end of the room. I had seen him before: a short, stocky man of clearly imperial bearing. A circle of lords and ladies surrounded him. He seemed gracious, sophisticated, relaxed in manner, the true heir to the Caesars, the defender of civilization in these dark times. At Leo's insistence I was presented to him. He greeted me warmly, crying out that the cousin of Metaxas was as dear to him as Metaxas himself. We talked for a while, the emperor and I; I was nervous, but I carried myself well, and Leo Ducas said, finally, "You speak with emperors as though you've known a dozen of them, young man."

I smiled. I did not say that I had several times glimpsed Justinian, that I had attended the baptisms of Theodosius II, Constantine V, the yet unborn Manuel Comnenus, and many more, that I had knelt in Haghia Sophia not far from Constantine XI on Byzantium's last night, that I had watched Leo the Isaurian direct the iconoclasms. I did not say that I was one of the many pluggers of the hungry hole of the Empress Theodora, five centuries previously. I looked shy and said, "Thank you, your grace."

46.

Byzantine parties consisted of music, a dance of slave-girls, some dining, and a great deal of wine. The night wore on; the candles burned low; the assembled notables grew tipsy. In the gathering darkness I mingled easily with members of the famed families, meeting men and women named Comnenus, Phocas, Skleros, Dalassenes, Diogenes, Botaniates, Tzimisces and Ducas. I made courtly conversation and impressed myself with my glibness. I watched arrangements for adultery being made subtly, but not subtly enough, behind the backs of drunken husbands. I bade goodnight to Emperor Alexius and received an invitation to visit him at Blachernae, just up the road. I fended off Metaxas' Eudocia, who had had too much to drink and wanted a quick balling in a back room. (She finally selected one Basil Diogenes, who must have been seventy years old.) I answered, evasively, a great many questions about my "cousin" Metaxas, whom everybody knew, but whose origins were a mystery to all. And then, three hours after my arrival, I found that I was at last speaking with Pulcheria.

We stood quietly together in an angle of the great hall. Two flickering candles gave us light. She looked flushed, excited, even agitated; her breasts heaved and a line of sweat-beads stippled her upper lip. I had never beheld such beauty before.

"Look," she said. "Leo dozes. He loves his wine more than most other things."

"He must love beauty," I said. "He has surrounded himself with so much of it."

"Flatterer!"

"No. I try to speak the truth."

"You don't often succeed," she said. "Who are you?"

"Markezinis of Epirus, cousin to Metaxas."

"That tells me very little. I mean, what are you looking for in Constantinople?"

I took a deep breath. "To fulfill my destiny, by finding the one whom I am meant to find, the one whom I love."

That got through to her. Seventeen-year-old girls are susceptible to that kind of thing, even in Byzantium, where girls mature early and marry at twelve. Call me Heathcliff.

Pulcheria gasped, crossed her arms chastely over the high mounds of her breasts, and shivered. I think her pupils may have momentarily dilated.

"It's impossible," she said.

"Nothing's impossible."

"My husband—"

"Asleep," I said. "Tonight—under this roof—"

'No. We can't."

"You're trying to fight destiny, Pulcheria."

"George!"

"A bond holds us together—a bond stretching across all of time—"

"Yes, George!"

Easy, now, great-great-multi-great-grandson, don't talk too much. It's cheap timecrime to brag that you're from the future.

"This was fated," I whispered. "It had to be!"

"Yes! Yes!"

"Tonight."

"Tonight, yes."

"Here."

"Here," said Pulcheria.

"Soon."

"When the guests leave. When Leo is in bed. I'll have you hidden in a room where it's safe—I'll come to you—"

"You knew this would happen," I said, "that day when we met in the shop."

"Yes. I knew. Instantly. What magic did you work on me?"

"None, Pulcheria. The magic rules us both. Drawing us together, shaping this moment, spinning the strands of destiny toward our meeting, upsetting the boundaries of time itself—"

"You speak so strangely, George. So beautifully. You must be a poet!"

"Perhaps."

"In two hours you'll be mine."

"And you mine," I said.

"And for always."

I shivered, thinking of the Time Patrol swordlike above me. "For always, Pulcheria."

47.

She spoke to a servant, telling him that the young man from Epirus had had too much to drink, and wished to lie down in one of the guest chambers. I acted appropriately woozy. Metaxas found me and wished me well. Then I made a candlelight pilgrimage through the maze of the Ducas palace and was shown to a simple room somewhere far in the rear. A low bed was the only article of furniture. A rectangular mosaic in the center of the floor was the only decoration. The single narrow window admitted a shaft of moonlight. The servant brought me a washbasin of water, wished me a good night's rest, and let me alone.

I waited a billion years.

Sounds of distant revelry floated to me. Pulcheria did not come.

It's all a joke, I thought. A hoax. The young but sophisticated mistress of the house is having some fun with the country cousin. She'll let me fidget and fret in here alone until morning, and then send a servant to give me breakfast and show me out. Or maybe after a couple of hours she'll tell one of her slavegirls to come in here and pretend she's Pulcheria. Or send in a toothless crone, while her guests watch through concealed slots in the wall. Or—

A thousand times I considered fleeing. Just touch the timer, and shoot up the line to 1204, where Conrad Sauerabend and Palmyra Gostaman and Mr. and Mrs. Haggins and the rest of my tourists lie sleeping and unguarded.

Clear out? Now? When everything had gone so neatly so far? What would Metaxas say to me when he found out I had lost my nerve?

I remembered my guru, black Sam, asking me, "If you had a chance to attain your heart's desire, would you take it?"

Pulcheria was my heart's desire; I knew that now.

I remembered Sam Spade telling me, "You're a compulsive loser. Losers infallibly choose the least desirable alternative."

Go ahead, great-great-multi-great-grandson. Skip out of here before the luscious primordial ancestress can offer her dark musky loins to you.

I remembered Emily, the helix-parlor girl with the gift of prophecy, crying shrilly, "Beware love in Byzantium! Beware! Beware!"

I loved. In Byzantium.

Rising, I paced the room a thousand times, and stood at the door listening to the faint laughter and the far-off songs, and then I removed all of my clothing, carefully folding each garment and placing it on the floor beside my bed. I stood naked except for my timer, and I debated removing that too. What would Pulcheria say when she saw that tawny plastic band at my waist? How could I explain it?

I unfastened the timer too, separating myself from it for the first time in my career up the line. Waves of real terror burst over me. I felt more naked than naked, without it; I felt stripped down to my bones. Without my timer around my hips I was the slave of time, like all these others. I had no means of quick escape. If Pulcheria planned some cruel joke and I was caught without my timer in easy reach, I was doomed.

Hastily I put the timer back on.

Then I washed myself, meticulously, everywhere, cleansing myself for Pulcheria. And stood naked beside the bed, waiting another billion years. And thought longingly of the dark swollen tips of Pulcheria's full breasts, and the softness of the skin inside her thighs. And my manhood came to life, rising to such extravagant proportions that I was both proud and embarrassed.

I didn't want Pulcheria to walk in and find me like this, beside the bed with this tree of flesh sprouting between my legs. I looked like a tipped tripod; to greet her this way was too blunt, too direct. Quickly I dressed again, feeling foolish. And waited a billion years more. And saw dawnlight beginning to blend with moonlight in my slit of a window.

And the door opened, and Pulcheria came into the room, and bolted the door behind her.

She had wiped away her heavy makeup and had taken off all her jewelry except a single gold pectoral, and she had changed from her party clothes into a light silken wrap. Even by the dim light I saw she was nude beneath it, and the soft curves of her body inflamed me almost to insanity. She glided toward me.

I took her in my arms and tried to kiss her. She didn't understand kissing. The posture one must adopt for mouth-to-mouth contact was alien to her. I had to arrange her. I tilted her head gently. She smiled, puzzled but willing.

Our lips touched. My tongue wiggled forth.

She quivered and flattened her body tight against mine. She picked up the theory of kissing in a hurry.

My hands slid down her shoulders. I drew off her wrap; she trembled a little as I bared her.

I counted her breasts. Two. Rosy pink nipples. I measured her hind cheeks with my outspread hands. A good size. I ran fingertips over her thighs. Excellent thighs. I admired the two deep dimples in the small of her back.

She was at once shy and wanton, a superb combination.

When I undressed, she saw the timer and touched it, plucked at it, but asked for no explanation, and her hands slipped lower. We tumbled down together on the bed.

You know, sex is really a ridiculous thing. The physical act of it, I mean. What they call "making love" in twentieth-century novels; what they call "sleeping together." I mean, consider all the literary effort that has gone into writing rhapsodies to screwing. And what does it all amount to, anyway?

You take this short rigid fleshy rod and you put it into this lubricated groove, and you rub it back and forth until enough of a charge is built up so that discharge is possible. Like making a fire by twirling a stick against a plank.

Really, there's nothing to it; Stick Tenon A into Mortise B. Vibrate until finished.

Look upon the act and you *know* it's preposterous. The buttocks humping up and down, the thrashing legs, the muffled groans, the speedings up and slowing down—can anything be sillier, as a central act governing human emotions?

Of course not. Yet why was this sweaty transaction with Pulcheria so important to me? (And maybe to her.)

My theory is that the real significance of sex, good sex, is a symbolic one. It's something beyond the fact that you get a tickle of "pleasure" for a short while during the ramming and butting. The same pleasure is available without the bother of finding a partner, after all, and yet it isn't the same, is it?

No, what sex is about is more than a twitch in the loins; it's a celebration of spiritual union, of mutual trust. We say to each other in bed, here, I give myself to you in the expectation that you'll give me pleasure, and I will attempt to give you pleasure too. The social contract, let's call it. And the thrill lies in the contract, not in the pleasure that is its payoff.

Also you say, here is my naked body with all its flaws, which I expose trustingly to you, knowing you will not mock it. Also you say, I accept this intimate contact with you even though I know you may transmit to me a loathsome disease. I am willing to take this risk, because you are you. And also the woman used to say—at least up until the nineteenth or early twentieth century—I will open myself to you even though there may be all sorts of biological consequences nine months from now.

All these things are much more vital than quick kickies. This is why mechanical masturbating devices have never replaced sex and never will.

This is why what happened between myself and Pulcheria Ducas on that Byzantine morning in 1105 was far more significant a transaction than what happened between myself and the Empress Theodora half a millennium earlier, and more significant than what had happened between myself and any number of girls a full millennium later. Into Theodora, into Pulcheria, and into those many girls down the line I poured roughly the same number of cubic centimeters of salty fluid; but with Pulcheria it was different. With Pulcheria, our orgasm was only the symbolic sealing of something greater. For me, Pulcheria was the embodiment of beauty and grace, and her easy surrender to me made me an emperor more mighty than Alexius, and neither the spurting of my jet nor her quiver of response mattered a tenth as much as the fact that she and I had come together in trust, in faith, in shared desire, in—love. There you have the heart of my philosophy. I stand revealed as a naked romantic. This is the profundity I've distilled from all my experience: sex with love is better than sex without love. Q.E.D. I can also show, if you like, that to be healthy is better than to be ill, and that having money is superior to being poor. My capacity for abstract thought is limitless.

48.

Nevertheless, even though we had proven the philosophical point quite adequately, we went on to prove it all over again half an hour later. Redundancy is the soul of understanding.

Afterward we lay side by side, glowing sweetly. It was the moment to offer my partner a weed and share a different sort of communion, but of course that was impossible here. I felt the lack.

"Is it very different where you come from?" Pulcheria asked. "I mean, the people, how they dress, how they talk."

"Very different."

"I sense a great strangeness about you, George. Even the way you held me in bed. Not that I am an expert on such things, you must understand. You and Leo are the only men I have ever had."

"Can this be true?"

Her eyes blazed. "You take me for a whore?"

"Well, of course not, but—" I floundered. "In my country," I said desperately, "a girl takes many men before she marries. No one objects to it. It's the custom."

"Not here. We are well sheltered. I was married at twelve; that gave me little time for liberties." She frowned, sat up, leaned across me to look in my eyes. Her breasts dangled enticingly over my face. "Are women really so loose in your country?"

"Truth, Pulcheria, they are."

"But you are Byzantines! You are not barbarians from the north! How can it be allowed, this taking of so many men?"

"It's our custom." Lamely.

"Perhaps you are not truly from Epirus," she suggested. "Perhaps you come from some more distant place. I tell you again, you are very strange to me, George."

"Don't call me George. Call me Jud," I said boldly.

"Jud?"

"Jud."

"Why should I call you this?"

"It's my inner name. My *real* name, the one I *feel.* George is just—well, a name I use."

"Jud. Jud. Such a name I have never heard. You *are* from a strange land! You *are!*"

I gave her a sphinxy smile. "I love you," I said, and nibbled her nipples to change the subject.

"So strange," she murmured. "So different. And yet I felt drawn to you from the first moment. You know, I've long dreamed of being as wicked as this, but I never dared. Oh, I've had offers, dozens of offers, but it never seemed worth the trouble. And then I saw you, and I felt this fire in me, this—this hunger. Why? Tell me why?. You are neither more nor less attractive than many of the men I might have given myself to, and yet you were the one. Why?"

"It was destiny," I told her. "As I said before. An irresistible force, pulling us together, across the—"

—centuries—

"—sea," I finished lamely.

"You will come to me again?" she said.

"Again and again and again."

"I'll find ways for us to meet. Leo will never know. He spends so much of his time at the bank—you know, he's one of the directors—and in his other businesses, and with the emperor—he hardly pays attention to me. I'm one of his many pretty toys. We'll meet, Jud, and we'll know pleasure together often, and—" her dark eyes flashed "—and perhaps you'll give me a child."

I felt the heavens open and rain thunderbolts upon me.

"Five years of marriage and I have no child," she went on. "I don't understand. Perhaps I was too young, at first—I was so young—but now, nothing. Nothing. Give me a child, Jud. Leo will thank you for it—I mean, he'll be happy, he'll think it's his—you even have a Ducas look about you, in the eyes, perhaps, there'd be no trouble. Do you think we made a child tonight?"

"No," I said.

"No? How can you be sure?"

"I have ways," I said. I stroked her silkiness. Let me go twenty more days without my pill, though, and I could plant babies aplenty in you, Pulcheria! And knot the fab-

ric of time beyond all unraveling. My own great-great-
multi-great-grandfather? Am I seed of my own seed? Did
time recurve on itself to produce me? No. I'd never get
away with it. I'd give Pulcheria passion, but not parturi-
tion. "Dawn's here," I whispered.

"You'd better leave. Where can I send messages to
you?"

"At Metaxas'."

"Good. We'll meet again two days hence, yes? I'll arrange everything."

"I'm yours, whenever you say it, Pulcheria."

"Two days. But now, go. I'll show you out."

"Too risky. Servants will be stirring. Go to your room,
Pulcheria. I can get out by myself."

"But—impossible—"

"I know the way."

"Do you?"

"I swear it," I said.

She needed some convincing, but at length I persuaded
her to spare herself the risk of getting me out of the palace. We kissed once more, and she donned her wrap, and
I caught her by the arm and pulled her to me, and released her, and she went out of the room. I counted sixty
seconds off. Then I set my timer and jumped six hours up
the line. The party was going full blast. Casually I walked
through the building, avoiding the room where my
slightly earlier self, not yet admitted to Pulcheria's joyous
body, was chatting with Emperor Alexius. I left the
Ducas palace unnoticed. In the darkness outside, beside
the sea wall along the Golden Horn, I set my timer again
and shunted down the line to 1204. Now I hurried to the
inn where I had left my sleeping tourists. I reached it less
than three minutes after my departure—seemingly so
many days ago—for Pulcheria's era.

All well. I had had my incandescent night of passion,
my soul was purged of longings, and here I was, back at

my trade once more, and no one the wiser. I checked the beds.

Mr. and Mrs. Haggins, yes.

Mr. and Mrs. Gostaman, yes.

Miss Pistil and Bilbo, yes

Palmyra Gostaman, yes.

Conrad Sauerabend, yes? No.

Conrad Sauerabend—

No Sauerabend. Sauerabend was missing. His bed was empty. In those three minutes of my absence, Sauerabend had slipped away.

Where?

I felt the early pricklings of panic.

49.

Calm. Calm. Stay calm. He went out to the *pissoir*, is all. He'll be right back.

Item One, a Courier must remain aware of the location of all of the tourists in his care at all times. The penalty—

I kindled a torch at the smoldering hearth and rushed out into the hall.

Sauerabend? Sauerabend?

Not pissing. Not downstairs rummaging in the kitchen. Not prowling in the wine cellar.

Sauerabend?

Where the devil are you, you pig?

The taste of Pulcheria's lips was still on my own. Her sweat mingled with mine. Her juices still crisped my short hairs. All the delicious forbidden joys of transtemporal incest continued to tingle in my soul.

The Time Patrol will make a nonperson out of me for this, I thought. I'll say, "I've lost a tourist," and they'll say, "How did it happen?" and I'll say, "I stepped out of the room for three minutes and he vanished," and they'll say, "Three minutes, eh? You aren't supposed to——" and I'll say, "It was only *three minutes*. Christ, you can't expect me to watch them twenty-four hours a day!" And they'll be sympathetic, but nevertheless they'll have to check the scene, and in the replay they'll discover me wantonly shunting out for some other point on the line, and they'll track me to 1105 and find me with Pulcheria, and see that not only am I guilty of negligence as a Courier, but also that I've committed incest with my great-great-multi-great——

Calm. Calm.

Into the street now. Flash the torch around. Sauerabend? Sauerabend? No Sauerabend.

If I were a Sauerabend, where would I sneak off to?

To the home of some twelve-year-old Byzantine girl? How would he know where to find one? How to get in? No. No. He couldn't have done that. Where is he, though? Strolling through the town? Out for fresh air? He should be asleep. Snoring. No. I realized that when I left he hadn't been asleep, hadn't been snoring; he'd been bothering Palmyra Gostaman. I hurried back to the inn. There wasn't any point in roaming Constantinople at random for him.

In mounting panic I woke up Palmyra. She rubbed her eyes, complained a little, blinked. Torchlight glittered off her flat bare chest.

"Where did Sauerabend go?" I whispered harshly.

"I told him to leave me alone. I told him if he didn't stop bothering me I'd bite his thing off. He had his hand right here, and he——"

"Yes, but where did he *go*?"

"I don't know. He just got up and went away. It was dark in here. I fell asleep maybe two minutes ago. Why'd you have to wake me up?"

"Some help you are," I muttered. "Go back to sleep."

Calm, Judson, calm. There's an easy solution to this. If you weren't in such a flutter, you'd have thought about it long ago. All you have to do is edit Sauerabend back into the room, the way you edited Marge Hefferin back to life.

It's illegal, of course. Couriers are not supposed to engage in time corrections. That's for the Patrol to do. But this will be such a small correction. You can handle it quickly and no one will be the wiser. You got away with the Hefferin revision, didn't you? Yes. Yes. It's your only chance, Jud.

I sat down on the edge of my bed and tried to plan my actions properly. My night with Pulcheria had dulled the edge of my intellect. Think, Jud. Think as you never thought before.

I put great effort into my thinking.

What time was it when you shunted up to 1105?

Fourteen minutes to midnight.

What time was it when you came back down the line to 1204?

Eleven minutes to midnight.

What time is it now?

One minute to midnight.

When did Sauerabend slip out of the room, then?

Somewhere between fourteen and *eleven to.*

Therefore, how far up the line must you shunt to intercept him?

About thirteen minutes. But if you jump back more than thirteen minutes, you will encounter your prior self, who will be getting ready to depart for 1105? That's the Paradox of Duplication. I've got to risk it. I'm in worse trouble than that already.

You'd better shunt, then, and get things fixed up.

Here I go.

I timed my shunt perfectly, going up the line thirteen minutes less a few seconds. I noticed with satisfaction that my earlier self had already departed, and that Sauerabend had not. The ugly fat bastard was still in the room, sitting up in his bed with his back to me.

It would be simplicity itself to stop him now. I simply forbid him to leave the room, and keep him here for the next three minutes, thus canceling his departure. The instant my prior self gets back—at eleven minutes to midnight—I shunt ten minutes down the line, resuming my proper place in the stream of time. Sauerabend thus will have been continuously guarded by his Courier (in one incarnation or another) throughout the whole dangerous period from fourteen minutes to midnight onward. There will be a very slight moment of duplication for me when I overlap my returning self, but I'll clear out of his time level so fast that he probably won't notice. And all will be as it should have been.

Yes. Very good.

I started across the room toward Sauerabend, meaning to block his path when he tried to leave. He pivoted, still sitting on his bed, and saw me.

"You're back?" he said.

"You bet. And I don't—"

He put his hand to his timer and vanished.

"Wait!" I yelled, ringing everybody up. "You can't do that! It's impossible! His timer doesn't—"

My voice trailed away. His timer doesn't—

Sauerabend was gone, time foolish-sounding gargle. Yelling at the place where he had been before my eyes. him back. The wiliness of the load wouldn't bring with his timer, boasting that he could working for him, somehow shorting the b! Fooling access to the control— it into

Now I was in a terrible mess of messes.

own tourists on the loose with an activated timer, jumping all over anywhen—what a monstrous botch! I was desperate. The Time Patrol was bound to pick him up, of course, before he could commit too many serious time-crimes, but beyond any doubt I'd be censured for letting him get away.

Unless I could catch him before he left.

Fifty-six seconds had elapsed since I had jumped here to keep Sauerabend from leaving.

Without hesitating further, I set my timer back sixty seconds, and shunted. There was Sauerabend again, sitting on his bed. There was my other self, starting across the room toward him. There were the other sleeping tourists, not yet awakened by my shout.

Okay now. We outnumber him. We've got him.

I launched myself at Sauerabend, meaning to grab his arms and keep him from shunting.

He turned as soon as I moved. With devilish swiftness he reached down to his timer.

He shunted. He was gone. I sprawled on his empty bed, numb with shock.

The other Jud glared at me and said, "Where in hell did you come from?"

"I'm fifty-six seconds ahead of you. I missed my first chance at collaring him, and jumped back to try a second time."

"And missed again, I see."

"So I did."

"And duplicated us, besides."

"At least that part can be fixed
time. "In another thirty seconds
onds yourself into the

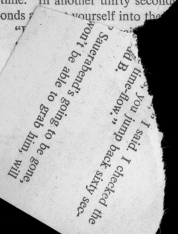

won't be able to grab him, will Sauerabend's going to be gone, B. time-flow," I said. I checked the you jump back sixty sec-

"But you've *got* to go," I said.

"Why?"

"Because it's what I did at that point in the flow."

"You had a reason for it," he said. "You had just missed Sauerabend, and you wanted to jump back a minute and try catching him then. But I haven't had a chance even to miss him. Besides, why worry about the timeflow? It's already been changed."

He was right. We had run out the fifty-six seconds. Now we were at the point when I had made my first try at blocking Sauerabend's exit; but Jud B, who presumably was living through the minute I had lived through just prior to Sauerabend's first disappearance, had lived through that minute in an altogether different way from me. Everything was messed up. I had spawned a duplicate who wouldn't go away and who had nowhere to go. It was now thirteen minutes to midnight. In another two minutes we'd have a third Jud here—the one who shunted down straight from Pulcheria's arms to find Sauerabend missing in the first place. *He* had a destiny of his own: to spend ten minutes in panicky dithering, and then to jump back from one-minute-to-midnight to fourteen-minutes-to-midnight, kicking off the whole process of confusions that culminated in the two of us.

"We've got to get out of here," Jud B said.

"Before *he* comes in."

"Because if he sees us, he may never get around ... shunt back to fourteen minutes to mid-

... you and me from existing."

... asked.

... three or four minutes ago,

... of us—the one who's

... way as soon as

"Right, ... to making his ... night, and that—

"But where do we go?"

"We could jump back ... and try to grab Sauerabend together ...

"No good. We'll overlap ... on his way to Pr ...

"So we ... we've ...

"Still no good. Because if we miss Sauerabend again, we'll induce still another change in the time-flow, and maybe bring on a third one of us. And set up a hall of mirrors effect, banging back and forth until there are a million of us in the room. He's too quick for us with that timer."

"You're right," I said, wishing Jud B had gone back when he belonged before it was too late.

It was now twelve minutes to midnight.

"We've got sixty seconds to clear out. Where do we go?"

"We don't go back and try to grab Sauerabend again. That's definite."

"Yes."

"But we *must* locate him."

"Yes."

"And he could be anywhen at all."

"Yes."

"Then two of us aren't enough. We've got to get help."

"Metaxas."

"Yes. And maybe Sam."

"Yes. And how about Capistrano?"

"Is he available?"

"Who knows? We'll try. And Buonocore. And Jeff Monroe. This is a *crisis!*"

"Yes," I said. "Listen, we've only got ten seconds now. Come on with me!"

We rushed out of the room and down the back way, missing the arrival of the eleven-minutes-to-midnight Jud by a few seconds. We crouched in a dark alcove under the stairs, thinking about the Jud who was two flights up discovering the absence of Sauerabend. I said, "This is going to call for teamwork. You shunt up the line to 1105, find Metaxas, and explain what's happened. Then call in reinforcements and get everybody busy tracing the time-line for Sauerabend."

"What about you?"

"I'm going to stay right here," I said. "Until one minute to midnight. At that point the fellow upstairs is going to shunt back a little less than thirteen minutes to look for Sauerabend—"

"—leaving his people unguarded—"

"—yes, and *somebody's* got to stay with them, so I'll go back upstairs as soon as he leaves, and slip back into the main Jud Elliott identity as their Courier. And I'll stay there, proceeding on a normal basis, until I hear from you. Okay?"

"Okay."

"Get going, then."

He got going. I huddled down in a little heap, shaking with fright. It all hit me in one mighty reaction. Sauerabend was gone, and I had spawned an alter ego by the Paradox of Duplication, and in the space of one evening I had committed more timecrimes than I could name, and—

I felt like crying.

I didn't realize it, but the mess was only beginning.

50.

At one minute to midnight I pulled myself together and went upstairs to take over the job of being the authentic Jud Elliott. As I entered the room I allowed myself the naive hope that I'd find everything restored to the right path, with Sauerabend in his bed again. Let it have been fixed retroactively, I prayed. But Sauerabend wasn't in the room.

Did that mean that he'd never be found?

Not necessarily. Maybe, to avoid further tangles, he'd be returned to our tour slightly down the line, say in the early hours of the night, or just before dawn.

Or maybe he'd be restored to the point he jumped from —thirteen minutes or so before midnight—but I somehow wouldn't become aware of his return, through some mysterious working of the Paradox of Transit Displacement, holding me outside the whole system.

I didn't know. I didn't even *want* to know. I just wanted Conrad Sauerabend located and put back in his proper position in time, before the Patrol realized what was up and let me have it.

Sleep was out of the question. Miserably I slumped on the edge of my bed, getting up now and then to check on my tour people. The Gostamans slept on. The Hagginses slept on. Palmyra and Bilbo and Miss Pistil slept on.

At half-past two in the morning there was a light knock at the door. I leaped up and yanked it open.

Another Jud Elliott stood there.

"Who are you?" I asked morosely.

"The same one who was here before. The one who went for help. There aren't any more of us now, are there?"

"I don't think so." I stepped out into the hall with him. "Well? What's been going on?"

He was grimy and unshaven. "I've been gone for a week. We've searched all up and down the line."

"Who has?"

"Well, I went to Metaxas first, in 1105, just as you said. He's terribly concerned for our sake. What he did, first of all, was to put all his servants to work, checking to see if anybody answering to Sauerabend's description could be found in or around 1105."

"It can't hurt, I guess."

"It's worth trying," my twin agreed. "Next, Metaxas went down to now-time and phoned Sam, who came flying in from New Orleans and brought Sid Buonocore with him. Metaxas also alerted Kolettis, Gompers, Plastiras, Pappas—all the Byzantium Couriers, the whole staff. Because of discontinuity problems, we're not notifying anyone who's on an earlier now-time basis than December 2059, but that still gives us a big posse. What we're doing now, what we've been doing for the past week, is simply moving around, year by year, hunting for Sauerabend, asking questions in the marketplace, sniffing for clues. I've been at it eighteen, twenty hours a day. So have all the others. It's wonderful, how loyal they are!"

"It certainly is," I said. "What are the chances of finding him, though?"

"Well, we assume that he hasn't left the Constantinople area, although there's nothing to prevent him from going down the line to 2059, hopping off to Vienna or Moscow, and vanishing up the line again. All we can do is plug away. If he doesn't turn up in Byzantine, we'll check Turkish, and then pre-Byzantine, and then we'll pass the word to now-time so Couriers on other runs can watch for him, and—"

He sagged. He was exhausted.

"Look," I said, "you've got to get some rest. Why don't you go back to 1105 and settle down at Metaxas' place for a few days? Then come back here when you're rested, and let me join the search. We can alternate that way indefinitely. Meanwhile, let's keep this night in 1204 as our reference point. Whenever you jump to me, jump to this night, so we don't lose contact. It may take us a couple of lifetimes, but we'll get Sauerabend back into the group before morning comes."

"Right."

"All clear, then? You spend a few days at the villa resting up, and come back here half an hour from now. And then I'll go."

"Clear," he said, and went down to the street to jump.

I returned to the room and resumed my melancholy vigil. At three in the morning, Jud B was back, looking like a new man. He had shaved, taken a bath or two, changed his clothes, obviously had had plenty of sleep. "Three days of rest at Metaxas' place," he said. *"Magnifique!"*

"You look great. *Too* great. You didn't, perhaps, sneak off to fool around with Pulcheria?"

"The thought didn't occur to me. But what if I had? You bastard, are you warning me to leave her alone?"

I said, "You don't have any right to—"

"I'm *you,* remember? You can't be jealous of yourself."

"I guess you can't," I said. "Stupid of me."

"Stupider of me," he said. "I *should* have dropped in on her while I was there."

"Well, now it's my turn. I'll put in some time on searching, then stop at the villa for rest and recuperation, and maybe have some fun with our beloved. You won't object to that, will you?"

"Fair's fair," he sighed. "She's yours as much as she's mine."

"Correct. When I've taken care of everything, I'll get back here at—let's see—quarter past three tonight. Got it?"

We synchronized our timetables for the 1105 end of the line to avoid discontinuities; I didn't want to get there while he was still there, or, worse, before he had ever arrived. Then I left the inn and shunted up the line. In 1105 I hired a chariot and was taken out to the villa on a golden autumn day.

Metaxas, bleary-eyed and stubble-faced, greeted me at the porch by asking, "Which one are you, A or B?"

"A. B's taking over for me at the inn in 1204. How's the search going?"

"Lousy," said Metaxas. "But don't give up hope. We're with you all the way. Come inside and meet some old friends."

51.

I said to them, "I'm sorry as hell to be putting you through all this trouble."

The men I respected most in the world laughed and grinned and chuckled and spat and said, "Shucks, 't'ain't nothin'."

They were frayed and grimy. They had been working hard and fruitlessly for me, and it showed. I wanted to hug all of them at once. Black Sambo, and plastic-faced Jeff Monroe, and shifty-eyed Sid Buonocore. Pappas, Kolettis, Plastiras. They had rigged a chart to mark off the places where they hadn't found Conrad Sauerabend. The chart had a lot of marks on it.

Sam said, "Don't worry, boy. We'll track him down."

"I feel so awful, making you give up free time—"

"It could have happened to any one of us," Sam said. "It wasn't your fault."

"It wasn't?"

"Sauerabend gimmicked his timer behind your back, didn't he? How could you have prevented it?" Sam grinned. "We got to help you out. We don't know when same'll happen to us."

"All for one," said Madison Jefferson Monroe. "One for all."

"You think you're the first Courier to have a customer skip out?" Sid Buonocore asked. "Don't be a craphead! Those timers can be rigged for manual use by anyone who understands Benchley Effect theory."

"They never told me—"

"They don't like to advertise it. But it happens. Five, six times a year, somebody takes a private time-trip behind his Courier's back."

I said, "What happens to the Courier?"

"If the Time Patrol finds out? They fire him," said Buonocore bleakly. "What we try to do is cover for each other, before the Patrol moves in. It's a bitch of a job, but we got to do it. I mean, if you don't look after one of your own when he's in trouble, who in hell will look after you?"

"Besides," said Sam, "it makes us feel like heroes."

I studied the chart. They had looked for Sauerabend pretty thoroughly in early Byzantium—Constantine through the second Theodosius—and they had checked out the final two centuries with equal care. Searching the middle had so far been a matter of random investigations. Sam, Buonocore, and Monroe were coming off search duty now and were going to rest; Kolettis, Plastiris, and Pappas were getting ready to go out, and they were planning strategy.

Everybody went on being very nice to me during the discussion of ways to catch Sauerabend. I felt a real sentimental glow of warmth for them. My comrades in adversity. My companions. My colleagues. The Time Musketeers. My heart expanded. I made a little speech telling them how grateful I was for all their help. They looked embarrassed and told me once again that it was a simple matter of good fellowship, the golden rule in action.

The door opened and a dusty figure stumbled in, wearing anachronistic sunglasses. Najeeb Dajani, my old tutor! He scowled, slumped down on a chair, and gestured impatiently to nobody in particular, hoping for wine.

Kolettis handed him wine. Dajani poured some of it into his hand and used it to wash the dust from his sunglasses. Then he gulped the rest.

"Mr. Dajani!" I cried. "I didn't know they had called you in too! Listen, I want to thank you for helping—"

"You stupid prick," said Dajani quietly. "How did I ever let you get your Courier license?"

52.

Dajani had just returned from a survey of the city in 630-650, with no luck at all. He was tired and irritated, and he obviously wasn't happy about spending his layoff searching for somebody else's runaway tourist.

He put out my sentimental glow in a hurry. I tried to foist on him my gratitude speech, and he said sourly, "Skip the grease job. I'm doing this because it'll reflect badly on my capabilities as an instructor if the Patrol finds out what kind of anthropoid I let loose as a Courier. It's my own hide I'm protecting."

There was a nasty moment of silence. A lot of shuffling of feet and clearing of throats took place.

"That's not very gratifying to hear," I said to Dajani.

Buonocore said, "Don't let him upset you, kid. Like I told you, any Courier's tourist is likely to gimmick his timer, and—"

"I don't refer to the loss of the tourist," said Dajani testily. "I refer to the fact that this idiot managed to duplicate himself while trying to edit the mistake!" He gargled wine. "I forgive him for the one, but not for the other."

"The duplication is pretty ugly," Buonocore admitted.

"It's a serious thing," said Kolettis.

"Bad karma," Sam said. "No telling how we'll cover that one up."

"I can't remember a case to match," declared Pappas.

"A messy miscalculation," Plastiras commented.

"Look," I said, "the duplication was an accident. I was so much in a sweat to find Sauerabend that I didn't stop to calculate the implications of—"

"We understand," Sam said.

"It's a natural error, when you're under pressure," said Jeff Monroe.

"Could have happened to anyone," Buonocore told me.

"A shame. A damned shame," murmured Pappas.

I started to feel less like an important member of a close-knit fraternity, and more like a pitied halfwit nephew who can't help leaving little puddles of mess wherever he goes. The halfwit's uncles were trying to clean up a particularly messy mess for him, and trying to keep the halfwit serene so he wouldn't make a worse mess.

When I realized what the real attitude of these men toward me was, I felt like calling in the Time Patrol, confessing my timecrimes, and requesting eradication. My soul shriveled. My manhood withered. I, the copulator with empresses, the seducer of secluded noblewomen, the maker of smalltalk with emperors, I, the last of the Ducases, I, the strider across millennia, I, the brilliant Courier in the style of Metaxas, I . . . I, to these veteran Couriers here, was simply an upright mass of perambulating dreck. A faex that walks like a man. Which is the singular of faeces. Which is to say, a shit.

53.

Metaxas, who had not spoken for fifteen minutes, said finally, "If those of you who are going are ready to go, I'll get a chariot to take you into town."

Kolettis shook his head. "We haven't allotted eras yet. But it'll take only a minute."

There was a buzzing consultation over the chart. It was decided that Kolettis would cover 700-725, Plastiras 1150-1175, and I would inspect 725-745. Pappas had brought a plague suit with him and was going to make a survey of the plague years 745-747, just in case Sauerabend had looped into that proscribed period by accident.

I was surprised that they trusted me to make a time-jump all by myself, considering what they obviously thought of me. But I suppose they figured I couldn't get into any worse trouble. Off we went to town in one of Metaxas' chariots. Each of us carried a small but remarkably accurate portrait of Conrad Sauerabend, painted on a varnished wooden plaque by a contemporary Byzantine artist hired by Metaxas. The artist had worked from a holophoto; I wonder what he'd made of *that*.

When we reached Constantinople proper, we split up and, one by one, timed off to the eras we were supposed to search. I materialized up the line in 725 and realized the little joke that had been played on me.

This was the beginning of the era of iconoclasm, when Emperor Leo III had first denounced the worship of painted images. At that time, most of the Byzantines were fervent iconodules—image-worshippers—and Leo set out to smash the cult of icons, first by speaking and preaching against them, then by destroying an image of Christ in the chapel of the Chalke, or Brazen House, in front of the Great Palace. After that things got worse; images and image-makers were persecuted, and Leo's son issued a proclamation declaring, "There shall be rejected, removed and cursed out of the Christian Church every likeness which is made out of any material whatever by the evil art of painters."

And in such an era I was supposed to walk around town holding a little painting of Conrad Sauerabend, asking people, "Have you seen this man anywhere?"

My painting wasn't exactly an icon. Nobody who looked at it was likely to mistake Sauerabend for a saint. Even so, it caused a lot of trouble for me.

"Have you seen this man anywhere?" I asked, and took out the painting.

In the marketplace.

In the bathhouses.

On the steps of Haghia Sophia.

Outside the Great Palace.

"Have you seen this man anywhere?"

In the Hippodrome during a polo match.

At the annual distribution of free bread and fish to the poor on May 11, celebrating the anniversary of the founding of the city.

In front of the Church of Saints Sergius and Bacchus.

"I'm looking for this man whose portrait I have here."

Half the time, I didn't even manage to get the painting fully into the open. They'd see a man pulling an icon from his tunic, and they'd run away, screaming, "Iconodule dog! Worshipper of images!"

"But this isn't—I'm only looking for—you mustn't mistake this painting for—won't you come back?"

I got pushed and shoved and expectorated upon. I got bullied by imperial guards and glowered at by iconoclastic priests. Several times I was invited to attend underground ceremonies of secret iconodules.

I didn't get much information about Conrad Sauerabend.

Still, despite all the difficulties, there were always some people who looked at the painting. None of them had seen Sauerabend, although a few "thought" they had noticed someone resembling the man in the picture. I wasted two days tracking one of the supposed resemblers, and found no resemblance at all.

I kept on, jumping from year to year. I lurked at the fringes of tourist groups, thinking that Sauerabend might prefer to stick close to people of his own era.

Nothing. No clue.

Finally, footsore and discouraged, I hopped back down to 1105. At Metaxas' place I found only Pappas, who looked even more weary and bedraggled than I did.

"It's useless," I said. "We aren't going to find him. It's like looking for—looking for—"

"A needle in a timestack," Pappas said helpfully.

54.

I had earned a little rest before I returned to that long night in 1204 and sent my alter ego here to continue the search. I bathed, slept, banged a garlicky slavegirl two or three times, and brooded. Kolettis returned: no luck. Plastiras came back: no luck. They went down the line to resume their Courier jobs. Gompers, Herschel, and Melamed, donating time from their current layoffs, appeared and immediately set out on the quest for Sauerabend. The more Couriers who volunteered to help me in my time of need, the worse I felt.

I decided to console myself in Pulcheria's arms.

I mean, as long as I happened to be in the right era, and as long as Jud B had neglected to stop in to see her, it seemed only proper. We *had* had some sort of date. Just about the last thing Pulcheria had said to me after that night of nights was, "We'll meet again two days hence, yes? I'll arrange everything."

How long ago had that been?

At least two weeks on the 1105 now-time basis, I figured. Maybe three.

She was supposed to have sent a message to me at Metaxas', telling me where and how we could have our second meeting. In my concern with Sauerabend I had forgotten about that. Now I raced all around the villa, asking Metaxas' butlers and his major domo if any messages had arrived from town for me.

"No," they said. "No messages."

"Think carefully. I'm expecting an important message from the Ducas palace. From Pulcheria Ducas."

"From whom?"

"Pulcheria Ducas."

"No messages, sir."

I clothed myself in my finest finery and clipclopped into Constantinople. Did I dare present myself at the Ducas place uninvited? I did dare. My country-bumpkin cover identity would justify my possible breach of etiquette.

At the gate of the Ducas palace I rang for the servants, and an old groom came out, the one who had shown me to the chamber that night where Pulcheria had given herself to me. I smiled in a friendly way; the groom peered blankly back. Forgotten me, I thought.

I said, "My compliments to Lord Leo and Lady

Pulcheria, and would you kindly tell them that George Markezinis of Epirus is here to call upon them?"

"To Lord Leo and Lady—" the groom repeated.

"Pulcheria," I said. "They know me. I'm cousin to Themistoklis Metaxas, and—" I hesitated, feeling even more foolish than usual at giving my pedigree to a groom. "Get me the major-domo," I snapped.

The groom scuttled within.

After a long delay, an imperious-looking individual in the Byzantine equivalent of livery emerged and surveyed me.

"Yes?"

"My compliments to Lord Leo and Lady Pulcheria, and would you kindly tell them—"

"Lady *who?*"

"Lady Pulcheria, wife to Leo Ducas. I am George Markezinis of Epirus, cousin to Themistoklis Metaxas, who only several weeks ago attended the party given by—"

"The wife to Leo Ducas," said the major-domo frostily, "is named Euprepia."

"Euprepia?"

"Euprepia Ducas, the lady of this household. Man, what do you want here? If you come drunken in the middle of the day to trouble Lord Leo, I—"

"Wait," I said. *"Euprepia? Not Pulcheria?"* A golden bezant flickered into my hand and fluttered swiftly across to the waiting palm of the major-domo. "I'm not drunk, and this is important. When did Leo marry this—this Euprepia?"

"Four years ago."

"Four—years—ago. No, that's impossible. *Five* years ago he married Pulcheria, who—"

"You must be mistaken. The Lord Leo has been married only once, to Euprepia Macrembolitissa, the mother of his son Basil and of his daughter Zoe."

The hand came forth. I dropped another bezant into it.

Dizzily I murmured, "His eldest son is Nicetas, who isn't even born yet, and he isn't supposed to have a son named Basil at all, and—my God, are you playing a game with me?"

"I swear before Christ Pantocrator that I have said no word but the truth," declared the major-domo resonantly.

Tapping my pouch of bezants, I said, desperate now, "Would it be possible for me to have an audience with the Lady Euprepia?"

"Perhaps so, yes. But she is not here. For three months now she has rested at the Ducas palace on the coast at Trebizond, where she awaits her next child."

"Three months. Then there was no party here a few weeks ago?"

"No, sir."

"The Emperor Alexius wasn't here? Nor Themistoklis Metaxas? Nor George Markezinis of Epirus? Nor—"

"None of those, sir. Can I help you further?"

"I don't think so," I said, and went staggering from the gate of the Ducas palace like unto one who has been smitten by the wrath of the gods.

55.

Dismally I wandered in a southeasterly way along the Golden Horn until I came to the maze of shops, market-places, and taverns near the place where there would one day be the Galata Bridge, and where today there is still a maze of shops, marketplaces, and taverns. Through those narrow, interweaving, chaotic streets I marched like a zombie, having no destination. I saw not, neither did I think; I just put one foot ahead of the other one and kept going until, early in the afternoon, kismet once more seized me by the privates.

I stumbled randomly into a tavern, a two-story structure of unpainted boards. A few merchants were downing their midday wine. I dropped down heavily at a warped and wobbly table in an unoccupied corner of the room and sat staring at the wall, thinking about Leo Ducas' pregnant wife Euprepia.

A comely tavern-slut appeared and said, "Some wine?"

"Yes. The stronger the better."

"A little roast lamb too?"

"I'm not hungry, thanks."

"We make very good lamb here."

"I'm not hungry," I said. I stared somberly at her ankles. They were very good ankles. I looked up at her calves, and then her legs vanished within the folds of her simple cloth wrap. She strode away and came back with a flask of wine. As she set it before me, the front of her wrap fell away at her throat, and I peered in at the two pale, full, rosy-tipped breasts that swung freely there. Then at last I looked at her face.

She could have been Pulcheria's twin sister.

Same dark, mischievous eyes. Same flawless olive skin. Same full lips and aquiline nose. Same age, about seventeen. The differences between this girl and my Pulcheria were differences of dress, of posture, and of expression. This girl was coarsely clad; she lacked Pulcheria's aristocratic elegance of bearing; and there was a certain pouting sullenness about her, the look of a girl who is living below her station in life and is angry about it.

I said, "You could almost be Pulcheria!"

She laughed harshly. "What kind of nonsensical talk is that?"

"A girl I know, who resembles you closely—Pulcheria, her name is—"

"Are you insane, or only drunk? *I* am Pulcheria. Your little game isn't pleasing to me, stranger."

"You—Pulcheria?"

"Certainly."

"Pulcheria Ducas?"

She cackled in my face. "Ducas, you say? Now I know you're crazy. Pulcheria Photis, wife of Heracles Photis the innkeeper!"

"Pulcheria—Photis—" I repeated numbly. "Pulcheria —Photis—wife—of—Heracles—Photis—"

She leaned close over me, giving me a second view of her miraculous breasts. Not haughty now but worried, she said in a low voice, "I can tell by your clothes that you're someone important. What do you want here? Has Heracles done something wrong?"

"I'm here just for wine," I said. "But listen, tell me this one thing: are you the Pulcheria who was born Botaniates?"

She looked stunned. "You know that!"

"It's true?"

"Yes," said my adored Pulcheria, and sank down next to me on the bench. "But I am a Botaniates no longer. For five years now—ever since Heracles—the filthy Heracles—ever since he—" She took some of my wine in her agitation. "Who are you, stranger?"

"George Markezinis of Epirus."

The name meant nothing to her.

"Cousin to Themistoklis Metaxas."

She gasped. "I *knew* you were someone important! I knew!" Trembling prettily, she said, "What do you want with me?"

The other patrons in the tavern were beginning to stare at us. I said, "Can we go somewhere to talk? Someplace private?"

Her eyes took on a cool, knowing look. "Just a moment," she said, and went out of the tavern. I heard her calling to someone, shouting like any fishwife, and after a moment a ragged girl of about fifteen came into the room. Pulcheria said, "Look after things, Anna. I'm going to be busy." To me she said, "We can go upstairs."

She led me to a bedchamber on the second floor of the building and carefully bolted the door behind us.

"My husband," she said, "has gone to Galata to buy meat, and will not be back for two hours. While the loathsome pig is away, I don't mind earning a bezant or two from a handsome stranger."

Her clothing fell away and she stood incandescently nude before me. Her smile was a defiant one, a smile that said that she retained her inner self no matter what stains of degration others inflicted on her. Her eyes flashed with lusty zeal.

I stood dazzled before those high, heavy breasts, whose nipples were visibly hardening, and before that flat, taut belly with its dark, mounded bush, and before those firm muscular thighs and before those outstretched, beckoning arms.

She tumbled down onto the rough cot. She flexed her knees and drew her legs apart.

"Two bezants?" she suggested.

Pulcheria transformed into a tavern whore? My goddess? My adored one?

"Why do you hesitate?" she asked. "Come, climb aboard, give the fat dog Heracles another pair of horns. What's wrong? Do I seem ugly to you?"

"Pulcheria—Pulcheria—I love you, Pulcheria—"

She giggled, shrill in her delight. She waved her heels at me.

"Come on, then!"

"You were Leo Ducas' wife," I murmured. "You lived in a marble palace, and wore silk robes, and went about the city escorted by a watchful duenna. And the emperor was at your party, and just before dawn you came to me, and gave yourself to me, and it was all a dream, Pulcheria, all a dream, eh?"

"You are a madman," she said. "But a handsome madman, and I yearn to have you between my legs, and I yearn also for your bezants. Come close. Are you shy? Look, put your hand here, feel how hot Pulcheria grows, how she throbs—"

I was rigid with desire, but I knew I couldn't touch her. Not this Pulcheria, this coarse, shameless, wanton, sluttish wench, this gorgeous creature who capered and pumped and writhed impatiently on the cot before me.

I pulled out my pouch and emptied it over her nakedness, dumping golden bezants into her navel, her loins, spilling them across her breasts. Pulcheria shrieked in astonishment. She sat up, clutching at the money, scrambling for it, her breasts heaving and swaying, her eyes bright.

I fled.

56.

At the villa I found Metaxas and said, "What's the name of Leo Ducas' wife?"

"Pulcheria."

"When did you last see her?"

"Three weeks ago, when we went to that party."

"No," I said. "You're suffering from Transit Displacement, and so am I. Leo Ducas is married to someone named Euprepia, and has two children by her, and a third on the way. And Pulcheria is the wife of a tavern-keeper named Heracles Photis."

"Have you gone spotty potty?" Metaxas asked.

"The past has been changed. I don't know how it happened, but there's been a change, right in my own ancestry, don't you see, and Pulcheria's no longer my ancestress, and God knows if I even exist any more. If I'm not descended from Leo Ducas and Pulcheria, then who am I descended from, and—"

"When did you find all this out?"

"Just now. I went to look for Pulcheria, and—Christ, Metaxas, what am I going to do?"

"Maybe there's been a mistake," he said calmly.

"No. No. Ask your own servants. *They* don't undergo Transit Displacement. Ask them if they've ever heard of a Pulcheria Ducas. They haven't. Ask them the name of Leo Ducas' wife. Or go into town and see for yourself. There's been a change in the past, don't you see, and everything's different, and—Christ, Metaxas! Christ!"

He took hold of my wrists and said in a very quiet tone, "Tell me all about this from the beginning, Jud."

But I had no chance to. For just then big black Sam came rushing into the hall, whooping and screaming.

"We found him! God damn, but we found him!"

"Who?" Metaxas said.

"Who?" I said simultaneously.

"*Who?*" Sam repeated. "Who the hell do you think? Sauerabend. Conrad F. X. Sauerabend himself!"

"You found him?" I said, limp with relief. "Where? When? How?"

"Right here in 1105," said Sam. "This morning, Melamed and I were in the marketplace, just checking around a little, and we showed the picture, and sure enough, some peddler of pig's feet recognized him. Sauerabend's been living in Constantinople for the past five or six years, running a tavern down near the water. He goes under the name of Heracles Photis—"

"No!" I bellowed. "No, you black nigger bastard, no, no, no, no, no! It isn't true!"

And I launched myself at him in blind fury.

And I drove my fists into his belly, and sent him reeling backward toward the wall.

And he looked at me strangely, and caught his breath, and came toward me and picked me up and dropped me. And picked me up and dropped me. And picked me up a third time, but Metaxas made him put me down.

Sam said gently, "It's true that I *am* a black nigger bastard, but was it really necessary to say so that loudly?"

Metaxas said, "Give him some wine, somebody. I think he's going off his head."

I said, seizing control of myself somehow, "Sam, I didn't mean to call you names, but it absolutely cannot be the case that Conrad Sauerabend is living under the name of Heracles Photis."

"Why not?"

"Because—because—"

"I saw him myself," Sam said. "I had wine in his tavern no more than five hours ago. He's big and fat and red-faced, and thinks a great deal of himself. And he's got this little hot-ass Byzantine wife, maybe sixteen, seventeen years old, who waits on table in the place, and waves her boobies at the customers, and I bet sells her tail in the upstairs rooms—"

"All right," I said in a dead man's voice. "You win. The wife's name is Pulcheria."

Metaxas made a choking sound.

Sam said, "I didn't ask about her name."

"She's seventeen years old, and she comes from the Botaniates family," I went on, "which is one of the important Byzantine families, and only Buddha knows what she's doing married to Heracles Photis Conrad Sauerabend. And the past has been changed, Sam, because up until a few weeks ago on my now-time basis she was the wife of Leo Ducas and lived in a palace near the imperial palace, and it happened that I was having a love affair with her, and it also happens that until the past got changed she and Leo Ducas were my great-great-multi-great-grandparents, and it seems to have happened that a very stinking coincidence has taken place, which I don't comprehend the details of at all, except that I'm probably a nonperson now and there's no such individual as Pulcheria Ducas. And now, if you don't mind, I'm going to go into a quiet corner and cut my throat."

"This isn't happening," said Sam. "This is all a bad dream."

57.

But, of course, it wasn't. It was as real as any other event in this fluid and changeable cosmos.

The three of us drank a great deal of wine, and Sam gave me some of the other details. How he had asked about in the neighborhood concerning Sauerabend/Photis, and had been told that the man had arrived mysteriously from some other part of the country, about the year 1099. How the regulars at his tavern disliked him, but came to the place just to get a view of his beautiful wife. How there was general suspicion that he was engaged in some kind of illegal activity.

"He excused himself," Sam said, "and told us that he had to go across to Galata to do some marketing. But Kolettis followed him and found that he didn't go marketing at all. He went into some kind of warehouse on the Galata side, and apparently he disappeared. Kolettis went in after him and couldn't find him anywhere. He must have time-jumped, Kolettis assumed. Then this Photis reappeared, maybe half an hour later, and took the ferry back into Constantinople."

"Timecrime," Metaxas suggested. "He's engaged in smuggling."

"That's what I think," said Sam. "He's using the early twelfth century as a base of operations, under this cover identity of Photis, and he's running artifacts or gold coins or something like that down the line to now-time."

"How did he get mixed up with the girl, though?" Metaxas asked.

Sam shrugged. "That part isn't clear yet. But now that we've found him, we can trace him back up the line until we find the point of his arrival. And see exactly what he's been up to."

I groaned. "How are we ever going to restore the proper sequence of events?"

Metaxas said, "We've got to locate the precise moment to which he made his jump out of your tour. Then we station ourselves there, catch him as soon as he materializes, take away that trick timer of his, and bring him back to 1204. That extricates him from the time-flow right where he came in, and puts him back into your 1204 trip where he belongs."

"You make it sound so simple," I said. "But it isn't. What about all the changes that have been made in the past? His five years of marriage to Pulcheria Botaniates—"

"Nonevents," said Sam. "As soon as we whisk Sauerabend from 1099 or whenever back into 1204, his marriage to this Pulcheria is automatically deleted, right? The time-flow resumes its unedited shape, and she marries whoever she was supposed to marry—"

"Leo Ducas," I said. "My ancestor."

"Leo Ducas, yes," Sam went on. "And for everybody in Byzantium, this whole Heracles Photis episode will never have happened. The only ones who'll know about it are us, because we're subject to Transit Displacement."

"What about the artifacts Sauerabend's been smuggling to now-time?" I asked.

Sam said, "They won't be there. They won't ever have been smuggled. And his fences down there won't have any recollection of having received them, either. The fabric of time will have been restored, and the Patrol won't be the wiser for it, and—"

"You're overlooking one little item," I said.

"Which is?"

"In the course of these shenanigans I generated an extra Jud Elliott. Where does *he* go?"

"Christ," Sam said. "I forgot about him!"

58.

I had now been running around 1105 for quite a while, and I figured it was time to get back to 1204 and let my alter ego know something of what was going on. So I made the shunt down the line and got to the inn at quarter past three on that same long night of Conrad Sauerabend's disappearance from 1204. My other self was slouched gloomily on his bed, studying the ceiling's heavy beams.

"Well?" he said. "How goes it?"

"Catastrophic. Come out into the hall."

"What's happening?"

"Brace yourself," I said. "We finally tracked Sauerabend down. He shunted to 1099, and took a cover identity as a tavernkeeper. A year later he married Pulcheria."

I watched my other self crumble.

"The past has been changed," I went on. "Leo Ducas married somebody else, Euprepia something, and has two and a half children by her. Pulcheria's a serving wench in Sauerabend's tavern. I saw her there. She didn't know who I was, but she offered to screw me for two bezants. Sauerabend is smuggling goods down the line, and—"

"Don't tell me any more," he said. "I don't want to hear any more."

"I haven't told you the good part yet."

"There's a good part?"

"The good part is that we're going to unhappen all of this. Sam and Metaxas and you are going to trace Sauerabend back from 1105 to the moment of his arrival in 1099, and unarrive him, and shunt him back here into this evening. Thus canceling the whole episode."

"What happens to us?" my other self asked.

"We discussed that, more or less," I said vaguely. "We aren't sure. Apparently we're both protected by Transit Displacement, so that we'll continue to exist even if we get Sauerabend back into his proper time flow."

"But where did we come from? There can't be creation of something out of nothing! Conservation of mass—"

"One of us was here all along," I reminded him. "As a matter of fact, I was here all along. I brought you into being by looping back fifty-six seconds into your time-flow."

"Balls," he said. "I was in that time-flow all along, doing what I was supposed to do. You came looping in out of nowhere. You're the goddam paradox, buster."

"I've lived fifty-six seconds longer than you, absolute. Therefore I must have been created first."

"We were both created in the same instant, on October 11, 2035," he shot back at me. "The fact that our time lines got snarled because of your faulty thinking has no bearing on which of us is more real than the other. The question is not who's the real Jud Elliott, but how we're going to continue to operate without getting in each other's way."

"We'll have to work out a tight schedule," I said. "One of us working as a Courier while the other one's hiding out up the line. And the two of us never in the same time at once, up or down the line. But how——"

"I have it," he said. "We'll establish a now-time existence in 1105, the way Metaxas has done, only for us it'll be continuous. There'll always be one of us pegged to now-time in the early twelfth century as George Markezinis, living in Metaxas' villa. The other one of us will be functioning as a Courier, and he'll go through a trip-and-layoff cycle——"

"——taking his layoff anywhen but in the 1105 basis."

"Right. And when he's completed the cycle, he'll go to the villa and pick up the Markezinis identity, and the other one will go down the line and report for Courier duty——"

"——and if we keep everything coordinated, there's no reason why the Patrol should ever find out about us."

"Brilliant!"

"And the one who's being Markezinis," I finished, "can always be carrying on a full-time affair with Pulcheria, and she'll never know that we're taking turns with her."

"As soon as Pulcheria is herself again."

"As soon as Pulcheria is herself again," I agreed.

That was a sobering thought. Our whole giddy plan for alternating our identities was just so much noise until we straightened out the mess Sauerabend had caused.

I checked the time. "You get back to 1105 and help Sam and Metaxas," I said. "Shunt here again by half past three tonight."

"Right," he said, and left.

59.

He came back on time, looking disgusted, and said, "We're all waiting for you on August 9, 1100, by the land wall back of Blachernae, about a hundred meters to the right of the first gate."

"What's the story?"

"Go and see for yourself. It makes me sick to think about it. Go, and do what has to be done, and then this filthy lunacy will be over. Go on. Jump up and join us there."

"What time of day?" I asked.

He pondered a moment. "Twenty past noon, I'd say."

I went out of the inn and walked to the land wall, and set my timer with care, and jumped. The transition from late-night darkness to midday brightness left me blinded for an instant; when I stopped blinking I found myself standing before a grim-faced trio: Sam, Metaxas—and Jud B.

"Jesus," I said, "Don't tell me we've committed another duplication!"

"This time it's only the Paradox of Temporal Accumulation," my alter ego said. "Nothing serious."

I was too muddled to reason it through. "But if we're both here, who's watching our tourists down in 1204?"

"Idiot," he said fiercely, "think four-dimensionally! How can you be so stupid if you're identical to me? Look, I jumped here from one point in that night in 1204, and you jumped from another point fifteen minutes

away. When we go back, we each go to our proper starting point in the sequence. I'm due to arrive at half past
three, and you aren't suppose to be there until quarter to
four, but that doesn't mean that neither of us is there
right now. Or all these others of us."

I looked around. I saw at least five groups of Metax-
as-Sam-me arranged in a wide arc near the wall. Obviously they had been monitoring this time point closely,
making repeated short-run shunts to check on the sequence of events, and the Cumulative Paradox was building up a multitude of them.

"Even so," I said dimly, "it somehow seems that I'm
not correctly perceiving the linear chain of—"

"*Stuff* the linear chain of!" the other Jud snarled at me.
"Will you look over there? There, on the far side of the
gate!"

He pointed.

I looked.

I saw a gray-haired woman in simple clothes. I recognized her as a somewhat younger version of the woman
whom I had seen escorting Pulcheria Ducas into the shop
of sweets and spices that day, seemingly so long ago, five
years down the line in 1105. The duenna was propped up
against the city wall, giggling to herself. Her eyes were
closed.

A short distance from her was a girl of about twelve,
who could only have been Pulcheria's younger self. The
resemblance was unmistakable. This girl still had a child's
unformed features, and her breasts were only gentle
bumps under her tunic, but the raw materials of Pulcheria's beauty were there.

Next to the girl was Conrad Sauerabend, in Byzantine
lower-middle-class clothes.

Sauerabend was cooing in the girl's ear. He was dangling before her face a little twenty-first century gimcrack,
a gyroscopic pendant or something like that. His other
hand was under her tunic and visibly groping in the vicin-

ity of her thighs. Pulcheria was frowning, but yet she wasn't making any move to get the hand out of her crotch. She seemed a little uncertain about what Sauerabend was up to, but she was altogether fascinated by the toy, and perhaps didn't mind the wandering fingers, either.

Metaxas said, "He's been living in Constantinople for a little less than a year, and commuting frequently to 2059 to drop off marketable artifacts. He's been coming by the wall every day to watch the little girl and her duenna take their noontime stroll. The girl is Pulcheria Botaniates, and that's the Botaniates palace just over there. About half an hour ago Sauerabend came along and saw the two of them. He gave the duenna a floater and she's been up high ever since. Then he sat down next to the girl and began to charm her. He's really very slick with little girls."

"It's his hobby," I said.

"Watch what happens now," said Metaxas.

Sauerabend and Pulcheria rose and walked toward the gate in the wall. We faded back into the shadows to remain unobserved. Most of our paradoxical duplicates had disappeared, evidently shunting to other positions along the line to monitor the events. We watched as the fat man and the lovely little girl strolled through the gate, into the countryside just beyond the city boundary.

I started to follow.

"Wait," said Sam. "See who's coming now? That's Pulcheria's older brother Andronicus."

A young man, perhaps eighteen, was approaching. He halted and stared in broad disbelief at the giggling duenna. We saw him rush toward her, shake her, yank her to her feet. The woman tumbled down again, helpless.

"Where's Pulcheria?" he roared. *"Where is she?"*

The duenna laughed.

Young Botaniates, desperate, rushed about the deserted sunbaked street, yelling for his maiden sister. Then he hurried through the gate.

"We follow him," Metaxas said. Several other groups of us were already outside the gate, I discovered when we got there. Andronicus Botaniates ran hither and thither. I heard the sound of girlish laughter coming from, seemingly, the wall itself.

Andronicus heard it too. There was a breach in the wall, a shallow cavelike opening at ground level, perhaps five meters deep. He ran toward it. We ran toward it too, jostling with a mob that consisted entirely of our duplicated selves. There must have been fifteen of us—five of each.

Andronicus entered the breach in the wall and let out a terrible howl. A moment later I peered in.

Pulcheria, naked, her tunic down near her ankles, stood in the classic position of modesty, with one hand flung across her budding breasts and the other spread over her loins. Next to her was Sauerabend, with his clothes open. He had his tool out and ready for business. I suppose he had been in the process of maneuvering Pulcheria into a suitable position when the interruption came.

"Outrage!" cried Andronicus. "Foulness! Seduction of a virgin maiden! I call you all to witness! Look at this, this monstrosity, this criminal deed!"

And he caught Sauerabend by one hand and his sister by the other, and tugged them both out into the open.

"Bear witness!" he bellowed. We got out of the way before Sauerabend could recognize us, although I think he was too terrified to see anyone. Pitiful Pulcheria, trying to hide all of herself at once, was huddled into a ball at her brother's feet; but he kept pulling her up, exposing her, crying, "Look at the little whore! Look at her! Look, look, look!"

And a considerable crowd came to look.

We moved to one side. I felt like throwing up. That

vile molester of children, that Humbert of stockbrokers
—exposing his swollen red thing to Pulcheria, involving
her in this scandal—

Now Andronicus had drawn his sword and was trying
to kill either Sauerabend or Pulcheria or both. But the
onlookers prevented him, bearing him to the ground and
taking away his weapon. Pulcheria, in frantic dismay at
having her nakedness exposed to such a multitude,
grabbed a dagger from someone else and attempted to kill
herself, but was stopped in time; finally an old man threw
his cloak about her. All was confusion.

Metaxas said calmly, "We followed the rest of the sequence from here before you arrived, then doubled back
to wait for you. Here's what happened: The girl was engaged to Leo Ducas, but of course it was impossible for
him to marry her after half of Byzantium had seen her
naked like this. Besides, she was considered tainted, even
though Sauerabend didn't actually have time to get into
her. The marriage was called off. Her family, blaming her
for letting Sauerabend charm her into taking off her
clothes, disowned her. Meanwhile, Sauerabend was given
the choice of marrying the girl he dishonored, or suffering
the usual penalty."

"Which was?"

"Castration," said Metaxas. "And so, as Heracles Photis, Sauerabend married her, changing the pattern of history at least to the extent of depriving you of your proper
ancestral line. Which we're now going to correct."

"Not me," said Jud B. "I've seen all I can stand. I'm
going back to 1204. I'm due there at half past three in
the morning to tell this guy to come back here and watch
things."

"But—" I said.

"Never mind figuring out the paradoxes," Sam said.
"We've got work to do."

"Relieve me at quarter to four," said Jud B, and
shunted.

Metaxas and Sam and I coordinated our timers. "We go up the line," said Metaxas, "by exactly one hour. To finish the comedy." We shunted.

60.

And with great precision and no little relief, we finished the comedy.

In this fashion:

We shunted to noon, exactly, on that hot summer day of the year 1100, and took up positions along the wall of Constantinople. And waited, trying hard to ignore the other versions of ourselves who passed briefly through our time level on snooping missions of their own.

The pretty little girl and the watchful duenna came into view.

My heart ached with love for young Pulcheria, and I ached in other places as well, out of lust for the Pulcheria who would be, the Pulcheria whom I had known.

The pretty little girl and the unsuspecting duenna, keeping close together, strolled past us.

Conrad Sauerabend/Heracles Photis appeared. Discordant sounds in the orchestra; twirling of mustaches; hisses. He studied the girl and the woman. He patted his bulging belly. He drew forth a snubby little floater and checked its snout. Leering enthusiastically, he came forward, planning to thrust the floater against the duenna's arm and, by giving her an hour of the giggling highs, to gain unimpeded access to the little girl.

Metaxas nodded to Sam.

Sam nodded to me.

We approached Sauerabend on a slanting path of approach.

"Now!" said Metaxas, and we went into action.

Huge black Sam lunged forward and clasped his right forearm across Sauerabend's throat. Metaxas seized Sauerabend's left wrist and bent his entire arm backward, far from the controls of the timer that could whiz him from our grasp. Simultaneously, I caught Sauerabend's right arm, jerking it up and back and forcing him to drop the floater. This entire maneuver occupied perhaps an eighth of a second and resulted in the effective immobilization of Sauerabend. The duenna, meanwhile, had wisely fled with Pulcheria at the sight of this unseemly struggle.

Sam now reached under Sauerabend's clothing and deprived him of his gimmicked timer.

Then we released him. Sauerabend, who undoubtedly thought that he had been set upon by bandits, saw me and grunted a couple of shocked monosyllables.

I said, "You thought you were pretty clever, didn't you?"

He grunted some more.

I said, "Gimmicking your timer, slipping away, thinking you could set up in business for yourself as a smuggler. Eh? You didn't believe we'd catch you?"

I didn't tell him of the weeks of hard work that we had put in. I didn't tell him of the timecrimes we ourselves had committed for the sake of detecting him—the paradoxes we had left strewn all up and down the line, the needless duplications of ourselves. I didn't tell him that we had just pinched six years of his life as a Byzantine tavernkeeper into a pocket universe that, so far as he was concerned, had no existence whatever. Nor did I tell him of the chain of events that had made him the husband of Pulcheria Botaniates in that pinched-off universe, depriving me of my proper ancestry. All of those things had now unhappened. There now would be no tavernkeeper

named Heracles Photis selling meat and drink to the Byzantines of the years 1100-1105.

Metaxas produced a spare timer, ungimmicked, that he
had carried for the purpose.

"Put it on," he said.

Sullenly, Sauerabend donned it.

I said, "We're going back to 1204, more or less to the
time you set out from. And then we're going to finish our
tour and go back down the line to 2059. And God help
you if you cause any more trouble for me, Sauerabend. I
won't report you for timecrime, because I'm a merciful
man, even though an unauthorized shunt like yours is
very definitely a criminal act; but if you do anything
whatever that displeases me in the slightest between now
and the moment I'm rid of you, I'll make you roast for it.
Clear?"

He nodded bleakly.

To Sam and Metaxas I said, "I can handle this from
here on. Thanks for everything. I can't possibly tell you—"

"Don't try," said Metaxas, and together they shunted
down the line.

I set Sauerabend's new timer and my own, and drew
forth my pitch-pipe. "Here we go," I said, and we
shunted into 1204.

61.

At quarter to four on that very familiar night in 1204 I
went once more up the stairs of the inn, this time with
Sauerabend. Jud B paced restlessly just within the door of

the room. He brightened at the sight of my captive. Sauerabend looked puzzled at the presence of two of me, but he didn't dare say anything.

"Get inside," I said to him. "And don't monkey with your goddam timer or you'll suffer for it."

Sauerabend went in.

I said to Jud B, "The nightmare's over. We grabbed him, took away his timer, put a regulation one on him, and here he is. The whole operation took just exactly four hours, right?"

"Plus who remembers how many weeks of running up and down the line."

"No matter now. We got him back. We start from scratch."

"And there's now an extra one of us," Jud B pointed out. "Do we work that little deal of taking turns?"

"We do. One of us stays with these clowns, takes them on down to 1453 as scheduled, and back to the twenty-first century. The other one of us goes to Metaxas' villa. Want to flip a coin?"

"Why not?" He pulled a bezant of Alexius I from his pouch, and let me inspect it for kosherness. It was okay: a standing figure of Alexius on the obverse, an image of Christ enthroned on the reverse. We stipulated that Alexius was heads and Jesus was tails. Then I flipped the coin high, caught it with a quick snap of my hand, and clapped it down on the back of my other hand. I knew, from the feel of the concave coin's edge against my skin, that it had landed heads up.

"Tails," said the other Jud.

"Tough luck, amigo." I showed him the coin. He grimaced and took it back from me.

Gloomily he said, "I've got three or four days left with this tour, right? Then two weeks of layoff, which I can't spend in 1105. That means you can expect to see me showing up at Metaxas' place in seventeen, eighteen days absolute."

"Something like that," I agreed.

"During which time you'll make it like crazy with Pulcheria."

"Naturally."

"Give her one for me," he said, and went into the room.

Downstairs, I slouched against a pillar and spent half an hour rechecking all of my comings and goings of this hectic night, to make sure I'd land in 1105 at a non-discontinuous point. The last thing I needed now was to miscalculate and show up there at a time prior to the whole Sauerabend caper, thereby finding a Metaxas to whom the entire thing was, well, Greek.

I did my calculations.

I shunted.

I wended my way once more to the lovely villa.

Everything had worked out perfectly. Metaxas embraced me in joy.

"The time-flow is intact again," he said. "I've been back from 1100 only a couple of hours, but that was enough to check up on things. Leo Ducas' wife is named Pulcheria. Someone named Angelus runs the tavern Sauerabend owned. Nobody here remembers a thing about anything. You're safe."

"I can't tell you how much I—"

"Skip it, will you?"

"I suppose. Where's Sam?"

"Down the line. He had to go back to work. And I'm about to do the same," Metaxas said. "My layoff's over, and there's a tour waiting for me in the middle of December, 2059. So I'll be gone about two weeks, and then I'll be back here on—" He considered it. "—on October 18, 1105. What about you?"

"I stay here until October 22." I said. "Then my alter ego will be finished with his post-tour layoff and will replace me here, while I go down the line to take out my next tour."

"Is that how you're going to work it? Turns?"

"It's the only way."

"You're probably right," said Metaxas, but I wasn't.

62.

Metaxas took his leave, and I took a bath. And then, really relaxed for the first time in what seemed like several geological epochs, I contemplated my immediate future.

First, a nap. Then a meal. And then a journey into town to call on Pulcheria, who would be restored to her rightful place in the Ducas household, and unaware of the strange metamorphosis that had temporarily come over her destinies.

We'd make love, and I'd come back to the villa, and in the morning I'd go into town again, and afterward—

Then I stopped hatching further plans, because Sam appeared unexpectedly and smashed everything.

He was wearing a Byzantine cloak, but it was just a hasty prop, for I could see his ordinary down-the-line clothes on underneath. He looked harried and upset.

"What the hell are you doing here?" I asked.

"A favor to you," he said.

"Huh?"

"I said I'm here as a favor to you. And I'm not going to stay long, because I don't want the Time Patrol after me too."

"Is the Time Patrol after me?"

"You bet your white ass it is!" he yelled. "Get your

things together and clear out of here, fast! You've got to hide, maybe three, four thousand years back, somewhere. Hurry it up!"

He began collecting a few stray possessions of mine scattered about the room. I caught hold of him and said, "Will you tell me what's going on? Sit down and stop acting like a maniac. You come in here at a million kilometers an hour and—"

"All right," he said. "All right. I'll spell it all out for you, and if I get arrested too, so be it. I'm stained with sin. I *deserve* to be arrested. And—"

"Sam—"

"All right," he said again. He closed his eyes a moment. "My now-time basis," he said hollowly, "is December 25, 2059. Merry Christmas. Several days ago on my time-level, your other self brought your current tour back from Byzantium. Including Sauerabend and all the rest of them. Do you know what happened to your other self the instant he arrived in 2059?"

"The Time Patrol arrested him?"

"Worse."

"What could be worse?"

"He vanished, Jud. He became a nonperson. He ceased ever to have existed."

I had to laugh. "The cocksure bastard! I *told* him that I was the real one and that he was just some kind of phantom, but he wouldn't listen! Well, I can't say that I'm sorry to see—"

"No, Jud," Sam said sadly. "He was every bit as real as you, when he was back here up the line. And you're every bit as unreal as he is now."

"I don't understand."

"You're a nonperson, Jud, same as he is. You have retroactively ceased to exist. I'm sorry. You never happened. And it's our fault as much as yours. We moved so fast that we slipped up on one small detail."

He looked frighteningly somber. But how else are you

supposed to look, when you come to tell somebody that he's not only dead but never was born?

"What happened, Sam? What detail?"

"It's like this, Jud. You know, when we took Sauerabend's gimmicked timer away, we got him another one. Metaxas keeps a few smuggled spares around—that tricky bastard has everything."

"So?"

"Its serial number, naturally, was different from the number of the timer Sauerabend started his tour with. Normally, nobody notices something like that, but when this tour checked back in, it just happened that the check-in man was a stickler for the rules, and he examined serial numbers. And saw there was a substitution, and yelled for the Patrol."

"Oh," I said weakly.

"They questioned Sauerabend," Sam said, "and of course he was cagey, more to protect himself than you. And since he couldn't give any explanation of the switch, the Patrol got authorization to run a recheck on the entire tour he had just taken."

"Oh-oh."

"They monitored it from every angle. They saw you leave your group, they saw Sauerabend skip out the moment you were gone, they saw you and me and Metaxas catch him and bring him back to that night in 1204."

"So all three of us are in trouble?"

Sam shook his head. "Metaxas has pull. So have I. We wiggled out of it on a sympathy line, that we were just trying to help a buddy in trouble. It took all the strings we could pull. But we couldn't do a thing for you, Jud. The Patrol is out for your head. They looked in on that little routine in 1204 by which you duplicated yourself, and they began to realize that you were guilty not only of negligence in letting Sauerabend get away from you in the first place, but also of various paradoxes caused in your unlawful attempts to correct the situation. The charges against you were so serious that we couldn't get them dropped, and we tried, man, we *tried*. The Patrol thereupon took action against you."

"What kind of action?" I asked in a dead man's voice.

"You were removed from your tour on that evening in 1204 two hours prior to your original shunt to 1105 for your tryst with Pulcheria. Another Courier replaced you in 1204; you were plucked from the time-flow and brought down the line to stand trial in 2059 for assorted timecrimes."

"Therefore—"

"Therefore," Sam swept on, "you never did slip away to 1105 to pay that call on Pulcheria. Your whole love affair with Pulcheria has become a nonevent, and if you were to visit her now, you'd find that she has no recollection of having slept with you. Next: since you didn't go to 1105, you obviously didn't return to 1204 and find Sauerabend missing, and anyway Sauerabend had never been part of your tour group. And thus there was no need for you to make that fifty-six-second shunt up the line which created the duplication. Neither you nor Jud B ever came into being, since the existence of both of you dates from a point later than your visit to Pulcheria, and you never made that visit, having been plucked out of the time-flow before you got a chance to do it. You and Jud B are nonpersons and always have been. You happen to be protected by the Paradox of Transit Displacement, as long as you stay up the line; Jud B ceased to be protected the moment he returned to now-time, and disappeared irretrievably. Got that?"

Shivering, I said, "Sam, what's happening to that other Jud, the—the—the *real* Jud? The one they plucked, the one they've got down there in 2059?"

"He's in custody, awaiting trial on timecrime charges."

"What about me?"

"If the Patrol ever finds you, you'll be brought to now-time and thus automatically obliterated. But the Patrol doesn't know where you are. If you stay in Byzantium, sooner or later you'll be discovered, and that'll be the end for you. When I found all this out, I shot back here to warn you. Hide in prehistory. Get away into some period earlier than the founding of the old Greek Byzantium—earlier than 700 B.C., I guess. You can manage there. We'll bring you books, tools, whatever you need. There'll be people of some sort, nomads, maybe—anyway, company. You'll be like a god to them. They'll worship you, they'll bring you a woman a day. It's your only chance, Jud."

"I don't want to be a prehistoric god! I want to be able to go down the line again! And to see Pulcheria! And—"

"There's no chance of any of that," Sam said, and his words came down like the blade of a guillotine. "You don't exist. It's suicide for you ever to try to go down the line. And if you go anywhere near Pulcheria, the Patrol will catch you and *take* you down the line. Hide or die, Jud. Hide or die."

"But I'm real, Sam! I *do* exist!"

"Only the Jud Elliott who's currently in custody in 2059 exists. You're a residual phenomenon, a paradox product, nothing more. I love you all the same, boy, and that's why I've risked my own black hide to help you, but you aren't real. Believe me. Believe me. You're your own ghost. Pack up and clear out!"

63.

I've been here for three and a half months now. By the calendar I keep, the date is March 15, 3060 B.P. I'm living a thousand years before Christ, more or less.

It's not a bad life. The people here are subsistence farmers, maybe remnants of the old Hittite empire; the Greek colonists won't be getting here for another three centuries. I'm starting to learn the language; it's Indo-European and I pick it up fast. As Sam predicted, I'm a god. They wanted to kill me when I showed up, but I did a few tricks with my timer, shunting right before their eyes, and now they don't dare offend me. I try to be a kindly god, though. Right now I'm helping spring to arrive. I went down to the shore of what will someday be called the Bosphorus and delivered a long prayer, in English, for good weather. The locals loved it.

They give me all the women I want. The first night they gave me the chief's daughter, and since then I've rotated pretty well through the whole nubile population of the village. I imagine they'll want me to marry someone eventually, but I want to complete the inspection first. The women don't smell too good, but some of them are impressively passionate.

I'm terribly lonely.

Sam has been here three times, Metaxas twice. The others don't come. I don't blame them; the risks are great. My two loyal friends have brought me floaters, books, a laser, a big box of music cubes, and plenty of

other things that are going to perplex the tails off some
archaeologists eventually.

I said to Sam, "Bring me Pulcheria, just for a visit."

"I can't," he said. And he's right. It would have to be a
kidnapping, and there might be repercussions, leading to
Time Patrol troubles for Sam and obliteration for me.

I miss Pulcheria ferociously. You know, I had sex with
her only that one night, though it seems as if I knew her
much better than that. I wish now that I'd had her in the
tavern, while she was Pulcheria Photis, too.

My beloved. My wicked great-great-multi-great-grandmother. Never to see you again! Never to touch your
smooth skin, your—no, I won't torture myself. I'll try to
forget you. Hah!

I console myself, when not busy in my duties as a
deity, by dictating my memoirs. Everything now is recorded, all the details of how I maneuvered myself into
this terrible fix. A cautionary tale: from promising young
man to absolute nonperson in sixty-two brief chapters. I'll
keep on writing too, now and then. I'll tell what it's like
to be a Hittite god. Let's see, tomorrow we'll have the
spring fertility festival, and the ten fairest maidens of the
village will come to the god's house so that we—

Pulcheria!

Why am I here so far from you, Pulcheria?

I have too much time to think about you, here.

I also have too much time to think unpleasant thoughts
about my ultimate fate. I doubt that the Time Patrol will
find me here. But there's another possibility.

The Patrol knows that I'm hiding somewhere up the
line, protected by displacement.

The Patrol wants to smoke me out and abolish me, because I'm a filthy spawn of paradox.

And it's in the power of the Patrol to do it. Suppose
they retroactively discharge Jud Elliott from the Time
Service prior to the time he set out on his ill-starred last
trip? If Jud Elliott never ever got to Byzantium that time

at all, the probability of my existence reaches the zero point, and I no longer am protected by the Paradox of Transit Displacement. The Law of Lesser Paradoxes prevails. Out I go—poof!

I know why they haven't done that to me yet. It's because that other Jud, God bless him, is standing trial for timecrime down the line, and they can't retroactively pluck him until they've found him guilty. They have to complete the trial. If he's found guilty, I guess they'll take some action of that sort. But court procedures are slow. Jud will stall. Sam's told him I'm here and have to be protected. It might be months, years, who knows? He's on his now-time basis, I'm on mine, and we move forward into our futures together, day by day, and so far I'm still here.

Lonely. Heartsick.

Dreaming of my forever lost Pulcheria.

Maybe they'll never take action against me.

Or maybe they'll end me tomorrow.

Who knows? There are moments when I don't even care. There's one comforting thing, at least. It'll be the most painless of deaths. Not even a flicker of pain. I'll simply go wherever the flame of the candle goes when it's snuffed. It could happen at any time, and meanwhile I live from hour to hour, playing god, listening to Bach, indulging in floaters, dictating my memoirs, and waiting for the end. Why, it could even come right in the middle of a sentence, and I'd